D1550377

UNIVERSE 8

UNIVERSE 8

Edited by TERRY CARR

All of the characters in this book
are fictitious, and any resemblance
to actual persons, living or dead,
is purely coincidental.

 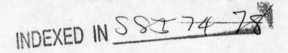
Library of Congress Cataloging in Publication Data

Main entry under title:
Universe 8.

    CONTENTS: Bishop, M. Old folks at home.—Felice, C.
David and Lindy.—Eklund, G. Vermeer's window. [etc.]
    1. Science fiction, American. I. Carr, Terry.
PZ1.U64 [PS648.S3]   813'.0876
ISBN: 0-385-12479-1
Library of Congress Catalog Card Number 77-82932

CONTENTS

Science fiction has usually dealt with the adventures of young people, and that's not surprising, since youth is a time of vigor and imagination. But the human life span is steadily increasing, so shouldn't we be giving some thought to what life will be like for the long-lived people of the future? Especially since, if we're lucky, they'll be us?

Michael Bishop, who is currently in his thirties and one of science fiction's best "young authors," here considers a new life style for the seniors of tomorrow. They'll be people who remember our time but who must adjust to future changes: it will give them a unique perspective on the world of the twenty-first century.

OLD FOLKS AT HOME
Michael Bishop

1 *"sold down the river"*

At a stilly six o'clock in the morning Lannie sat looking at the face of her visicom console in their sleeper-cove, Concourse B-11, Door 47, Level 3. Nausea was doing its stuff somewhere down in her plumbing: bubbles and fizzes and musical flip-flops. And Sanders—Sanders, her blue-jowled lummox—he lay sprawled snoring on their bed; if Levels 1 and 2 fell in on them, he'd still sleep, and he didn't have to get up for another hour. But Lannie intended to fight it; she wasn't going to the bath booth yet, no matter how tickly sick she began to feel.

That would wake Zoe, and she wasn't ready for Zoe yet, maybe not for the rest of the day.

Putting her arms across her stomach, Lannie leaned over the glow-

ing console and tapped into the *Journal/Constitution* newstapes. Day
13 of Winter, 2040, New Calendar designation. Front page, edito-
rials, sports: peoplenews, advertisements, funnies.

Then, in among the police calls and obituaries, a boxed notice:

> *WANTED: Persons over sixty to take part in the second phase
> of a five-year-old gerontological study funded by the URNU
> HUMAN DEVELOPMENT COMMISSION. Health and sex
> of applicants of no consequence; our selections will be based on
> a consideration of both need and the individual interest of each
> case. Remuneration for the families of those applicants who are
> selected. Contact DR. LELAND TANNER, or his repre-
> sentative, UrNu Human Development Tower.*

Lannie, still clutching her robe to her middle, held this "page" on
the console. After two or three read-throughs she sat back and gazed
at the room's darkened ceiling. "Eureka," she whispered at the
acoustical punctures up there. "Eureka."

Sanders, turning his mouth to the pillow, replied with a beluga-like
whistling.

She wasn't deceived, Zoe wasn't. She read the newstapes, too,
maybe even more closely than they did, and if Melanie and Sanders
thought they could wool-eye her with this casual trip to the UrNu
Human Development Tower, they needed to rethink their clunky
thinking. I wasn't born yesterday, Zoe thought. Which was so ludicrous a musing that right there in the quadrangle, on the gravel path
among the boxed begonias and day lilies, Sanders craning his head
around like a thief and Melanie drawing circles in the gravel with the
toe of her slipper, Zoe chuckled: *Clucka-clucka-cluck.*

"Mother, hush!"

"'Scuse me, Lannie, 'scuse me for living." Which was also reasonably funny. So she *clucka-clucked* again.

Sanders said, "What does he want to meet us out here for? How
come he can't conduct this in a businesslike fashion?" Sanders was a
freshman investment broker. He had had to take the afternoon off.

"Not everyone runs their business like you do," Melanie answered.
She was a wardrobe model for Consolidated Rich's.

It was 2:10 in the afternoon, and the city's technicians had dialed
up a summery 23° C. in spite of its being the month Winter. The grass
in the quadrangle, as Zoe had already discovered by stepping off the

path, was Astroturf; and for sky the young Nobles and Melanie's mother had the bright, distant geometry of Atlanta's geodesic dome. On every side, the white towers of that sector of the Human Development complex called the Geriatrics Hostel. Many of the rooms had balconies fronting on the garden, and at various levels, on every side but one (the intensive-care ward), curious faces atop attenuated or bloated bodies stared down on them, two or three residents precariously standing but many more seated in wheel chairs or aluminum rockers. Except for these faces, the Nobles and the old woman had the carefully landscaped inner court to themselves.

"Home, sweet home," Zoe said, surveying her counterparts on the balconies. Then: "Sold down the river, sold down the river."

"Mother, for God's sake, stop it!"

"Call it what you want to, Lannie, I know what it is."

"Leland Tanner," a young man said, surprising them. It was as if he had been lying in wait for them behind a bend in the path, the concealing frond of a tub-rooted palm.

Leland Tanner smiled. More than two meters tall, he had a horsy face and wore a pair of blue-tinted glasses whose stems disappeared into shaggy gray hair. A pleasant-looking fellow. "You're Zoe Breedlove," he said to her. "And you're the Nobles. . . . I thought our discussion might be more comfortable out here in the courtyard." He led them to a ginkgo-shaded arbor on one of the pathways and motioned the family to a stone bench opposite the one he himself took up. Here, they were secure against the inquisitive eyes of the balcony-sitters.

"Zoe," the young man said, stretching out his long legs, "we're thinking of accepting you into our community."

"Dr. Tanner, we're very—" Melanie began.

"Which means I'm being sold down the river."

"Damn it, Mother!"

The young man's eyes, which she could see like clear drops of sapphire behind the colored lenses, turned toward her. "I don't know what your daughter and your son-in-law's motives are, Zoe, but it may be that—on down the Chattahoochee, so to speak—you'll find life a little better than it was on the old plantation. You may be freer here."

"She's as free as she wants to be with us," Sanders said, mounting his high horse. "And I don't think this plantation metaphor's a bit necessary." His foot always got caught in that wide, loose stirrup: his mouth.

Only the young doctor's eyes moved. "That may be true, Mr. Noble," he said. "In the Urban Nucleus everyone's freedoms are proscribed equally."

"The reason they're doing it," Zoe said, putting her hands on her papery knees (she was wearing a disposable gown with clip-on circlets of lace at sleeves and collar), "is 'cause Lannie's gone and got pregnant and they want me out of the cubicle. They're not gonna get off Level 3 anytime soon, and four rooms we've got. So they did this to get me out."

"Mother, we didn't *do it* to get you out."

"I don't know why we did it," Sanders said, staring at the gravel.

Zoe appealed to the intent, gracefully lounging young doctor. "It could sleep in my room, too, that's the shame of it: it could sleep in my room." Then, chuckling again, "And they may be sorry they didn't think of that before hauling me up here. Like two sneaky Simon Legreedies, Lannie and Sandy."

"Dr. Tanner," Melanie said, "we're doing this for her as much as for ourselves and the baby. The innuendoes about our motives are only—"

"Money," Zoe said, rubbing her fingers against her thumb like a usurer. "I read that box in the newstapes, you know. You're auditioning for old people, aren't you?"

"Sort of like that," Leland Tanner said, standing. "Anyway, Zoe, I've made up my mind about you." Under a canopy of ginkgo leaves he stared down at the group huddled before him, his eyes powerful surrogates for the myopic ones on the balconies.

"Don't take me," Zoe said, "it'll serve them right."

"From now on," the young man said, "we're going to be more interested in serving *you* right. And in permitting you to serve."

Sanders, her son-in-law, lifted his head and squinted through the rents in the foliage. "It's supposed to be Winter," he said. "I wish they'd make it rain." But an even, monochromatic afternoon light poured down, and it was 23° C.

She was alone with young Leland in a room opening onto the garden, and he had pulled the curtain back so that she could see out while they talked. A wingback chair for her, with muted floral-print upholstery. Her feet went down into a pepper-and-salt shag carpet. Tea things on a mahogany coffee table, all of the pieces a dainty robin's-egg blue except for the silver serving tray.

Melanie and Sanders had been gone thirty minutes, but she didn't miss them. It didn't even disturb her that it might be a long while—a good long while—before she saw them again. The ginkgo trees in the garden turned their curious oriental leaves for her examination, and the young man was looking at her like a lover, although a cautious one.

"This is a pretty room," she said.

"Well, actually," he said, "it's a kind of decompression chamber, or air-lock, no matter what the comfortable trappings suggest. Usually I'm not so candid in my explanation of its function; most prospective residents of the Geriatrics Hostel must be introduced into their new environment slowly, without even a hint that a change *is* occurring. But you, Zoe, not only realize from the outset what's going on, you've also got the wit to assimilate the change as if it were no more significant than putting on a new pair of socks."

"That's not so easy any more, either."

He tilted his head. "Your response illustrates what I'm saying. I judge you to be a resilient woman; that, along with my interview with your family, induces me to select you as a candidate for the second stage of our study. I can use a term like *air-lock* to describe this sitting room without flustering you. Because, Zoe, if you decide to stay with us, and to press your candidacy, you'll be very much like an astronaut going from the cramped interior of a capsule—via this room, your air-lock—into the alien, but very liberated realm of outer space."

"First a sold-down-the-river darkie. Now a spaceman." Zoe shook her head and looked at the damp ring her teacup had made on the knee of her gown. "Well, I'm old, Mr. Leland, but I'm still around. More than you can say for slaves and astronauts, thank goodness in the one case, too bad in the other."

Young Mr. Leland's violet eyes (he had taken those hideous

glasses off), twinkled like St. Nick's, but he didn't laugh, not with his voice. Instead he said, "How old are you, Zoe?"

"Sixty-seven. Didn't *they* tell you?"

"They told me. I wanted to see if you would."

"Well, that's correct. I was born in 1973, before the domes ever was, and I came into Atlanta from Winder, Georgia, during the First Evacuation Lottery. Barely twenty-two, virgin and unmarried, though in those days you'd best not admit to the first condition any more than you had now. Met my husband, Rabon Breedlove, when the dome wasn't even a third finished. But a *third* of my life—my entire youth, really—I spent in the Open, not even realizing it was dangerous, the city politicians even said traitorous, to be out there." A few bitter, black leaves adhered to the robin's-egg-blue china as she turned her empty cup.

"And how old is Melanie, then?"

"Twenty-eight or -nine. Let's see." She computed. "Born in 2011, a late child and an only one. Rabon and me had tried before, though. Four times I miscarried, and once I was delivered of a stillborn who went into the waste converters before we had a chance to put a name on it. Boy or girl, they didn't tell us. Then Melanie, a winter baby, when we thought we'd never have one. All the other times was forgotten, a pink and living tadpole we had then, Rabon and me."

"Your husband died when she was eight?"

"Embolism."

Young Mr. Leland stood up and went to the window drapes. She saw how the shag lapped over his work slippers, even though his feet were big: good and big. "The Geriatrics Hostel has two parts, Zoe, one a nursing home and hospital, the other an autonomous community run by the residents themselves. You don't need the first, but you can choose to be a candidate for the second."

"I got a choice, huh?"

"We coerce no one to stay here—but in the case of those committed to the hostel's nursing sector it's often impossible for the residents to indicate choice. Their families make the decisions for them, and we then do the best we can to restore their capacity for reasoned, self-willed choice."

"What does it mean, I'm a 'candidate'?"

"If you so decide, you'll go into one of our self-contained communities. Whether you remain with that group, however, is finally up to you and the members of the group themselves."

"S'pose the old fuddy-duddies don't like me?"

"I view that as unlikely. If so, we find you another family or permit you to form one of your own. No losers here, Zoe."

Very quietly she said, "Hot damn." Young Mr. Leland's eyebrows went up. "An expression of my daddy's."

And came down again into an expression amusingly earnest. "Your husband's been dead twenty years. How would you like to get married again?"

"You proposin'?"

Well, he *could* laugh. With his voice as well as his eyes. She was hearing him. "No, no," he said, "not for myself. For the first septigamic unit we want to introduce you to. Or for the six remaining members of it, that is. You'll have six mates instead of one, Zoe. Three husbands and three wives, if those terms mean anything at all in such a marriage covenant. The family name of the unit is Phoenix. And if you join them your legal name will be Zoe Breedlove-Phoenix, at least within the confines of the Geriatrics Hostel itself. Elsewhere, too, if things work out as we wish."

"Sounds like a bridge group that's one short for two tables."

"You'll be doing more than playing bridge with these people, Zoe. No false modesty, no societally dictated inhibitions. And the odd number is a purposive stipulation, not merely a capricious way of messing up card games. It prevents pairing, which can sometimes occur on an extremely arbitrary basis. The old NASA programmers recognized this when they assigned *three* men to the Apollo missions. The same principle guides us here."

"Well, that's fine, Mr. Leland. But even with those astronauts, you'll remember, only two of 'em went down honeymooning."

His horsy face went blank, then all his cheek- and jawbones and teeth worked together to split the horsiness with a naughty-boy grin. He scratched his unkempt hair: shag on top, shag around his shoes. "Maybe I ought to renege on the Phoenix offer and propose for myself, Mrs. Breedlove. All I can say to answer you is that honeymooning needn't be what tradition only decrees. For the most part, the septigamic covenant has worked pretty well these last five years at the hostel. And your own wit and resilience make me believe that you can bring off your candidacy and marry with the Phoenix. Do you wish to become a candidate, Zoe?"

Zoe put her cup on the silver serving tray. "You know, Mr. Leland, you shoulda been a comedy straight man." By which she

didn't mean to imply that he was even half so humorless as Sanders
Noble. No, sir. That Sanders could stay sour in a room full of laughing gas.

"Missed my calling. But do you want to?"

"Oh, I do," Zoe said, taking what he'd served up. "I do."

3   helen, and the others

Dr. Leland Tanner made a call on an intercom unit in the sitting
room. Then, leaning over Zoe so that she could smell the sharp co-
logne on him, he kissed her on the forehead. "I'm going out now,
Zoe. If you decide to stay, you'll see me only infrequently; your new
family will occupy your time and your attention. There's no interdict,
however, on associating with the culturally immature. If you like, you
can see me or anyone else younger than yourself. Just let me know."

"Then I s'pose I shall, Mr. Leland."

" 'By," and he strode through the whipping shag, saluted at the
sliding glass doors, and went out into the quadrangle. In only a moment he was lost to Zoe on one of the foliage-sheltered paths, and the
calm, curious ginkgo trees held her amazed interest until an inner
door opened and a thin woman with close-cropped gray hair came in
to her.

"Zoe Breedlove?" A Manila envelope clasped in front of her, the
newcomer looked *toward* the wingback but not exactly *at* it. A handsome, frail woman with silvery opaque eyes and an off-center smile.

"That's me," Zoe said. The other's eyes focused on her then, and
the smile firmed up. The woman navigated through waves of carpet
to a chair opposite Zoe's, and they faced each other across the tea
service.

"I'm Helen," the woman said. "Helen Phoenix. Parthena and Toodles wanted another man, I think, but I'm happy Leland found somebody who won't have to compete with our memories of Yuichan.
That would have been unfair to you."

"Yui-chan?" The word sounded foreign, particularly to a dome-
dwelling Georgia girl. Whereas Helen's accent marked her as no native to Atlanta. New York? Something cosmopolitan, anyhow: once.

"Yuichan Kurimoto-Phoenix. He was born in Kyoto, but he behaved like a raving Italian. Had execrable taste in everything; not a
bit subtle. There's an unpainted plaster-of-Paris squirrel on the bole

of one of the trees in the garden: Yuichan's doing." Helen lowered her head. "A lovely man; just lovely."

"Well, I hope the others don't think I'm even going to try to take Yoo-chi's place. I don't even know anything about China."

The woman's smile died at the corners of her mouth, then slowly grew back. "Nevertheless," she said, "you may be more like Yuichan than you know. Which is all to the good: a bonus for us. And the question of your competing with Yuichan's memory won't enter into our appreciation of you at all. I'm sure of that. Toodles only favored another man, I'm sure, because she's a voluptuary and thinks Paul and Luther inadequate for our servicing."

Servicing: that probably meant exactly what she thought it did. Zoe leaned over the coffee table. "Would you like some of this tea Mr. Leland left with me?"

"Please. And if you'll push the service to one side, Zoe—may I call you Zoe?—I'll introduce you to the others even before we go upstairs. That's an advantage you'll have over them, but probably the only one. We hardly begrudge it."

"Good. I could use an evener." And it was after pushing the tea service aside and while watching Helen take the photographs and printouts out of the Manila envelope that Zoe realized Helen was blind. The opaque eyes worked independently of her smile and her hands: the eyes were beautiful, somehow weightless ball bearings. Mechanical moving parts in a body that was all Siamese cat and animal silver. Without fumbling, Helen's small hands laid out the pictures and the data sheets. Reminiscently, Zoe touched one of the photographs.

"You can examine it all while I drink my tea, Zoe. I won't bother you."

The top sheet on the pile was neatly computer-typed. Zoe held it up and tilted it so that she could read it.

THE PHOENIX SEPTIGAMOKLAN

Covenant Ceremony:

>*Day 7 of Spring, 2035, New Calendar designation.*

Septigamoklanners:

>M. L. K. Battle (Luther). *Born July 11, 1968, Old Calendar designation. No surviving family. Last employer:*

McAlpine Construction and Demolition Company. Septi-gamoklan jack-o-trades and activity-planner. Ortho-Urbanist, lapsed, age-exempted. Black.

Parthena Cawthorn. *Born November 4, 1964, o.c.; Madison, Georgia. A son Maynard, a daughter-in-law, and three grandchildren: enfranchised UrNu citizens. Last employer: Inner Earth Industries. Sgk artisan and folklorist. Ortho-Urbanist, semiactive. Black.*

Paul Erik Ferrand. *Born October 23, 1959, o.c.; Bakersfield, California. Family members (children, grandchildren, great-grandchildren) in the Urban Nuclei of Los Angeles and San Francisco. Last employer: (?). Unclassifiable Mystic, age-exempted. White.*

Yuichi Kurimoto (Yuichan). *Born May 27, 1968, o.c.; Kyoto, Japan. Children, grandchildren, great-grandchildren alive in Kyoto and Tokyo. Last employer: Visicomputer Enterprises, Atlanta branch. Sgk legislator. Neo-Buddhist, lapsed, nationality-exempted. Oriental.*

Joyce Malins (Toodles). *Born February 14, 1971, o.c.; Savannah, Georgia. No surviving family. Last employer: Malins Music, Voice, and Dance. Sgk musician. Ortho-Urbanist, lapsed, age-exempted. White.*

Helen Mitchell. *Born July 11, 1967, o.c.; Norfolk, Virginia. A son in the Washington UrNu, a daughter in the Philadelphia UrNu. Last employer: UrNu Civil Service, Atlanta branch. Sgk mediator. Ortho-Urbanist, semiactive. White.*

Jeremy Zitelman (Jerry). *Born December 9, 1970, o.c. No surviving family. Last employer: University of Georgia, Urban Extension, Astronomy Department. Sgk historian. Recidivist Jew, age-exempted. White.*

A mixed lot, Zoe decided: a party assortment. Over the capsule-biography of Yuichi Kurimoto the word DECEASED was stamped in large, double-lined red letters which did not conceal the information under them. Zoe looked at the photographs and tried to match them up with the résumés (they weren't very good photographs); she got them all matched up, but it was pretty apparent that some of the pictures had been taken years ago. For instance, Paul Erik Ferrand, supposedly just over eighty, was a rakish, lupine man wearing a style of cravat that hadn't been fashionable in two decades. Before their names and faces meant anything Zoe would have to meet these people: in the flesh.

"Is that what I'll be—a septigamoklanner—if y'all like me?"

"That's an institute word, Zoe, made up by someone who didn't know what to call a family like ours. Don't worry. None of us use it. You see, these information sheets contain only passed-upon, UrNu-validated 'facts': impersonal and bureaucratic. Jerry or I, either one, could have put a little pizzazz into the sketches. . . . Unfortunately, civil service sachems frown on pizzazz. . . ." Helen's voice trailed off.

"Well, that's encouraging—'cause I think I'd have a hard time thinking of myself as a . . . *septigamoklansperson.*" A mouthful, that. "But in Yoo-chi's biography here, it says he was the family legislator. Does that mean, since I'm coming in for him, I have to put on his shoes and be a legislator?"

"No, no. On these official data sheets everyone's given a position, as if we were baseball players or chess pieces. Really, though, we do whatever we do best, and by defining ourselves in that way we become ourselves to the others. Later, someone will probably put a label on what you are. It won't be a Phoenix who does it, though."

"Mr. Leland?"

"Perhaps. A study is going on here, though we're mostly oblivious to it, and studies demand statistics and labels. A cosmic law, like gravitation and magnetism and whatnot."

"Well, if it was *age-exempted,* even an apple might not have to fall."

Helen's opaque eyes locked on her face. "An appropriate observation. But we do have a chance to do some naming of our own. Phoenix was our own choice, you know. Some of the other families in the Tower are Cherokee, Piedmont, O'Possum, and Sweetheart."

"Oh, those are good ones, too." They were, too; had what Helen would probably call pizzazz.

"Yes," Helen said, pleased. "Yes, they are."

Zoe met them all at supper that evening. They ate in a room decorated with a quilted wall banner, and with several potted plants that Joyce Malins (Toodles) said she had bought from a slum-area florist in a place called the Kudzu Shop.

The Phoenix family had an entire suite of rooms, including a kitchen, on the Geriatrics Hostel's fourth floor, and this evening Luther, Toodles, and Paul had shared the cooking: corn bread, frozen vegetables, and pasta with a sauce of meat substitutes. Better than Lannie managed after two hours of sloozying around in new clothes for the lechers at Consolidated Rich's; better than Zoe usually did for herself, come to that. The table was round, and wooden, and big enough for seven people, a metal pitcher of cold, sweetened tea, and several china serving dishes. No attendants waited on them, Zoe noted, no nurses, no white-smocked young men with pursed lips. A biomonitor cabinet, to which they were all linked by means of pulse-cued silver bracelets, was the only alien presence in the dining room, and it kept quiet. (The people downstairs had a hookup to the monitor, though, she was sure of that.) Zoe self-consciously turned her own new bracelet, a handsome thing in spite of its being, also, a piece of medical equipment. Plugged in already she was, a rookie Phoenix.

Helen had introduced her. She was sitting between Helen and Jerry. Then clockwise beyond Helen: Parthena, Paul, Luther, and Toodles. Jerry was sitting in a wheel chair, a lap robe over his knees. The others, like Helen, looked pretty mobile—even the eighty-year-old Paul, whose eyes resembled a Weimaraner dog's and whose mouth still knew how to leer.

"How old are you, Zoe?" he asked, after the opening small talk had faded off into mumbles and spoon-rattling.

Helen said, "Paul!" Like Lannie shushing her, Zoe; only nicer.

"Bet she ain't as old as me. Three-to-one odds. Place your bets." He smacked his lips.

"No one's so old as that," Jerry said. Jerry's hair was a dandelion puffball: just that round, that gray, that delicate. His face was red.

"I'm sixty-seven," Zoe said. Second time today. But saying so didn't age you, just worrying about it.

"Young blood," the wide-faced black man said: Luther. His hair (she was comparing now) was the kind of white you see on a photograph negative, a darkness turned inside out. His hands, on either side of his plate, looked like the mallets on sledgehammers. "Hooooi! Old folks, we're being transfused, we're gettin' new blood."

"Toodles ain' the baby no mo'," Parthena said out of a tall, stern Zulu mask of a face. Plantation accent, Zoe noticed. Luther sounded more like Paul or Toodles than he did Parthena; except for that *Hooooi!* Except for that.

"How 'bout that, Toodles?" Paul said. "Puttin' your foot on the bottom rung of Jacob's ladder at last. I'm up the highest, but you've finally climbed on." Toodles, whose mouth was a red smear, a candy heart (even though no one wore lip ices or eye blacking any more), lowered a forkful of squash to reply, but crazy old Paul turned to Zoe again: "I'm up the highest, but I'm never gonna die. I was born in California."

"Which is your typical Ferrand-Phoenix *non sequitur*," Jerry said.

"I've never made an issue of being the youngest one here," Toodles interjected. "And I'm not disturbed by losing that position, either." Her jowly face swung toward Zoe. "Zoe, I bought that fuchsia and the coleus for your arrival today. Parthena and I walked into that jungle off New Peachtree and haggled with the little Eurasian shopkeeper over prices. Then we carried our purchases back, pots and all, no help from these noble gentlemen."

"Course," Parthena said, "that 'fo' she knew how old you was." Her Zulu mask smiled: perfect dentures. Taller than anyone else in the room, Parthena, even seated, loomed.

"Parthena, damn your black hide, you know that wouldn't've made any difference! It wouldn't've!" Toodles dropped her fork, her mouth silently working itself into a multiplex variety of lopsided O's.

"Joke," Parthena said. "Jes' funnin'."

"Well, what the hell's funny about my being younger than you old cadavers?" Her mascara, tear-moistened, was making crater holes out of her eyes. "What's so damn funny about that?!"

"What's she takin' on like this for?" Luther asked the table.

"Humor her," Jerry said, winking at Zoe from under his puffball. "She thinks she's in her period."

Which brought guffaws from Paul and Luther and pulled the roof down on everyone else. Rearing back as if bee-stung, Toodles knocked her chair over and stood glaring at each member of her family in turn. Not counting Zoe.

"Jackasses!" she managed. Then, more vehemently: "Limp ole noodles!" Her mouth had begun to look like a pattern on an oscilloscope. Zoe, in fact, saw that one of the miniature screens on the biomonitor cabinet was sending delicate, pale comets back and forth across its surface: Toodles pulsing into the hysterical.

In person, Toodles left off glaring and, without looking back, moved painfully, heavily, out of the dining room. A minute or two after her exit, the pale comets stopped whizzing. Not dead, Toodles wasn't; just out of range. Another cabinet would pick her up shortly.

"Silly biddy," Paul announced, chewing.

"Jerry's last remark was crude," Helen said. "A sort of crudity, Zoe, that he usually doesn't permit himself."

"Please believe that," the crimson-faced man said, wheeling himself back from the table. "Lately she's been upset. That she was on the verge, though, I didn't think. I'm sorry, I'm honestly sorry, you know." The chair powered him out the door.

"Hot damn," Zoe said. "Some debut."

"Ain' yo' fault," Parthena said. "She been eggcited. Las' two week, she knew we was gonna fine a 'placement for Yuichan, that's all."

"That's true," Helen said. "We argue like young married couples do sometimes, Zoe, but usually not before company and not very often. Ordinarily Toodles is a lovely woman. And the only explanations I can give for her behavior are the menfolk's bad manners and her excitement. Courting's always made her nervous; always."

"As for the sort of crudity you heard from *her*," Luther said, "that's her style. She don't mean nothin' by it, though, even when she's mad."

"Silly biddy," the time-blotched old Frenchman (or whatever he was) said. "Carry on like that, die before I will. . . . I ain't gonna die." He was the only one who finished eating what was on his plate. Once finished, long lips glistening, he let a red, translucent eyelid drop lasciviously over an amber eye: a wink. For Zoe.

5 *rotational reminiscence*

Two hours later. The roof court of the UrNu Human Development Tower, geriatrics wing. Temperature holding steady at 21° C.

Night had risen as the city's fluorescent suns had been gradually dialed down.

The Phoenix had patched things up among themselves and now sat in a semicircle at a tower railing overlooking the Biomonitor Agency on West Peachtree and, ten floors down, a floodlit pedestrian park. All the Phoenix but that oddie, Paul: he still hadn't come up. Zoe put that old codger out of her mind, though. The rooftop was open and serene, and she had never seen such a pretty simulated twilight. Not much chance on Level 3, *under*. Now, winking on across the city's dying-into-the-violet skyscape, a thousand faint points of light. The breath sucked away just at the glory of it.

Jerry Zitelman-Phoenix maneuvered his wheel chair into position beside her. (Ramps and lift-tubes made it possible for him to go anywhere at all inside the complex.) "I want to apologize, Zoe, for my uncalled-for remark in your presence."

"I always try to apologize to the person who needs it."

"Me, too. Look, you can see she's back." And she was, Toodles: sitting with Luther, Parthena, and Helen and animatedly narrating another episode of her afternoon's shopping. "But you, too, need an apology for the disruption I made," Jerry said, "so to you also I say, 'Sorry.' "

Zoe accepted this apology, and Jerry began talking. He told her that on Thursday nights—alternate ones, anyhow, and it was Thursday night that night—the Phoenix clan had this screened section of the rooftop for whatever purpose they wished. He told her that tonight it was a game they called "rotational reminiscence" and that they were waiting for Paul, who never participated but who insisted on attending every session. The rules, Jerry said, were simple and would become clear once they started. Then, pointing to the darkened, concave hollow overhead, the honeycombed shell in which they all lived, he told her that in his youth he had been an astronomer.

"Even now," he said, "I can look up there at night and imagine the constellations rolling by. Oh, Zoe, it's just as plain as day—which is one more of your typical Ferrand *non sequiturs,* Zitelman version thereof. But it's true, I can. There's Cassiopeia, there's Ursa Major, there's Camelopardalis. . . . Oh, all of them I can see. The dome is no impediment to me, Zoe, but it's certainly no joyous boon either. That it isn't."

He went on. He told her that the only advantage the dome offered him was that he could just as easily imagine the constellations

of the *Southern* Hemisphere passing in procession across its face.
Sometimes he so imagined: Canis Minor, Hydra, Monoceros. There
they all were, so dizzying in their splendor that he felt sure he would
one day power his wheel chair right up into their diamond-dusted
nets and connect the dots among them with the burning tip of a
raunchy, green cigar. "Cigars I'm not allowed any more," he said.
"Not even the neutered ones with no tobacco, no tar, and no taste.
And stars . . . ?" He pointed at the dome.
"Well," Zoe said, "we got three stars at least. And they move."
Jerry's puffball rolled back, his vein-blossomed cheeks shone with
wan, reflected light. "Ah, yes. Girder-cars is what we've got there,
Zoe. Torchlight repairs on the dome. So they send out the magnetized
girder-cars at night and let us pretend, with these insulting sops to
our memory, that the sky hasn't been stolen. Pretty, though, I grant
you." He was right. Artificial stars—only three—on a metal zodiac.
How did the men inside those topsy-turvy trolleys feel? What was
that old song? She mentally hummed a bit of it:

> *Would you like to ride on a star?*
> *Carry moonbeams home from afar?*

"Damn that old zombie!" Toodles suddenly said to them. "Let's
go on without Paul, he never contributes anyway."
"Yeah," Luther said. "Let's start."
Helen persuaded them to wait a few more minutes. OK with Zoe,
A-OK. She listened as Jerry related how he had been involved in a
bone-crushing, paralyzing automobile accident in 1989, when most of
the old "interstates" were falling into disuse: cracked pavements,
weed-grown shoulders, brambly medians. He hadn't walked since.
"When it happened, I'd never even had relations with a woman; impossible, after. At night, sometimes, I'd cry. Just like that fellow in
the Hemingway book—except his legs, they weren't crushed; it was
something else. So I never got married until Dr. Tanner accepted me
for the study here. Then three wives at once I got. Now, in my old
age, poor Yuichan dead, I'm helping my spouses court a fourth one.
Who can say it isn't a strange and wizardly life, our pains and
weaknesses notwithstanding?"
"Not me, Jerry," Zoe said. "Not me."
So Jerry went on and told her about how he had got his degree and
then moved into the dome and tried to teach astronomy by means of
textbooks, slide programs, and old films. He'd done it for almost

twenty years, at which point the city decided it was foolish to pay somebody to lecture about a subject with so limited an application to modern society. "Fffft!" Jerry said. "Fired. Me and others, too. A whole program, kaput!" He had had to live on Teachers' Retirement and future-secure benefits in a Level 6 cubicle until—

"Howdy," Paul said. "Ain't you started yet?"

"Sit down," Luther said. "What have you been up to?"

Paul, running his fingers through tatters of thin hair, lowered himself creakingly to the fore-edge of a chair between Parthena and Zoe. "Fetched up some night things for our fiancée. She didn't bring none with her." He looked at Zoe. And winked. "'Gainst my better judgment, too."

"You mighty sweet," Parthena said. "Now let's get on with it."

They did. The rules were these: 1) Silence while the person whose turn it was thought of a pre-Evacuation experience he wished to evoke for himself or, better, himself and the others. 2) An evocation of that experience in one word, the settled-upon word to be spoken, very clearly, only once. 3) An after-silence in which this word might resonate. 4) No repetitions from previous games. 5) An automatic halt after each Phoenix had had two turns. 6) In order to avoid a debilitating preoccupation with the past, no mention or replaying of any of the game's reminiscences before or after the sessions themselves.

Helen, a new Gardner-Crowell braille-writer in her hands, recorded the evening's twelve reminiscences and called down anyone who repeated any of the old shibboleths. As Zoe discovered, accusations of encroaching senility flew around the circle when this happened. No worries tonight, though. She had never played before, and there'd be no whistle-blowing no matter what words she spoke into the quiet ring of their anticipation.

"Three months," Toodles said. "It's been three months since we've done this. Back when Yuichan was ill."

"Go ahead, then," Helen said. "You start, Toodles."

The group's silence grew. The girder-cars above them slid in slow motion down the steeps of the dome. In three or four minutes Toodles dropped a word into the pooling dark, the well of their ancient breaths:

"*Fudgsicles,*" she said.

Paul, Zoe noticed, had his head thrown all the way back over the top of his chair, his eyes all goggly and shiny. The old man's mouth was open, too. If he hadn't already moved his butt back into the chair, he would have fallen to the roof tiles.

It was Parthena's turn. Three or four minutes after Toodles' reminiscence, the tall black woman said,

"*Scup'nins.*" Scuppernongs, that meant. A kind of grape.

When the word had echoed in their heads for a while, Luther said, "Paul isn't going to say nothin', Zoe. You go ahead now. It's your turn." No, he wasn't going to say anything, Paul: he was still mouthing Parthena's word.

As for Zoe, she was ready. She had thought of it while Jerry was explaining the rules to her. But it wouldn't do to blurt it out, it wouldn't do to show she'd been thinking ahead of the game. (Surely, they all did it, though.) So she waited. Then, leaning forward to look into the pedestrian park below, she gave the word to her new family:

"*Fireflies. . . .*"

6   mount fujiyama and the orpianoogla

In their suite on the fourth floor the Phoenix slept in a circular common room, their beds positioned around a hub where the self-locomoting biomonitor cabinet (the first of three on the floor) had already taken up its brooding watch. Each bed had a nightstand, an effects-bureau, and an easy chair in its vicinity, as well as plasti-cloth dividers that, at a finger's touch, would roll automatically into place. Since no one seemed to use these, Zoe, grateful to Paul for having fetched her a nightgown, got ready for bed in front of the others.

Like having six Rabons in the room with you. Well, five: Jerry had powered himself off somewhere. "Like some time to himself 'fo' turnin' in," Parthena said. But even five Rabons was plenty, even if they were decent enough not to devour you with their eyes. (Rabon never had been.) Old Paul, of the five, excepted. Again.

Anyhow, it didn't take this creaky crew long to start plying the waters of Nod. No, sir. Everyone off, it seemed, but Zoe herself. She even heard Jerry come whirring back into the snore-ridden room and hoist himself out of the wheel chair onto his bed. In five or ten minutes he, too, was rowing himself under. Only Zoe had her head clear, her whole, fatigued body treading against the desire to be drowned in sleep. My sweet lord, what a day! Every bit of it passed in front of her eyes.

Then Zoe heard the sobs. For a long time she listened to them. It was Toodles, two beds away, heart-troubled Toodles.

Feeling for slippers that weren't there, Zoe got out of bed. She walked barefooted to the easy chair beside Toodles, sat down, and smoothed back the woman's moist, frizzly bangs. "Can you tell me what it is?"

Unnhuh; nope. Strangled, desperate noises.

"Is it about that supper-time business, Toodles? Hope not. Up against you I look like the . . . the Wicked Witch of the North." Which was a Glinda-the-Good lie if she'd ever told one: white lie, though.

Subsiding strangles—"It . . . isn't . . . that"—trailing off into hiccups. "Really . . . it . . . isn't . . . that." Apparently to prove this contention, Toodles pulled herself up to a sitting posture. Across her rumpled lap she reeled in, inch by hand-wrung inch, a dressing gown that had been spread out over her bedclothes. A corner of it went to her throat, and was held there.

"What, then? Can you say?"

A modicum of control now. "Yuichan," Toodles said. "I was thinking of Yuichan. You see this robe, Zoe. . . . He gave me this robe." It was too dark to see well, but Toodles turned the robe toward her and displayed it anyway, an occasional hiccup unsteadying her hands. All Zoe got was a musty whiff of a familiar, kidneylike odor.

"Here," Zoe said, and punched on the reading light on Toodle's headboard. A circle of paleness undulated on the dressing gown. Execrable taste, Helen had said. And rightly: On one side of the robe, an embroidered, snow-covered peak; on the other (once Toodles had lifted the limp lapel so that she could see them), the words *Mount Fujiyama*. An ugly and smelly garment, no matter how you hemmed or whiffed it.

"Oh, I know it's not to everybody's taste," Toodles said. "But it reminds me of Yuichan. He mail-ordered it from San Francisco four years ago when he learned that there was a very sick Japanese woman in the nursing section of the hostel. That was just like Yuichan. He gave the robe to that poor woman. A coupla years later, when the woman died and her son threw away almost all of her effects, Yuichan brought the gown back and gave it to me. Oh, it was tight on me and it smelled like urine, all right, but I knew what spirit Yuichan gave it in and I had it washed and washed—till I was afraid it'd fall apart in the water." Toodles spread the dressing gown over her knees. "And tonight . . . tonight . . . it reminds me of him . . . of Yuichan . . . just ever so much." And propped her elbows on her shrouded knees and lowered her face into her hands.

The consolation Zoe gave Toodles was that of sitting beside her until the poor, blowsy woman, mascara long since washed away, fell into a sleep as mortally shallow as the crater holes of her eyes.

But the next afternoon, in the room they called the recreation center, Toodles sat at the battery-powered orpianoogla and led them all in a songfest: thin, strained vocal cords reaching for notes those cords couldn't remember. In fact, only Toodles had an unimpaired range, a bravura contralto that could soar like an undercourse glissador or tiptoe stealthily through a pianissimo lullaby. With one arm she led their singing, with her free hand she rippled the keys, punched buttons, flipped toggles, and mixed in the percussion. Nor did her heavy legs keep her from foot-pedaling like an unbeliever on burning coals. The whole suite of rooms reverberated with Toodles' music, and Zoe, clapping and croaking with the rest, wondered dimly if she had dreamed, only dreamed, the midnight despair of this boisterous Phoenix.

"Very good!" Toodles would shout at them between choruses. "Ain't you glad we're too old for them jackasses who passed the Retrenchment Edicts to come in here and shut us up?!"

Zoe was. Outlawed music they were souling on, outlawed lyrics and proscribed morals-corrupting rhythms. Old times. As they clapped and sang, Helen told Zoe that Toodles had once been a renaissance-swing headliner in a New Orleans hookah club. "Turn of the century and a few years after," Helen stage-whispered in her ear as they all clapped to the rumbling orpianoogla. "When she was forty she was doing a bushman, pop-op-rah review in D.C. Forty! Quite professional, the old newsfax say." Since '35, when the ward reps and urban councilmen panicked, those kinds of performances had been totally *nyetted,* at least in Atlanta. Who knew, these days, what other cities did?

"All right!" Toodles shouted. "This one's 'Ef Ya Gotta Zotta!' Way back to twenny-awht—tooo, evvverbodddy!"

So they all sang, the orpianoogla singlehandedly—literally single-handedly—sounding like the entire defunct, blown-away, vinylscrutchy Benny Goodman Orchestra of a century ago. Or Glenn Miller's, maybe. This was the chorus:

> *Ef ya gotta zotta*
> *Thenna zotta wa me:*
> *Durnchur lay ya hodwah*
> *On tha furji Marie.*
> *Ef ya gotta zotta,*
> *Then ya gotta zotta wa me!*

My sweet lord! Zoe remembered the whole song, every kaporni word of all seven verses. She and Rabon had danced to that one; they'd done the buck-and-wing jitters in the remodeled Regency lobby ballroom. My sweet lord, she thought: "Ef Ya Gotta Zotta!"

But after the last sing-through of the chorus, Toodles barreled out of the renaissance-swing retrospective and into a hard, hard computer-augmented tour of late-twenties/early-thirties racked-and-riled terrorism. With the advent of this deliberate cacophony, old Paul stopped stomping and let his mouth fall open, just as it had during the rotational reminiscence. The others, like Zoe, irresistibly fell to swaying in their chairs.

Toodles sang the ominous lyrics, and sang them so certainly that you could look at her full, jowly face and see that despite the sags, and wens, and ludicrous, smeared lips, she was living every note, vivisecting every lurid word and dragging its guts out for the purpose of feeding her own and her listeners' irrational fears. (Which was fun: a musical horror movie.) Toodles sang, and sang, and sang. She sang "Walnut Shell Nightmare," "Tomb of the Pharaohs," "Crimson Clay Tidal Wave," and "Outside Sky." When the last note of the or-pianoogla died away, a rain of bravos fell down on the (incredibly) beginning-to-blush Miz Joyce "Toodles" Malins-Phoenix. Even Paul joined in, though he stomped like a jackass rather than hallooed.

"Her first concert since Yuichan died," Helen whispered.

"Encore!" Jerry shouted. "That we wish more of!"

"Hooooi!" Luther said. "I ain't heard her sing or play so well since Year-end Week in '38."

"I'm in as fine a voice as I was thirty years ago," Toodles said, turning on her stool. "It's hard to believe and it sounds like bragging, but by God! it's the gospel truth."

"Damn straight," Luther said.

"You ain' done, though," Parthena said. "Finish out now like we awways do, 'fo' we have to go eat."

Toodles, turning back to the keyboard, honored this request. Ignoring the buttons, switches, and resonator pins on the console, she played with both hands: an old melody, two hundred years almost. Everyone sang, everyone harmonized. Zoe found that, just as with "Ef Ya Gotta Zotta," she remembered the words—every word, each one called to her lips from a time-before-time that had nothing to do with the Urban Nucleus, or with Sanders and Lannie, or with Mr. Leland and the Geriatrics Hostel. And it wasn't timesickness or nostalgia that fed her recollection of the lyrics (some things you don't ever want to go back to), but instead a celebration of the solidity of the present: this present: the moment itself. They all sang:

> *'Way down upon the Swanee River*
> *Far, far away,*
> *There's where my heart is turning ever,*
> *There's where the old folks stay.*

They even sang the stanza about the old plantations and the plaintive line "Oh, darkies, how my heart grows weary," Luther and Parthena too, and none of what they sang distressed them. Stephen Foster somehow was and wasn't Stephen Foster when interpreted by an orpianoogla. Sticks and stones, Zoe thought, and names can never . . .

Why, only a week ago her own daughter had called her, during a moment of ill-concealed morning sickness, a mummified witch. Zoe had chuckled: *Clucka-clucka-cluck.* What else could she do? When you're two steps from the finish line, you laugh at the self-loathing insults of also-rans. You have to. Even in the melancholy performance of a nigh-on dead-and-gone work of a sure-enough dead-and-gone composer, Toodles' whole body laughed. Toodles was two steps from the finish line. They all were. And it certainly wasn't death they were running at, not as Zoe saw it. No, sir. Something else altogether; something else.

7   parthena

That evening, after the orpianoogla-assisted songfest, Parthena, Helen, and Jerry saw to the cooking of supper. And after supper Zoe

helped these three clean up in the galley beside the dining room
(whereas, downstairs, three levels under, Lannie and Sanders had
only a kitchen board in their cubicle and no dining room at all). A
beautiful day it had been, a zippity-doo-dah day if she'd ever lived
one. Not since Rabon . . .

"You quilt?" Parthena asked her as they put the last of the china
away. But Zoe's attention was momentarily elsewhere. Jerry, in his
wheel chair, was handing the plates to Helen, and the blind woman
was stacking them cleanly in the hanging plastic cabinet over the
sink. Before beginning, Helen had produced a pair of miniature black
goggles, or binoculars, from a dress pocket and snapped these on
over her eyes with seemingly only a thin metal bridge-piece to support them. With these in place she moved as if sighted. And yet this
was the first time she had worn the goggles in Zoe's presence.

"Hey, Zoe," Parthena said again. "You quilt?"

"You mean stitch squares together? Sew? Maybe. Things with my
hands I could always bluff through. I'm a bluffer."

"Shoot, we ain' even axed you yet what you good at. Where you
work 'fo' you got put on the Ole Folk Dole Role?"

"Photography," Zoe said. "I took pitchurs. Still ones and moving
ones. And I was good, too, you know. If you want to know the truth,
some of my still pitchurs are pretty moving."

They all laughed. Zoe told them how she and Rabon had been a
team for both the *Journal/Constitution* combine and one of the vis-
ual-media affiliates; neither wrote copy ("I didn't have the schooling
and Rabon hadn't put his to use that way"), but they could both
wield cameras, video portables, and the instant-print-making varie-
ties. She had been better than Rabon was, but from '01 to '09 she
had been taken out of action four times by the onset of motherhood
and he had got more commissions by virtue of his being insuscepti-
ble, as he put it, to pregnancy. But it had all been planned, and after
Melanie was born the UrNu Sitter Mission Program had freed them
both to pursue their careers. Sort of. They got docked an incredi-
ble number of earnies to have Lannie mission-sat for four hours a
day, four days a week, she and Rabon splitting up the remaining
hours and working less frequently as a team. But they'd done it, she
and Rabon, and maybe it was only Lannie's having been their only
child that had caused her to grow up a gimme girl and a sometimes-
sweet, more-usually-petulant young woman. What lovely portraits Zoe
had made of her when she was little, ole sweet-treat Lannie. In a

telecom to her that morning Zoe had asked her daughter to bring
from her sleeper-cove only the few clothes she had there and the photographs on the walls, and Melanie had said she would bring them:
maybe Mr. Leland had them already.

"Well, if you can shoot pitchurs," Parthena said, "you can he'p us
knock off that new wall banner what you seen on the quiltin' frame in
the rec center. So you c'mon now, Zoe."

They were finished in the galley. Parthena led them out of there
and down the corridor: seventy-six years old and as straight and
skinny as a broom handle.

"Other work I got this evening," Jerry said. "If you all will excuse
me." And he zoomed around them in his winged chair and disappeared into a room Zoe hadn't been in yet. A closetlike alcove between the rec center and the dining room.

Luther and Toodles were already at the quilting frame when they
got there: a monstrous, plastic contraption over which the layer of
sewn squares, the synthetic cotton batting, and the underlining had
all been tautly spread and whipped down. Zoe had seen this thing—"a
Wright brothers plane made of sewing scraps"—during their afternoon songfest, but it had been behind them and partially hidden by a
moving screen and no one had volunteered to explain its purpose or
its function to her.

Now the screen had been shoved back against the wall, and Toodles and Luther were sitting at opposite ends of the frame pushing
and pulling their needles through the three layers of material. Helen,
still wearing her goggles, sat down between them, and Parthena and
Zoe took up chairs on the other side of the frame, which was tilted
like an aileron. It was 1903, and they were Orville and Wilbur,
crazy-quilt pilots at a Kitty Hawk where the sands of time had trans-
mogrified into linoleum tile.

"Helen," Zoe blurted, "with those goggles on you look like you're
gonna fly us right out of here—right up to the dome." Ooops. Was
that the right thing to say to a blind person?

Helen raised her head and stared at Zoe. Straight on, the goggles—
or glasses, or binoculars—gave her the look not of a biplane pilot but
of an unfriendly outerspace critter. "Aren't they hideous?" Helen
said. "I'd wear them all the time except for the way they look." And,
expertly, she began plunging her own needle into the layers of cloth
and forcing it back through.

Parthena showed Zoe how to do it, giving her a needle and thimble and making her watch her technique. "I taught us all how to quilt— but Paul he don' like it and use his weekend to think on keepin' him- sef a-live for awways. Jerry he got real bidness to tend to. Otherwise, he 'most awways here. Now you keep yo' thumb in that thimble, gal, or that needle it gonna bite you. Look here—"

Well, Zoe had sewn before and she'd always been pretty handy anyway. Easy, take it easy, she told herself, and pretty soon she was dipping in and digging out as well as any of them, stitching those jaunty, colored squares—yellow, green, and floral-print blue in a step- pin'-'round-the-mountain pattern—to batting and lining alike. Much concentration to begin with, like a pilot taking off; then, the hang of it acquired, free, relaxing flight. Nobody talked, not anyone.

When had she ever felt so serene and at peace? Serene and at peace, yes, but with a tingle of almost physical pleasure throwing off cool little sparks up and down her backbone. The quiet in the room was a part of this pleasure.

Then Parthena began to talk, but not so that it violated the silence they were working in: "I use to do this up in Bondville, when my son Maynard jes' a little flea and the dome ain' even half finished yet. Oh, the wind it blow then, it didn' have no dome to stop it, and we use these quilts to sleep unner, not to hang up on them ole broke-up plasser walls of ours. I still 'member how Maynard, when I was workin', would get himsef up unner the frame—a wooden un my hus- ban' made—and walk back and fo'th like a sojer so that all you could see was the bump of his head goin' from one end of that frame to the other, up and down, till it seem he warn' ever gonna wear out. Laugh? Lord, I use to laugh him into a resentful meanness 'cause he didn' unnerstan' how funny his ole head look."

She laughed in a way that made Zoe join her. "Now he got three babies of his own—Georgia, Mack, and Moses—and a wife what can do this good as me; better maybe, she so spry."

They quilted for an hour. When they broke off, Parthena insisted that Zoe come back to the dormitory common room and see the "pitchurs of my gran'babies. Shoot, you like pitchurs and babies, don' you?" So Zoe went. She sat in the easy chair while Parthena, having lowered her bed to an accommodating height, sat like an ebony stork on its edge.

"This one my pert Georgie," Parthena said, handing her a picture of a handsome little black girl. "She twelve now and one sassy fas' chile. She gonna get out of Bondville all by hersef, jes' on charm and speed." The two boys were older and a little meaner-looking; they probably had to be. None of them were babies. "I jes' want you to see I had me a fam'ly 'fo' the Phoenix. I ain' like Luther and po' Toodles what suffer till they was pas' sixxy without finin' a real home. Now, though, they got us an' we got them—but they come a long road, Zoe, a long road. Jerry, too. Sometime I jes' lif' up a prayer for how lucky I been."

"I never did pray much," Zoe said, "but I know what the urge is like." Like loving somebody in a way that didn't permit you to tell them: Zoe remembered.

They talked while some of the others got ready for bed. Parthena showed Zoe a set of dentures that had been made for her in 2026; she even made Zoe take them in her hand and examine them as if they were the teeth of an australopithecine. "They clean," she said. "I ain' wore 'em since '29. The reason I show 'em to you is 'cause they made by Dr. Nettlinger."

"Who?"

"Gee-rard Nettlinger. You 'member, Zoe. He that fellow what shot Carlo Bitler. Stood up in the middle of the Urban Council meetin' and shot that tough, holy man. The day I heard that, I took out them dentures and never put 'em in again. They shoddy-made, anyhow. Only keep 'em so Maynard can sell 'em one day. People go all greedy-crazy over doodads what b'long to 'sassins. People crazy."

"Yep," Zoe agreed. "My daddy said it was the new idolatry."

"It idle, awright. Don' make a mussel-shell worth o' sense."

Then, somehow, their conversation got around to why the original family members had chosen Phoenix—rather than something light like Sweetheart or O'Possum—as the group's surname. Zoe said she had supposed it was because Atlanta was sometimes called the Phoenix City, having risen again from its own ashes after the Civil War (which Zoe's grandfather, even in the 1980s, had insisted on calling the War Between the States—as if that made some kind of significant difference). And when the dome went up in that decade linking the old century with the new one, Atlanta had undergone still another incarnation. Were those part of the group's original reasons?

"They part of 'em awright," Parthena said. "But jes' part. Another one is, we all come out of our own ashes when we 'greed to the cov'nant. We all bone again, Zoe, like in Jesus."

"Well, I thought that, too, you know. That's what makes the name so good."

"Yeah. But Paul he like it 'cause the phoenix a 'Gyptian bird what was im-ortal, you see. It only *look like* it die, then it spurt back up jes' as feathery and fine as befo'. He a mean man on that pint, Paul is."

"He ought to be happy with the Ortho-Urban Church, then. It says the same sort of thing happens to *people* after they die."

"Ain' the same, though, Paul say. 'Cause people do die, no lookin'-like in it, and they don' get a body back at all. Paul he hung up on the body."

"You don't say? It's good to know he's not just a Dirty Old Man."

"Oh, he that, too, he sho' is." They chuckled together. "But it the other thing keep him thinkin' and rockin' and figgerin'. The Phoenix lucky. Mos' of us still got our mines. But Paul he eighty-some-odd and his been goin' ever since we marry. Mr. Leland awmos' didn' 'cept him in this program five year back, you see. Res' of us made him say yes. So Mr. Leland fine'ly 'cepted him, hopin' we could haul him back on the road. We done it, too. Pretty much."

"Did Paul suggest the name?"

"No. Maybe. I don' 'member zackly. What I do 'member is that the name fit, it fit fo' all kinds o' reasons. One other, and maybe the bes' un, was a story my gran'daddy tole that his own daddy tole him. It was 'bout a slave chile, a little gal, what was made to watch the two-year-ole baby of the boss man, the 'marster' as gran'daddy say his daddy say.

"Well, that little baby fell down the steps while the slave gal was watchin' it: she took her eye away a minute and it bumped down them ole steps and took on a-hollerin'. Scared, you know, but not kilt. Well, when the white mistresses in the house heard this, they took on a-cryin' and carryin' on terrible—jes' like that baby been murdered. They kep' on till the marster himsef come strollin' in and axed them what it was. When they tole him, he pick up a board and hit that little slave gal in the head. Kilt her. Then he gathered 'round him a bunch of niggers (my gran'daddy he tole it this way, now) and ordered 'em to thow the gal in the river. The gal's mama begged and prayed and axed him to spare the gal fo' buryin', but he paid her no mine and made 'em thow the chile in.

"Now this where the story get magical, Zoe. The little girl's name was Phoebe, and five slaves and the girl's mama went down to the river with her—the biggest nigger in front, carryin' little Phoebe with her bloody head hangin' down, mournful and cold. This big nigger he

thew the gal in like the marster order him to, Phoebe's mama jes'
moanin' and beatin' on hersef, and then he walk right in affer the girl
and hole himsef unner water till he drown. The others they resolve to
do the same. And they do it too, the mama goin' in las' and prayin' to
God they all be taken up together.

"One night later, the white folks from the big house is walkin' by
the river and all at once they see seven small, ugly birds fly up outa
the water and go sailin' straight at the moon. The higher they get, the
brighter and purtier and bigger they get too—till at las' they stop in
the sky like stars and stay still over the big house where them white
folks live. A new constellation they become, which evvyone on that
plantation call the Phoenix—'cep' this constellation don' move like it
s'posed to but jes' sit with its wings spread, wide and haughtylike,
over the marster's house.

"And that the story, Zoe. Jerry he say he never heard of no constellation call the Phoenix. But with that dome up there who gonna
'member zackly how the sky look? Nobody; not nobody.

"An' I believe it still up there somewhere."

8 *flashforward: at the end of winter*

Almost three old-style months after entering the Geriatrics Hostel, not as patient or prisoner but as a genuine, come-and-go-as-you-
please resident, Zoe sat on the roof one evening and recalled the steps
of her slow immersion in the Phoenix clan. Supper was eaten: a
calming warmth in her stomach and bowels.

Pretty soon the family would decide. When you're streaking toward either seventy or eighty—as well as that something else that isn't
death—long courtships are as foolish as whirlwind ones. Three
months is plenty to decide in, maybe too much. Anyhow, they were
formally going to pass on her, and it might be that in giving her this
hour of solitude, this retrospective moment on the darkening rooftop,
they were already engaged in the process of their decision. Was it in
doubt? And hadn't they been so engaged all along, every day that
Zoe had lived among them sharing their lives?

One girder-car tonight, and a flight of pigeons wheeling together in
great loops in front of a huge, neon Coca-Cola sign.

Look what had happened in these three old-style months: For one
thing, she had found out that the septigamoklans in the Tower

weren't living there as welfare recipients solely, as so many helpless
mendicants on the Old Folk Dole Role. Most of them had spent their
lives paying into the medicaid and future-secure programs of the city;
since 2035, the year young Mr. Leland's study had begun, the quarterly benefits of all the people in the hostel had been pooled and
invested. This was done with permission from the residents, only a
scant number of whom denied the UrNu Human Development Commission the legal administration of their estates. And against these
holdouts, no penalty at all. In any event, the dividends on these
pooled investments and the interest on several well-placed accounts
financed the feeding and the sheltering of the residents and even provided them with personal funds to draw on. They also helped remu-
nerate the surviving families of those who came into the study.

Each family had a budgeter: Helen was the Phoenix budgeter,
and, wearing those little, black, vision-assisting binoculars, she kept
books like a born-and-bred C.P.A. (which was C.U.A. now, Zoe
remembered). Other times, she used her braille-writer. Anyhow, they
weren't dole-riders, the people in the Tower—although Zoe had to
admit that the hostel's system was dependent upon the good offices
and business acumen of those who administered their benefits. This
drawback was partially offset by the budgeter of each septigamoklan's having a seat on the Commission Board of Financial
Planners, as well as by the judicious appeal to market-forecasting
computers.

Down on Level 3 with Sanders and Melanie, Zoe's quarterly allot-
ments—only a day or two after the future-secure printout chit arrived
—had been eaten up like nutmeg-sprinkled oatmeal. The Nobles gar-
nisheed the entire value of the chit, without even so much as a coun-
tersignature, for granting Zoe the privilege of living with them. Only
the coming of their child and the prospect of a lump-sum reward
from the commission had induced them to hand Zoe over. Just like a
prisoner-exchange, or the sale of a decrepit and recalcitrant slave.
Yessir, Zoe thought: Sold down the river. But a river out of which it
was possible to fly like a sleek bird, dripping light as if it were water.
An old bird, Zoe was; a bird of fire being reborn in the Lethe of
Sanders and Melanie's forgetfulness and neglect.

"A pox on self-pity," Zoe said aloud, surprising herself. Overhead,
the torchlit girder-car had almost reached the acme of the dome.

Well, what else? What else? Lots of things. She had met members
of other septigamoklans, the O'Possums and the Cadillacs and the

Graypanthers and oh! all the others, too. There'd been a party one Saturday night in the garden, with food and music and silly paper decorations. Hostel attendants had closed the patio windows and pulled the acoustical draperies in the intensive-care rooms, and everyone else had gone to town. Young Mr. Leland, at their invitation, had been there, and nobody but Paul of all the Phoenix went to bed before 4 A.M. Sometime after midnight Toodles led everybody in a joyful, cacophonous version of "Ef Ya Gotta Zotta."

Then there were Sunday afternoons, alone with Paul or Luther or maybe, just maybe, one of the girls. During the week, field trips to the Atlanta Museum of Arts ("Boring as hell," said Paul) and Consolidated Rich's and the pedestrian-park flea markets. Two different excursions to the new theatre-in-the-round opera house, where they had watched a couple of interesting, council-sanctioned hologramic movies. They were OK, sort of plotless and artsy, but OK. Back in their own fourth-floor suite, though, they could show old-fashioned, two-dimensional movies; and just since Zoe had been there, the Phoenix had held a Rock Hudson festival and a mock seminar in the "Aesthetic of Late Twentieth-century X-rated Cinema," during which Jerry had turned off the sound tracks and lectured to quite humorous effect with the aid of a stop-action button and a pointer.

After one such lecture, when the rooftop was theirs, Luther and Zoe had laid out a croquet course; and, except for Jerry, in 23° C. weather (the internal meteorologists had given them one or two cold days, though) they had all played without their clothes! Nude, as Helen said. And that had been one of those rare occasions *not* requiring meticulous attention to detail—quilting, putting away dishes, keeping books—when Helen wore her goggle-binoculars. And, not counting the pulse-cued bracelet, *only* the goggle-binoculars. The idea, lifted from an old book of short stories, had been Toodles', but Paul had given it a vigorous seconding. And so Zoe, like a girl going skinny-dipping in the before-the-dome countryside, shed her paper gown, her underthings, her inhibitions, and let the temperate air swaddle her sensitive flesh and her every self-conscious movement. Much merriment. And no repugnance for their blotched and lignifying bodies; instead, a strange tenderness bubbling under the surface merriment.

What, after all, did the bunions, and the varicosities, and the fleshy folds signify? Zoe could answer that: the onset of age and their emphatic peoplehood, male and female alike. Finally, that day, she forgot the sensuous stirrings of the dome winds, lost herself in the game, and became extremely angry when Parthena sent her ball careening off into an unplayable position. Yessir, that had been an all-fun day.

And what else? Well, the Phoenix had given her a still camera, and for the first time in ten or fifteen years she had begun taking pictures again. The camera was an old but still beautifully operable Double-utility Polaroid, and the first project Zoe undertook was the capturing in stark black and white of the faces of her new family. Posed photographs, candid ones, miniatures, darkroom enlargements: group portraits, singles, double-exposure collages, meditative semiabstracts. The best of these went up in the rec center. The Wall of the Phoenix, this gallery became, and it was framed on both sides by bright, quilted wall banners.

Paul and Toodles both grew quite vain about certain of these portraits and occasionally got caught staring at their favorites: teen-agers ogling themselves in a mirror. Vanity, vanity, saith somebody or other, Zoe remembered. But Helen never donned her little binoculars to look at her own photographed image, even though she had more justification than either Paul or Toodles. One day Zoe asked her why. "I haven't looked at my own face since I was thirty," she said, "because I am quite content with the self-deluding vision of my thirty-year-old one that still resides up here." She tapped her head. Then she showed Zoe an old photograph of herself, one that glinted in the common room's fluorescents and revealed a woman of disgusting, not-to-be-gainsaid beauty. "I can *feel* what I look like now," Helen said. "I don't have to *look*." Even so, Zoe's portraits of Helen did her no disservice; in fact, they launched a thousand tiresome accolades from the men, Paul in particular—when, that is, he wasn't mesmerized by his own amber-eyed, celluloidally distanced self. Well, why not? Zoe's pitchurs were damn good, if she did say so herself, just by way of echoing the others.

The month Spring was coming on. What else could she recall about Winter in the hostel? Visits by Melanie and Sanders. The prospect of a grandchild. This last excited her, tickled her like air on her naked body, and for it alone did she anticipate the biweekly drop-ins of her daughter and son-in-law. No, that wasn't true. Lannie she always had a hankering to see, whether a baby was growing in her womb or not. Her daughter Lannie was, her own flesh and that of dead Rabon: her daughter. Only fatuous Sanders did she have difficulty tolerating, and he had never once called her anything as brutal as a mummified witch, not ever in his life. So what did you do?

Zoe, for her part, never visited them in their Level 3 cubicle, and when they came to see her, thereby perfunctorily carrying out their filial duty, she always greeted them in the quadrangle where they had first put her on the block. That made Sanders uncomfortable: he scuffed his street slippers in the gravel and craned his neck around as if looking for the one mean old codger in the hostel who would use his balcony advantage to shoot him, Paul, with a blowgun or pellet rifle. Minor sport for Zoe, watching her son-in-law sidelong as she asked Melanie how she felt—if the morning sickness had gone away yet ("There are pills for that, Mother!")—what sex the Jastov-Hunter test had said the child would be—other things that Lannie was at last willing to talk about.

But she never used her freedom to visit them on Level 3, and they never extended her such an invitation. No, sir. Not once.

Zoe tilted her head back and saw that the girder-car she had been following was nowhere in sight. My sweet lord, hadn't she been up on the Tower roof a long time? And hadn't the time flown by? They were reaching a decision on her, the Phoenix were. That was it.

Was the outcome in doubt? Would Mr. Leland send her into another incomplete septigamoklan (if one existed) because of a single person's snide, blackballing veto? As Mr. Leland had explained it, they could easily do that, blackball her. How would she feel if they did? As far as that went, did she herself want to marry with the Phoenix, to join with them in a new covenant?

Well, the answer to that was an easy one. The answer was yes; yes, she wanted to marry with Luther, Parthena, Toodles, Paul, Helen, and Jerry. And her reason for wanting to was a simple one, too: she was in love.

9   spending the afternoon with luther

On her first Sunday among the Phoenix, Toodles told Zoe that although it was her, Toodles', turn to spend the afternoon with Luther, she would be happy to yield to Zoe. "I don't feel all that good," she explained, "and, besides, it's the only really hospitable way for me to behave, don't you think?" Propped up in bed, Yui-chan's awful Fujiyama robe bundled about her shoulders, Toodles was eating a breakfast roll that a cartlike servo-mechanism had wheeled into the common room from the galley. A hairline smear of artificial-peach jelly rode Toodles' upper lip like a candied mustache, and Zoe wanted to take a tissue and daub it away.

"If you don't feel well, should you be eating jelly rolls?"

Toodles winked. "You know the ole saying: jelly rolls is medicine. But I'm having mine this morning and don't need a dose this afternoon."

"Does 'spend the afternoon' mean what the young drakes and duckies call 'bodyburning'?" Why was she asking? She already knew the answer. Parthena and Helen were off to an Ortho-Urban service somewhere on West Peachtree, Paul was asleep across the room from them, and Jerry and Luther had both got up early and gone down the hall toward the rec center. Zoe had declined an invitation to attend services with Parthena and Helen. Now she wished she were with them.

"You ain't slow, Zoe," Toodles said. "I'da been blunter, but it embarrasses Errol."

"Errol?"

Flipping up the bed linen and extending a heavy leg, Toodles put one bunion-afflicted foot on the tray of the servo-cart. "Errol," she reiterated. The cart hummed and backed up, but Toodles got her leg off the tray in time to avoid a nasty spill. A doughnut did drop to the floor, though. "Temperamental, Errol is. . . . You're not thinking of saving yourself for after the covenant ceremony, are you?"

"Well, if I am, I been saving myself so long that my interest's now a whole lot greater than my principles." That was the punch line of a joke Rabon used to tell. It didn't suit Zoe's mood, which was cautious and a bit skeptical, but it perfectly suited Toodles'—she was delighted. I always play to my audience, Zoe thought; can't seem to help it. Aloud, attempting to recover, "I never was one to kiss on the first date, Toodles; just not the sort."

"Oh, I always said that, too. Anyhow, you've already slept in the same room with the Phoenix, you know. It's not like you'd be sacking out with some bulgy-britches thugboy." And at last she wiped the peach-jelly mustache off her upper lip. "Please say yes. Luther's liable to be hurt." And with her little, gold remote-con box Toodles beckoned Errol (who, Zoe noted with some annoyance, was something of a whiner) closer to the bed so that she could pick up another breakfast pastry.

"OK," Zoe answered, almost as if it were someone else: not her.

So that afternoon she and Luther walked through the pedestrian courts outside the Geriatrics Hostel and stopped to eat lunch at a little restaurant that seemed to be made entirely of plate glass; it was nestled under the stone eaves of a much taller building, though, and had green, reed-woven window shades to keep out the glare of the dome's day lamps. Atmosphere, Rabon would have said the shades gave the place.

They sat in a simulated-leather booth with potted ferns on both sides of them to cut off their view to the front door and drank scotch and water while waiting for the steward to bring them their meal. A Sunday drink. Well, that was something the Retrenchment Edicts hadn't outlawed. You could get one right after your favorite Ortho-Urban services, which was what half the people in this place, it looked like, were doing. The other half were sharing table hookahs and letting the thin smoke coil away from them through the decorative ferns.

"Good food," Luther said. "They do know how to throw together good food here." He was a little nervous, Zoe could see. He kept putting his malletlike hands on the table, dropping them to his lap, taking a sip of his drink, then sticking those heavy, purplish hands back on the table. "You ain't disturbed that Toodles pushed you into this, are you now?" he said, his brow comically corrugating.

"Luther, my daughter and son-in-law *pushed* me into this, not Toodles. And they don't even know when they're doing me a favor."

That loosened him, more than the scotch even. He asked her questions about her family, he told her about himself. Their meal came—a vegetable dinner featuring hydroponically grown snapbeans, zucchini, tomatoes (stewed), and some sort of hybrid greens—and Luther, between bites, kept on talking. A warm rumble.

"I was born the same year Dr. King was assassinated," he said at one point. "That's how I got my name. The shame of it is, I lived to see that sort of business over and over before the cities went undercover—and then after the doming, too. I wasn't quite six when I saw a young man shoot Mrs. Martin Luther King, Sr., and several other people right in the old man's own church. My church, too. Then. More died after the dome was up. That young Bitler he was the last one, and it's been eleven years since we've had to walk our hungry-children miles to some good man's grave.

"You know, I was so sick I almost shot myself that year, I almost took a razor to my wrists. Back when you could breathe, when you could look up and see a sun or a moon, some men used to be born in the year a comet come through and wait their whole lives till it come back again so that they could die. That year, I was so down I knew it had been written that Luther Battle was supposed to come in and go out with another man's assassination.

"But I was in my thirty-second year with McAlpine Company in '29, and we had a lot of work that year. Bitler had done made a lot of people angry, he had got a lot of ole dead asses movin'. After he was shot, there was all kind of uproar to tear down the surfaceside slums and stick up some kind of halfway decent housing on top of the streets instead of under 'em. I was on McAlpine's demolition crews, not the construction ones. Sixty years old and I was workin' off my anger and grief by wreckin' ole tenements; it was the only way they let us make anything of our own. I bossed the demolition of fifteen buildings that year, workin' it all out so that walls come down clean and the guts got hauled off neat. Cranes, cats, tractors, trucks, all of 'em doin' this and doin' that 'cause of how I told 'em to go. Only thing that kep' me sane, Zoe: tearin' down another century's toilets and doin' it with that century's equipment. Then the uproar quieted off, the work contracts run out, and the Urban Council didn't do nothin' to start 'em up again. We still got some damn ghettos in Atlanta, no matter what the ward reps say. Bondville, one of the worst. Parthena's boy and her gran'chillun still live there. . . . But that bad year was over, and I had survived it, Zoe.

"Retired, then. Lived alone on 7, *under,* just like I had all the years I was with McAlpine. The company had been my family since all the way back to '97. My mama and daddy was lucky: they died before they had to see a dome go up over their heads. Me, I wasn't lucky: I had to sign on with McAlpine and help build that damn thing up there."

"You helped build the dome?" Zoe said. She'd never met anyone who had, not anybody who'd admit to it at least.

"I did. They was twelve different outfits, different companies, workin' to do it, everybody goin' from blueprints they had run off a computer somewhere up East or maybe in California. We were a year behind New York and Los Angeles, McAlpine told us, and we had to catch up. He was still sayin' this in '97, the year I come on, three after the Dome Projec' started; and no one ever asked why the hell we had to catch up with this foolishness that New York and L.A. was pursuin'. Most of us hadn't had any kinds of jobs at all before the projec', so we shut up and did what all of a sudden the city was givin' us money to do. Yessir, Zoe. We started in a-buildin' a pyramid, a great ole tomb to seal ourselves into and never come out of again. Slaves in Egypt might have to work twenty years to build a House of the Dead for Pharaoh, but they didn't have to lie down in it themselves. We was more advanced. We done ours in ten and managed it so we could put the lid on ourselves from the *inside*. No Moses anywhere to say, 'Hey! wait a minute, you don't want to live in this place forever!' But we were pullin' down some decent cash, even if they was UrNu dollars, and didn't think there'd ever be a day you couldn't see at least a little square of sky somewhere, at least enough blue to make denim for a workingman's britches. It was an adventure. Nobody thought he was just another one of Pharaoh's slavin' niggers. I didn't, anyhow. Even when I first come on with McAlpine, I felt like *I* was the chief mucketymuck myself."

"How come?"

"Well, we had to go up to the sections of the dome's gridwork that we'd completed, and we always went up in girder-cars, just like the ones you see comb-crawlin' along after dark with their torches alight. You worked on platforms or from harnesses on the girder-car, and you was always right out there over the whole damn state, you could see everything—even when the wind was streamin' by you like it wanted to shake all your hard labor into rubble and scrap. Stone Mountain. All kinds of lakes. The mountains up by Gainesville.

"And kudzu, Zoe, kudzu like you've never seen or can even remember. That ole madman vine ran itself over everything, telephone poles and broken-down barns and even some of them cheapjack townhouses and condo-minny-ums they hammered up all las' century. The whole world was green, dyin' maybe 'cause of that kudzu but so green it made your eyes ache. And up there above the whole world Luther Battle felt like Kheops himself, or King Tut, or whichever one of them mean bastards built the bigges' tomb. And I never did say, 'Hoooi! Luther, why are we doin' this?' "

After their meal, Zoe and Luther went back to the hostel and rode the Tower lift-tube up to the fourth floor. Although she hadn't let him do it in the pedestrian courts on the walk home, in the lift-tube she gave him her hand to hold. Ten years after retiring from the McAlpine Company, he still had calluses on his palm, or the scars of old calluses. In the lift-tube he didn't talk. He was embarrassed again, as if his talking at lunch had been a spiritual bleeding which had left him weak and uncertain of his ground. Well, she was embarrassed too. Only Luther had an advantage: a blush on him wasn't so all-fired conspicuous as it was on her.

In the common room, which was unoccupied by group design and agreement, Luther took her to his bed and made the automatic room dividers roll into place. Bodyburning, the young people called it now. That's what it was for her, too, though not in the way the term was supposed to suggest and not because Luther was a snorting dragon in the act. No, it had been a long time. Rabon was the last, of course, and this ready compliance to the rule of the Phoenix surprised her a little. For years she had been (what was Melanie's amusing vulgarity?) *mummifying,* and you couldn't expect to throw off the cerements, vaporize the balms and preservatives, and come back from your ages-long limbo in one afternoon.

So that afternoon Zoe experienced only the dull excitement of pain; that, and Luther's solicitude. But each Sunday—the next one with Paul, the one after with Luther, the following one with Paul, and so on, depending on inclination and a very loose schedule—it got better. Since she had never really been dead, it didn't take so long as might the hypothetical, attempted resurrection of a Pharaoh. Not anywhere near so long as that. For she was Zoe, Zoe Breedlove, and she no longer remembered her maiden name.

10 *jerry at his tricks*

What did Jerry do in that mysterious alcove between the rec center and the dining room? Zoe wondered because whenever Jerry had a moment of free time—after dinner, before bed, Sunday morning —his wheel chair, humming subsonically, circled about and went rolling off to that little room. And Jerry would be gone for fifteen minutes, or thirty, or maybe an hour, whatever he could spare. What provoked her curiosity was the midnight vision of his puffball hairdo and his sad hollow eyes floating out of the corridor's brightness and into the darkened common room after one of these recurrent disappearances.

On the Sunday night (more properly, the Monday morning) after her conversations, both social and carnal, with Luther, Zoe had this vision again and heard the crippled man unmindfully whistling to himself as he returned from that room: "Zippity-Doo-Dah," it sounded like. And up to his unmade bed Jerry rolled.

Jerry rolls in at night, Zoe thought, and jelly rolls in the afternoon. A muddled, word-fuzzy head she had. It all had something to do with Toodles. And Helen, Parthena, and Luther. Only Paul left out, to date anyway. But these members of the Phoenix were all sleeping.

Sitting up and lowering her feet to the floor she said, "Jerry?"

"Who is it?" She couldn't see his eyes any more, but the macrocephalic helmet of his silhouette turned toward her, dubiously. "Is it Zoe?"

"Yep," she said. "It's me. Can't sleep." She pulled on her dressing gown (Sanders had brought most of her things to the hostel on Saturday afternoon, but had not come up to see her) and walked barefooted on the cold floor over to Jerry's territory.

The Phoenix could certainly saw wood. No danger of these buzz saws waking up; it was enough to make you wish for impaired hearing. Except that each one of the sounds was different, and interesting: an orchestra of snorers. There, a tin whistle. There, a snooglehorn. Over there, a tubaphone. That one, a pair of castanets. And . . .

Jerry grinned quizzically at her and scratched his nose with one finger. "Can't sleep, heh? Would you like to go to the galley for a drink? Maybe some wine. Wine's pretty good for insomnia."

"Wine's pretty good for lots of things," Zoe said. "What I wanted to ask was, what are you up to when you get all antisocial on us and shut yourself up in that closet out there?" She nodded toward the door.

"You're a nice lady. You get a multiple-choice test. A) I'm concocting an eternal-youth elixir. B) I'm perfecting an antigravity device which will spindizzy all of Atlanta out into the stars. C) I'm performing unspeakable crimes of passion on old telescope housings and the jellies in Petri dishes. Or D) I'm . . . I'm . . . My wit fails me, dear lady. Please choose."

"D," Zoe said.

"What?"

"I choose D. You said multiple-choice. That's what I choose."

As if struck with an illuminating insight (for instance, the key to developing an antigravity device), Jerry clapped his hands together and chuckled. "Ah. Even at this late hour, *your* wit doesn't fail *you*," he said. "I am bested."

"Not yet. You haven't given me a real answer yet, and I've been talking to you for almost two minutes."

"Oh ho! In that case, dear Zoe lady, come with me." Jerry Zitel-man-Phoenix circled about in his subsonically humming chair and went rolling through the common room door. Zoe followed.

Down the corridor Jerry glided, Zoe now more conscious of the raw slapping of her feet than of his wheel chair's pleasant purr. Which stopped when he reached the mysterious room. "I would have preferred to wait for tomorrow, you know. But over the years I have learned to honor the moods of insomniac ladies. And, besides, what I have been working on is finished. It won't hurt for you to get a foreglimpse of the issue of my labors. It won't hurt *me*, anyway. *You,* on the other hand, may merely aggravate your sleepless condition."

At two in the morning, if it wasn't later than that, Jerry was a caution, a nonstop caution. Not much like Thursday night on the roof when he had talked about unseeable stars and his lifelong paralysis. Fiddle! Zoe knew better: he was just like he was Thursday night, if you were talking about the underneath part of him; the seeming change was only in his approach to the revelation of this self. Then, candor. Now, a camouflage that he stripteased momentarily aside, then quickly restored. Oh, it wasn't hard to undress this man's soul. You just had to warn yourself not to destroy him by letting him know that you could see him naked. Nope. Keep those pasties in place, wrap up the emotional overflow in an old G-string. And smile, smile, smile.

Because he was funny, Jerry was. In spite of his tricks.

They went into the little room, and he hit the light button. Zoe, standing just inside the door, saw a counter with some sort of duplicating machine on it, reams of paper, an IBM margin-justifying typer (they had had those in the offices of the *Journal/Constitution* combine), and a stack of bright yellow-orange booklets. There were little inset docks in the counter (put there by Luther) so that Jerry could maneuver his wheel chair into comfortable working positions.

Booklets. You didn't see booklets very often. One good reason: The Retrenchment Edicts of '35 had outlawed private duplicating machines. Everyone had a visicom console and better be glad he did. The Phoenix had two such consoles in the rec center, though Zoe couldn't recall seeing anyone use either of them. Why, since she'd been at the hostel, she hadn't tapped into one at all. And now she was seeing booklets: *booklets!*

"I always wondered where Atlanta's pamphleteers holed up," Zoe said. "You preachin' the overthrow of our Urban Charter?"

Jerry put a hand to his breast. "Zoe lady, the name is Zitelman, not Marx, and I am first—no, not first, but last and always—a Phoenix." He took a copy of one of the booklets from the counter and handed it to Zoe, who had moved deeper into his crowded little den of sedition. "This issue, which has been in preparation for three or four weeks now, nay, longer, is for you. Not just this copy, mind you, but the whole issue."

Zoe looked at the booklet's cover, where on the yellow-orange ground a stylized, pen-and-ink phoenix was rising from its own ashes. The title of the publication was set in tall, closely printed letters on the bottom left: *Jerry at His Tricks.* Beneath that: Volume VI, No. 1. "What is it?" she asked.

"It's our famzine," Jerry said. "All the septigamoklans have one. *Fam*ily maga*zine,* you see. Of which I am the editor and publisher. It is the True History and Record of the Phoenix Septigamoklan, along with various creative endeavors and pertinent remarks of our several spouses. One day, dear Zoe, you will be represented herein."

Leafing through the famzine, Zoe said, "Don't count your chickens . . ."

"Well, as an egghead who has already hatched his personal fondnesses, I am now seriously counting." He pointed a wicked, crooked finger at her. "One," he said in a burlesque, Transylvanian accent. "One chicken."

She laughed, patting him on top of his wiry puffball. But it was not until the next day, before breakfast, that she had a chance to read through the booklet—the advance copy—that Jerry had given her. In it she found artwork signed by Parthena, Helen, and Paul, and articles or poems by everyone in the family. Several of these were tributes, brief eulogies, to the dead Yuichan Kurimoto. The issue concluded with a free verse poem welcoming Zoe Breedlove as a candidate for marriage with the Phoenix. It was a flattering but fairly tastefully done poem. It was signed J. Z-Ph., and at the bottom of this last page was the one-word motto of the clan:

Dignity.

It was all too ridiculously corny. How did they have the nerve to put that word there? Zoe had to wipe her eyes dry before going into the dining room for breakfast.

Of all of them Paul was the hardest to get to know. Parthena had spoken rightly when she said that part of the difficulty was that his mind was going, had been going for a long time. He seemed to have a spiritual umbilicus linking him to the previous century and the time before the domes. He had been nine years old at the time of the Apollo 11 moon landing, thirteen at the time of the final Apollo mission, and he remembered both of them.

"Watched 'em on TV," he said. "Every minute I could of the first one. Just enough of the last one to say I saw it."

And he talked considerably more lucidly about his boyhood in California than he did about everyday matters in the hostel. His other favorite subject was the prospect of attaining, not in a dubious and certainly vitiated afterlife, but in the flesh, immortality. His only real grounding in the present, in fact, was the unalloyed joy he took in Sunday afternoons, at which time he performed creditably and behaved like a mature human being. The leers and the winks, it seemed, were almost involuntary carry-overs from a misspent youth.

"He gone sklotik up here"—Parthena tapped her head—"from the life he led as much as from jes' gettin' ole." (*Sklotik,* Zoe figured out, was *sclerotic.*) "Drugs, likker, womens, card playin'. Brag on how he never had a real job, jes' gamble for his keep-me-up. Now Mr. Leland 'fraid to use on him them new medicines what might stop his brain cells a-dyin'. Easy to see, he done los' a bunch."

And with his washed-out, Weimaraner eyes and raw, long lips Paul sometimes seemed like his own ghost instead of a living man. But he could still move around pretty good; he drifted about as effortlessly as a ghost might. And one day, three weeks after Zoe's arrival, he drifted up to her after dinner in the rec center (she was making a photo-display board) and pulled a chair up next to hers. She turned her head to see his raw lips beginning to move.

"It's time for one of my services," he said. "You don't go to the Ortho-Urbanist ones with Helen and Parthena, so I expect you're a fit body for one of mine. This Sunday morning, right in here."

"What sort of services?"

"My sort." A wink, maybe involuntary. "The True Word. Once every quarter, once every new-style month, I preach it."

"The True Word on what? Everybody's got his own true word, you know."

"On how not to die, woman. The basis of every religion."

"No," Zoe said. "Not every one of them; just the ones that don't know exactly what to do with the here-and-now."

His long lips closed, his eyes dilated. She might just as well have slapped him. In eighty years no one had told him that an ontological system didn't have to direct its every tenet toward the question of "how not to die." Or if someone had, Paul had forgotten. Even so, he fought his way back from stupefaction. "The basis," he said archly, "of every *decent* religion."

Jerry, who had overheard, powered himself up to the work table. "Rubbish, Paul. And besides, if tomorrow we were all granted everlasting life, no better than struldbrugs would we be, anyhow."

Zoe raised her eyebrows: *struldbrugs?* Paul kept silent.

"That's someone," Jerry explained, "who can't die but who nevertheless continues to get older and more infirm. Two hundred years from now we'd all be hopelessly senile immortals. Spare me such a blessing."

That ended the conversation. A ghost impersonating a man, Paul got up and drifted out of the room.

On Sunday morning, though, Luther went down to the rec center and took a box of aluminum parts, the largest being a drumlike cylinder, out of the closet where they kept the dart boards, the croquet equipment, and the playing cards, and assembled these aluminum pieces into . . . a rocking horse, one big enough for a man.

It was a shiny rocking horse, and its head, between its painted eyes, bore the representation of a scarab beetle pushing the sun before it like a cosmic dung ball. Zoe, who was in the rec center with all the Phoenix but Paul, went up to the metal critter to examine it. The scarab emblem was so meticulously wrought that she had to lean over to see what this horse had crawling on its forehead. A blue bug. A red ball. Well, that was different: funny and mysterious at once. "What's this?" she asked Luther, who, mumbling to himself, was trying to wedge the cardboard box back into the closet.

"Pulpit," he said. He thought she meant the whole thing. No sense in trying to clarify herself, he was still shoving at the box. But *pulpit* was a damn funny synonym for *rocking horse*.

After wedging the parts box back into place, Luther dragged a tall metal bottle from the closet and carried it over to the biomonitor cabinet next to Toodles' orpianoogla. Then he set it down and came back to the ring of chairs in front of the rocking horse. A silly business, every bit of it. Zoe put a single finger on the horse's forehead, right on the blue bug, and pushed. The horse, so light that only its weighted rockers kept it from tipping, began to dip and rise, gently nodding. No one was talking. Zoe turned to the group and shrugged. It looked like you'd have to threaten them all with premature autopsy to get anyone to explain.

"Don't ask," Jerry said finally. "But since you're asking, it's to humor him. He asked for the horse the second month after our covenant ceremony in '35, and Dr. Tanner said OK, give it to him. Now, four times a year, he plays octogenarian cowboy and rides into the sunset of his own dreams right in front of everybody. It's not so much for us to listen to him, you know."

Zoe looked at the five of them sitting there afraid she wouldn't understand: five uncertain, old faces. She was put off. They had been dreading this morning because they didn't know how she would react to the living skeleton in their family closet: the *de*-ranged range-rider Paul Erik Ferrand-Phoenix. Well, she was put off. All somebody'd had to do was tell her, she was steamingly put off. "O ye of little faith," she wanted to say, "go roast your shriveled hearts on Yuichan's hibachi. All of it together wouldn't make a meal." But she didn't say anything, she sat down with the group and waited. Maybe they didn't think she had Yuichan's compassion, maybe they didn't think she was worthy to replace their dear departed Jap . . .

Just then Paul came drifting in: an entrance. Except that he didn't seem to be at all aware of the impression he was making; he was oblivious of his own etiolated magnificence. Dressed in spotless white from head to foot (currently fashionable attire among even the young, matched tunic and leggings), he wandered over to the metal horse without looking at them. Then, slowly, he climbed on and steadied the animal's rocking with the toe tips of his white slippers.

He was facing them. Behind him, as backdrop, one of the quilted wall banners: a navy-blue one with a crimson phoenix in its center, wings outspread. Zoe couldn't help thinking that every detail of Paul's entrance and positioning had been planned beforehand. Or maybe it was that this quarterly ritual had so powerfully suffused them all that the need for planning was long since past. Anyhow, knowing it all to be nonsense, Zoe had to acknowledge that little pulses of electricity were moving along her spine. Like the time she had first quilted with the group.

Slowly, mesmerizingly slowly, Paul began to rock. And softly he began to preach the True Word. "When we were young," he said, "there was fire, and sky, and grass, and air, and creatures that weren't men. The human brain was plugged into this, the human brain was run on the batteries of fire and sky and all of it out there."

"Amen!" Luther interjected, without interrupting Paul's rhythm, but all Zoe could think was, The city still has creatures that aren't men: pigeons. But the rocking horse began to move faster, and as it picked up speed its rider's voice also acquired momentum, a rhythmic impetus of its own. As Paul spoke on, preached on, an "Amen!" or a "Yessir, brother!" occasionally provided an audible asterisk to some especially strange or vehement assertion in his text. All of it part of the ritual. But then Zoe was caught up in it in a way that she could see herself being caught up. Very odd: she found herself seconding Paul's insane remarks with "Amen!" or "All praises!" or some other curiously heartfelt interjection that she *never* used. This increased as the rocking horse's careering grew more violent and as Paul's eyes, the horse going up and down, flashed like eerie strobes.

"Then before our lives was half over, they put us in our tombs. They said we was dead even though we could feel the juices flowin' through us and electricity jumpin' in our heads. Up went the tombs, though, up they went. It didn't matter what we felt, it didn't matter we was still plugged into the life outside our tombs, the air and fire and sky. Because with the tombs up, you really do start dyin', you really do start losin' the voltage you have flowin' back and forth between you and the outside. Just look at yourself, just look at all of us." —Could anything be more ridiculous than this reasoning?—"It's slippin' away, that current, that precious, precious juice. It's because our brains are plugged into the sun or the moon, one socket or the other, and now they've stuck us in a place where the current won't flow."

Even as she said "Yessir!" Zoe was thinking that he, Paul, must have been plugged into the moon: loony.

But in another way, an upside-down way, it made a kind of loony sense, too. Even though everybody knew the world had been going to hell in a handcar before the domes went up, it still made a loony kind of sense. Maybe, at a certain time in your life (which was already past for her), you learned how to pass judgment on others, even unfavorable ones, without condemning. Zoe was doing that now. She beheld the madly rocking Paul from two utterly opposed perspectives and had no desire to reconcile them. In fact, the reconciliation happened, was happening, without her willing it to. As it always had for her, since Rabon's death. It was the old binocular phenomenon at work on a philosophical rather than a physical plane. Long ago it had occurred in Helen, too, the Phoenix "mediator," and just as Helen's little black goggles brought the physical world into focus for her, this double vision Zoe was now experiencing brought the two galloping Pauls—the demoniac one and the human one—into the compass of her understanding and merged them. Since this had happened before for her, why was she surprised?

". . . And the key to not-dying, and preserving the body too, is the brain. That's where we all are. We have to plug ourselves into the sun again, the sun and the moon. No one can do that unless he is resurrected from the tomb we were put in even before our lives were half over. . . ."

The horse was rocking frenetically, and Paul's voice was swooping into each repetitive sentence with a lean, measured hysteria. The bracelet on Zoe's wrist seemed to be singing. She looked at the biomonitor cabinet beside the orpianoogla and saw the oscilloscope attuned both to Paul's brain waves and his heartbeat sending a shower of pale comets back and forth, back and forth, across its screen. The other six windows were vividly pulsing, too, and she wondered if someone downstairs was taking note of this activity. Well, they were certainly all alive: very much alive.

Now Paul's eyes had rolled back in his head and the rocking horse had carried him into a country of either uninterrupted childhood or eternally stalled ripeness. He was alone in there, with just his brain and the concupiscent wavelets washing back from his body. Still preaching, too. Still ranting. Until, finally, the last word came out.

Only then did Paul slump forward across the neck of his aluminum steed, spent. Or dead maybe.

Zoe stood up—sprang up, rather. Amazingly, the other Phoenix—Toodles, Helen, Jerry, and Parthena—were applauding. Luther exempted himself from this demonstration in order to catch Paul before he slid off the still rocking horse and broke his head open.

"That the bes' one he manage in a long time," Parthena said.

Since the applause continued, Zoe, feeling foolish, joined in too. And while they all clapped (did sermons always end like this, the congregation joining in a spontaneous ovation?), Luther carried Paul over to the biomonitor cabinet, laid him out, and administered oxygen from the metal bottle he had earlier taken out of the closet. After which the wraithlike cowboy lifted his head a bit and acknowledged their applause with a wan grin. Then Luther put him to bed.

"You have to let him hear you," Toodles said. "Otherwise the old bastard thinks you didn't like it."

But he wasn't much good for three days after the sermon. He stayed in the common room, sleeping or staring at the ceiling. Zoe sat with him on the first night and let him sip soup through a flexible straw. In a few minutes he waved the bowl away, and Zoe, thinking he wanted to sleep, got up to leave. Paul reached out for her wrist and missed. She saw it, though, and turned back to him. His hand patted the bed: *Sit down.* So she lowered herself into the easy chair there and took his liver-spotted hand in her own. For an hour she sat there and held it. Then the long, raw lips opened and he said, "I'm afraid, Zoe."

"Sometimes," she said carefully, "I am, too." Now and again she was, she had to admit it.

The mouth remained open, the Weimaraner eyes glazed. Then Paul ran his tongue around his long lips. "Well," he said, "you can get in bed with me if you want to."

And closed his eyes. And went to sleep.

12   somewhere over the broomstick

It had never been in doubt. Maybe a little, just a little, in jeopardy the first night when the menfolk insulted Toodles. Or maybe a bit uncertain with Paul, until after his rocking-horse oration and subsequent collapse. But never really perilously in doubt.

So when Luther came up to the rooftop on that evening at the end of Winter and said, "You're in, Zoe, you're in," her joy was contained, genuine but contained. You don't shout Hooray! until the wedding's over or the spacemen have got home safely. Zoe embraced Luther. Downstairs, she embraced the others.

On the morning after the group's decision, they had the covenant ceremony in the hostel quadrangle. Leland Tanner presided. Day 1 of Spring, 2040, New Calendar designation.

"All right," Mr. Leland said. "Each septigamoklan has its own covenant procedure, Zoe, since any way that it chooses to ratify its bond is legal in the eyes of the Human Development Commission. The Phoenix ceremony owes its origin to an idea of Parthena's." He looked at the group. They were all standing on a section of the artificial lawn surrounded by tubbed ginkgo trees. A table with refreshments was visible in the nearest arbor. "That's right, isn't it?"

"That right," Parthena said.

And then, of all crazy things, Mr. Leland brought a broom out from behind his back. He laid it on the wiry turf at his feet and backed up a few steps. "OK," he said. "What you all do now is join hands and step over the broomstick together." He reconsidered. "Maybe we better do it in two groups of three, Zoe, you making the fourth each time. Any objections?"

"No," Parthena said. "So long as she cross it in the same direction both times, so none of it get undone."

OK. That's the way they did it. Zoe went first with Helen, Toodles, and Luther, then a second go-round with Parthena, Paul, and Jerry. Jerry had to drive his wheel chair over one end of the broom handle.

"I pronounce you," Mr. Leland said, "all seven of you, married in the Phoenix. Six of you for a second time, one of you for the first." He took them all over to the arbor and passed out drinks. "Viva the Phoenix."

Zoe drank. They all drank. Toasts went around the group several times. It was all very fitting that when you were sold down the river, into freedom, you got married by jumping over a broomstick. How else should you do it? No other way at all. No other way at all.

Paul and Toodles, the oldest and the second youngest in the family, died in 2042. A year later Luther died. In 2047, two days short of her eightieth birthday, Helen died. In this same year Dr. Leland Tanner resigned his position at the Human Development Tower; he protested uninformed interference in a study that was then twelve years old. Upon his departure from the Geriatrics Hostel his programs were discontinued, the remaining members of the ten septigamoklans separated. In 2048 Jeremy Zitelman died in the hostel's nursing ward. Parthena and Zoe, by the time of his death, had been returned to their "surviving families," Parthena to a surfaceside Bondville tenement, Zoe to the Level 1 cubicle of Sanders and Melanie Noble. Oddly enough, these two last members of the Phoenix died within twelve hours of each other on a Summer day in

2050, after brief illnesses. Until a month or two before their deaths, they met each other once a week in a small restaurant on West Peachtree, where they divided a single vegetable dinner between them and exchanged stories about their grandchildren. Parthena, in fact, was twice a *great*-grandmother.

After the broomstick-jumping ceremony in the garden court Mr. Leland took Zoe aside and said that someone wanted to talk to her in the room that he had once called an "air-lock." His horsy face had a tic in one taut cheek, and his hands kept rubbing themselves against each other in front of his bright blue tunic. "I told him to wait until we were finished out here, Zoe. And he agreed."

Why this mystery? Her mind was other places. "Who is it?"

"Your son-in-law."

She went into the air-lock, the decompression chamber, whatever you wanted to call it, and found Sanders ensconced in one corner of the sofa playing with the lint on his socks. When he saw her he got up, clumsily, with a funereal expression on his face. He looked like somebody had been stuffing his mouth with the same sort of lint he'd been picking off his socks: bloated jowls, vaguely fuzzy lips. She just stared at him until he had worked his mouth around so that it could speak.

"Lannie lost the baby," he said.

So, after Lannie got out of the hospital, she spent a week in their Level 3 cubicle helping out until her daughter could do for herself. When that week was over, she returned to her new family in the Geriatrics Hostel. But before she left she pulled Sanders aside and said, "I've got some advice for you, something for you to tell Lannie too. Will you do it?"

Sanders looked at his feet. "OK, Zoe."

"Tell her," Zoe said, "to try again."

Telepathy is a theme that's fascinated science fiction writers and readers alike, for wouldn't it be wonderful to share our thoughts with others without the fetters of spoken language, and to perceive our friends' emotions directly?

Yet there could be dangers. Consider sharing a telepathic link with a friend who's dying, who can "speak" to no one but you . . . and who might be able to take over your mind. How strong can a friendship be?

Cynthia Felice, who wrote this suspenseful story about the implications of mind-sharing, spends most of her time managing a motel with her husband in Colorado; between check-ins, she pursues a beginning career as an author. Unless the business becomes too hectic, you'll see her by-line frequently, and prominently, in the future.

DAVID AND LINDY
Cynthia Felice

The *Nightwine* is faster than light, but, from the moment we received the report of Captain Linden's injuries, the damn ship moved like a horse in a tar pit. Lindy wasn't dead but he was dying. His ship had blown an unstable cargo and half the crew as well. While I worried only about Lindy, death notices were blinking throughout the universe. No guilt; I couldn't do anything for them but it was possible I could do something for Lindy: he's a telepath and so am I.

Finally, the *Nightwine* was falling in a tight elliptical orbit around a giant planet in Barnard's Star System, matching velocity with the *Dandelion*. Before the lights signaled "go" for transfer, I was in an eva-pod, the new ship's doctor waiting in another. Through relay cameras, I could see a dozen eva-pods on silver-coated lines, hauling plates from the *Dandelion*'s cargo hatch to replace damaged ones on the hull. Waldoes were being used to repair damaged sensors and telemetry. They'd tried to jettison the cargo before it blew up but had only half-succeeded, so now the tedious work of jury-rigging spare parts, billions of AU's from a supply depot, was underway. At least the burial pods were gone. They'd been shoved into a lower orbit and in a few years would wink out like meteorites as they passed through the planet's atmosphere.

Then it was "go." I latched Doc Varner's eva-pod with a waldoe and gave a long thrust with the cold-jet. Hauling the other pod's mass required several mid-course corrections, or maybe it was because I was aware of Lindy's thoughts by then—incomprehensible mumbo jumbo as if he were desperately trying to concentrate amid frantic interruptions. The pattern indicated fear and I couldn't get the word-thoughts. I could have broken through then and there, but the eva-pods are not to be trifled with, and I was catching subliminal alarms from the *Dandelion*'s crew about my deceleration. I stayed with the job at hand.

Once inside the *Dandelion*'s axis, the iris spiraled shut behind us and in a few minutes the safe-atmosphere light went on. I traced a comma on the labyrinth control, popping my pod's hatch, then floated in freefall, waiting for Doc Varner. He came out, too fast, arms flailing and face filled with bewilderment. I grabbed his belt before he hit the bulkhead and pulled him to the hatch, shoving him into the lighted tube beyond. He didn't feel confident until I'd manhandled him down to the hydroponic farm level where the tug of centrifugal force gave him something to base his bearings on. He grabbed the center pole and pushed past the succeeding levels until he could slide. At the outer rim, he stood again, signaled an "okay" to me, and ducked into the corridor. I was right behind him.

Jill, Lindy's wife, was waiting at the pole. She's a red-haired woman, freckle-skinned, with height that makes me feel like a dwarf. There were healing wounds on her arms and fresh ones in her mind. —Big fat question mark surrounded by anxiety.—

"He's there, Jill," I said. "I've been reading him during transfer." Her eyes moistened and I felt her anxiety give over to relief.

Uninhibited excitement turned my attention to the doc. —What does he say? Telepath, aware while in a coma. Computers and medics

inadequate . . . perhaps not really coma . . . confusion when deal-
ing with telepaths . . .—

The doc was athirst to see his patient in the clinic just meters away
though outwardly he was appropriately composed. I was pleased with
his mind's impatience; I've learned that most competent professionals
are exhilarated by their work. I gestured and we three went into the
clinic together.

Lindy lay amid stark white sheets with IV's feeding in and tubes I
couldn't identify draining out. He'd been shorn of his tight brown
curls and his skull skin was stitched together like a patchwork quilt.
But within the mind of the fallen giant was a brilliance: thoughts,
which were not stacked in his usual order of concentration but which
were somehow pasted into a collage, swirling in that same desperate
intentness I'd seen while in the eva-pod. What I did then was not like
comparing a shout to a normal speaking voice; it was like leaping and
hitting him with two feet square in the brain. It had to be quick for I
had to get back and catch my body before it collapsed with nothing
for support. —Lindy.—

The collage splintered. —David!—

My name was a sonic boom in my skull as I felt his joy. My own
pleasure was no small thing either. —I'm here, Lindy.—

The exchange went quickly without words to slow us down. In
minutes I knew of the agony he'd suffered by being trapped within his
own mind yet hearing Jill and the crew, picking up the medic's concern for the injured and himself, the grief of the funerals without
being able to communicate in any way. Fearing insanity, he'd worked
state vectors, doing the computer's work in his mind. When I understood what it was like for him to have only the deep complications of
his own mind for company, I perspired. Then I realized the doc was
talking to me:

"Can you read him?"

"Loud and clear; he's fine," I said.

Jill smiled but the doctor shook his head and went back to the
medical computer printouts he was studying.

Lindy, still content from my arrival, asked me almost light-
heartedly, —What's the latest prognosis?—

I tried to feel optimistic. —The doc has no confidence in computers.—

But it's difficult to keep a secret from Lindy. Lindy was listening
to the doc while listening to me, and the doc, who was fresh from

Earth and did not have command of the privacy request normals
develop when they live around telepaths, was spewing diagnosis like
a siren: —coma for sure . . . paralyzed even if he can be revived
. . . rapid deterioration . . .—

—Give the man a chance to think, Lindy. Thought processes are
not final conclusions.— But Lindy knew that.

Resignedly, he sighed. —Coma, the medic was right. It's less
difficult to accept with you here. At least I can communicate.—

—He may change his diagnosis when he's done examining you.—

Lindy laughed. —Right now he's thinking of the implications of an
aware telepathic mind while the body lies in a coma and about a
paper he will write.—

I glanced up at Doc Varner, seemingly involved only with the printouts. The paper was only a fringe thought; the human mind cannot
help exploring its thoughts even while pressing needs involve the conscious. I wished I had Lindy's ability to decipher simultaneous
thoughts. I had to shift from one person to the other. Lindy already
knew more than I.

—How's Jill taking it?— Lindy said.

I was aware that Jill's thoughts were drawn tight in privacy request. Telepaths honor normals' privacy because we've carefully cul-
tivated trust within the closed social system of the ships. Lindy
wouldn't breach the privacy pattern with any of his crew—except Jill,
whom he couldn't resist touching often. But he honored her request
now, fearing that her love had been replaced with pity she could not
hide from him. Yet he was asking me if pity was there.

—I don't know,— I said honestly. —She was relieved when I told
her I could read you. Beyond that I'm not sure. Why should pity
worry you? It's a normal reaction.—

—I don't want her pity and none from you either! There's enough
around the ship without yours and Jill's.—

—Been busy since you've had me to lean on, haven't you? Be nice,
or I'll stop listening . . .—

Lindy's mind screamed: —No!—

I regretted the jest immediately. I touched his hand. He couldn't
feel my touch with his body's nerves, but his mind felt the gesture.

—I'm sorry, David. I've had enough silence . . . perhaps more
than I can take. Don't leave me.—

—I won't. I'll stay.—

—Until the end?—

I was startled. —We don't know that you're going to die. The doc . . .—

—. . . is doubtful. I need the services of an Earth specialist but the planetfall would surely kill me even if Earth-eaters gave dispensation for surgery on a telepath. My body is wasting. Men have lived months, even years, in comas, but Varner sees only months for me.—

The doc was talking in muted tones to the medic. Sure enough, they were planning life-prolonging, not lifesaving, measures. Stricken, I turned back to Lindy. —To the end, then . . . but I'm not convinced you'll die. You know that.—

—Do I?—

Fringe thoughts. "Hey, Doc, give Captain Linden a frank report on his condition. Forget the bedside manner: it would be wasted."

He verbalized and his words were pretty close to the truth; "It's not good. On Earth, I would give him a fifty-fifty chance on the paralysis after surgery, but I'm just not sure about the coma. The symptoms hinge on each other. I'm not qualified to perform the surgery and we can't transport him to Earth because his spinal cord could be severed during atmospheric re-entry. I don't even want to subject him to the jolt necessary to exceed speed-of-light." The next part was almost a lie, designed to comfort the next of kin—Jill and me—and to keep up the patient's spirits. It helped only Jill. "I'm going to set up a temporary clinic on the hydroponic farm level. The lesser centrifugal force will help heal the bedsores and relieve nerve pressure. Then you'll have to decide if you want me to return to Earth and find a competent specialist."

"No decision involved, Doctor." It was Jill who spoke. "Of course you must go."

The doc had the good grace at least to try straight-line communication. He was clumsy, but I got the message. Time was the problem, a three-month round trip from Barnard's Star System to Sol, not including downtime in locating the right doctor. Lindy probably wouldn't last. There also were fringe thoughts about his paper and mental explorations about sending the medic to Earth while he remained with Captain Linden.

While Jill was looking at Lindy, I gave the doc a nod to let him know I understood. Then I went to the computer console and traced a spiral on the maze that put me in direct contact with the *Nightwine*'s bridge.

"Greenberg," I said, "this is David Atkins. "What's the fastest jump you can make to Earth, decelerating past Luna?"

"Past Luna? We can't. That's against the law . . ."

Earth's laws are archaic. Our equipment can slip into parking orbit right from speed-of-light, but Earth-eaters still worry about deep-space collisions on their slag pile. "The hell with the law," I said, "the captain's life hangs on time."

"Twenty days," Greenberg replied promptly. "He's communicating?"

"Yes," I said, regretting I'd forgotten to tell the crews earlier. With few exceptions these people had worked for Lindy for a long time. Their concern was genuine.

"And the captain agrees to risk Earth's law?" Greenberg said.

—No, I don't,— Lindy straight-lined to me. —Tell him to take time for proper deceleration.—

"Yes, he does," I told Greenberg, "but he says to be careful."

—Damn you, David. There's forty good crew on that ship!—

Earth-eaters would have to catch the *Nightwine* before they could arrest her crew. Never happen. —Shut up, Lindy. I'm in command.— I turned back to the doc. I'd given him enough time to finish exploring. "Can the medic make the jump?"

The doc was cautious, rechecked his data: —Printouts are accurate . . . no dud, this medic . . . give him a list of the best men . . . Linden Fleet rich enough to offer the right price . . . learn much for my paper by staying . . . be on hand to take more drastic measures than a medic might dare . . .— "Yes," he finally said. "I'll . . ."

I waved off his list of things to do. "Go do it, I know," I said. Then into the communicator: "Greenberg, I'm sending the medic to the *Nightwine*. You jump for Earth as soon as he gets there."

"We're transferring cargo, Mr. Atkins. Twenty hours of work . . ."

"Stow it."

"Yes, sir."

—They could do some business as long as the trip has to be made,— Linden said.

—And waste a day? Not on *your* life.— "Doc, I've got things to see to." It wasn't necessary for me to be in the same room with Lindy to keep him company and we both had ship worries on our minds that I could soothe with a little checking.

"Now? So soon? But we haven't talked. You haven't told me what

his reactions are!" Intoxicated excitement again: —Medical first . . .
brain alert . . . need David's co-operation to learn . . .—

"Later. Right now I'm going to take Jill back to the captain's
cabin."

The doc nodded resignedly. "The medic gave her some sedatives.
See that she takes one." He gave Jill a sideways glance.

—Tell him to give me one too,— Lindy said.

I responded with confusion.

—You're going to talk to Jill, aren't you?— he said.

—Yes.—

—I don't want to listen.—

He was anxious that he'd lost something with Jill. It had to do with
her faith in his strength and what Lindy got from that faith. It's just
the way it was between them; it was theirs and maybe, now, it was
gone. The doctor was still at my side by the console. "If you have
something that will make Captain Linden's brain relax, give it to
him."

He seemed to understand, for he nodded and left me with his mind
muttering about avoiding depression.

—Try to sleep, Lindy. I'll be waiting when you awaken.—

I took Jill's hand and led her out of the clinic and down the corridor. Her privacy request was ablaze. Even though she was exhausted,
it didn't skip. When I was sure Lindy wasn't fighting the shot the doc
gave him, I asked Jill: "Why won't you talk to Lindy?"

"I'm . . . shaken. I don't want him to see me this way. He's always
been the stronger, but now he can't help me. I need time to do it on
my own."

I nodded. Eventually Lindy would reach for Jill, and I hoped she
could carry it off when that time came. He'd need her strength. Role
reversal? No, that was what it always was. Her love was his strength.
We were standing in front of the captain's cabin. "Will you take the
sedative, Jill?"

She nodded. "I can rest now. You're here."

"Did you doubt I'd come?"

"No, but it should be me he needs . . ."

But those were fringe thoughts, verbalized. "He's sleeping now," I
told her. "You do the same."

Jill smiled tiredly, nodded, and let the labyrinth sense her body
warmth in the proper pattern. I watched until the iris closed between

us, then I turned to the bridge. The *Dandelion* had been orbiting without a captain for weeks. I had much to attend.

There are few telepaths in the universe, but Earth-eaters are scared of even a minute number. Lindy was one of Earth's first exiles, only ten years old when he was piped aboard a none-too-willing merchant ship as cabin boy. Twenty years later, I, a comfortably settled man with a nice job, a wife, and two kids, was discovered. I'd barely learned myself that I was telepathic and I wasn't too happy about leaving Earth. I couldn't see what all the fuss was about, didn't understand why I must be exiled to live the rest of my life in orbital tin cans. I wasn't piped aboard; they took me to Lindy's ship in a strait jacket.

Lindy was a compassionate teacher: I had tried to deny my telepathic abilities, for I thought if I wouldn't or couldn't use them, I'd be welcomed home with open arms. Lindy tried to explain that Earth-eaters are not dung beetles. When it didn't sink in, he showed me why. He put me in an eva-pod and shoved me out the air lock. The comm-system in the pod was inexplicably jammed and I couldn't operate the confusing labyrinth controls without direction. I learned a lot about my will to live and telepathy that day. For a long time I thought I knew what I hated: Lindy. It gave me something powerful on which to cling. Doesn't sound like much of a beginning for a friendship, but at that time Lindy knew my mind better than I. He'd seen what was in the fringes of my cortex, hammered there by Earth-eaters' hatred and fear, and he didn't let me alone until he'd pried the synapses that let out love, compassion, and joy.

That was a long time ago. Now there is a fleet of one hundred cargo and passenger ships, blinking between star systems, which is the Linden Fleet. Earth-eaters are suspicious about the cabin boy who became the head of the fantastic fleet. Success stories about telepaths make them tremble. Their fears are well founded; we are powerful and Lindy is ruthless. But he's also very shrewd, for he knows Earth's good will is our bread and butter. If there is a mercy trip to be made, the Linden Fleet can be counted on to do it at its own cost. If there is a dangerous cargo to be hauled, we do that too. . . .

After I'd seen the *Nightwine* change attitude and leave for Earth, finished going over the damage reports, checked death and injury compensations, revised the repair schedule, talked with the doc, and gone to bed, I felt Lindy's probe. I was tired, but I didn't resist his need for communication.

—Sorry to awaken you.—

—It's okay,— I lied, and Lindy knew I lied but such formalities are accepted at face value between telepaths.

—How's Jill?—

—Sleeping, I hope.— But I couldn't hedge with Lindy. —I don't know. She's scared for you and for herself as well.—

—Keeping her thoughts from you too?—

—affirmative—

—David, I want to try something . . . for Jill's sake. Let me borrow your body.—

I couldn't help flinching. Protests came unbidden. —She doesn't know of the method. It might not help the state she's in. We've rarely done it. It frightens me!—

Eagerness: —It's power, David, and power will destroy her pity. I can end her fears, and mine. Let me!—

—It requires my submission. I don't like that.—

—You fear I'd not release you?—

—No.— Too slow, the affirmative slipped through. I tried to explain. —I trust you, but I have a ship to run.—

Lindy laughed. —You forget, *I'm* the captain.—

I felt sheepish. —All right, Lindy, but be careful. She may not accept you in my body.—

—I know how to handle my own wife.—

I took my conscious and my doubts that anyone "handled" Jill into a far cozy corner of my mind before Lindy could sense them. Then it was like wading through a dream while he sought out my synapses and tripped the right ones in proper sequence. I felt cramped, but not uncomfortable when he began moving fully in my mind, using my body as if it were his own. But I was helpless where I waited. Lindy was in control until he chose to relinquish my body, or until he fell asleep. Briefly, I wondered if men in comas ever slept naturally or only under sedatives. I heard Lindy's good-humored reply and I relaxed. My fears, brief as they were, seemed groundless just then.

For all his forethought, Lindy reflexively traced the pattern on the labyrinth of his cabin's iris and he didn't realize what he'd done until Jill looked up from where she stood, drawing up her jumper. Her hands tried to cover her naked breasts and Lindy grinned in full appreciation.

Thrusting her arms into the jumper, she whirled to display backside fabric while she fastened the front out of his sight. Then she turned, redfaced and angry. "David!" was all she could manage.

Lindy was enjoying Jill's first display of modesty in years, but she was struggling between impulses to throw a boot at him and to reasonably await explanation.

He spoke when she reached for the boot. "It's Lindy, not David." Jill's eyes softened slightly. "You're relaying for him?"

"No. It's Lindy, first hand. I am possessing. David and I have experimented with possession. This seemed a good time to put the experiments into practical use."

Jill was nervous. "I don't know . . . I'm not sure." Then, with less suspicion. "Why?"

Lindy walked to his grip-chair, eager to enjoy its comforts again. It dwarfed my small body, the specially made contours didn't fit and he stood up again, looking around the cabin. It was one that a monk might live in: bed, chairs, and workbench by the computer extension. In ten years, Jill had made no changes except to add her own chair and hang her clothes in the closet. "I lay three weeks in black silence and you need to ask why?" He smiled. "It feels good to flex muscles again, even these small ones of David. But most of all, I needed to talk to you, directly."

"David is your friend. He would have relayed precisely what you wished," Jill said. "Lindy, is it truly you? Or is David Atkins perpetrating some macabre trick?"

"Would David walk in here without announcing himself?"

"Not ordinarily. But if it served some obscure purpose, Linden could have shown him the pattern."

"What purpose could it serve?" he said.

When Jill did not answer, Lindy, for the first time in a very long time, deliberately ignored her privacy pattern. He laughed aloud. "Do you really think David would dare seduce my wife? The thought has occurred to him, but he knows it would risk our friendship."

Jill frowned. "Nor would David invade my privacy."

Lindy still grinned. "No, he wouldn't."

Jill walked across the cabin, staring at David's face. —Linden? . . . tugs on a beard that isn't there, but I've seen the gesture in Lindy a million times . . . smooth fingers brushing across my cheekbone . . . don't pull my hair, Lindy! David would not touch me this way . . . your way.—

"Don't be afraid, Jill. It *is* me." When he saw Jill close her eyes, he drew her near and found his cheek on her breast. There were some compensations for being a short man that he'd not suspected, but it wasn't all pleasant surprises. He was less enthralled when Jill had to bend to kiss him. Lindy'd had enough with the height reversal and he leveled it. He picked up Jill, a heavier weight than he remembered but not an unreasonable burden for my strong body, and carried her to the bed.

I'm not a voyeur but I get bored going through state vectors like a computer—especially when there's something more interesting going on in my own body. . . .

I felt as anyone feels after missing sleep periods. Coffee helped but it was an effort to resist the temptation of going back to bed. I'd finished another session with the doc in the jury-rigged medical area on the hydroponic level where Lindy's body lay. The doc was pleased that the captain's depression had eased after a prolonged discussion with Jill—I didn't explain how that was accomplished—and pleased that Lindy was resting comfortably now. But the doc was unhappy with the rapid deterioration of Lindy's body. He was glad he'd stayed, for he'd come close to losing Lindy—unquestionably during the time he was possessing me. Lindy's kidneys were failing. I was compelled to put off rest for a while longer and tell Jill about his condition. I didn't even hesitate in front of the iris. I traced a pattern on the labyrinth and started through.

"Lindy!" Jill said when she saw me.

I stopped and the iris whooshed behind me. "No," I said quickly. "It's David." I glanced back at the iris, realizing that the day before I'd not known the operational pattern. "Sorry, Jill. I guess some things remain. I didn't give it a thought."

"What else remained?" I saw flickers of disgust and embarrassment.

"Don't worry about it. It's insignificant to me, less than a dream."

"You forget that I'm a computer programmer. I know how the storage systems work in the mechanical brains and I've had experience with the flesh ones too."

"Still, it's less than a dream," I insisted. "Perhaps there will be times when something will trigger a memory that is not of my own making, but it's not something I can do voluntarily." Certain lies comfort and I never hesitate to use them when I know things that are none of my business.

Jill sat in her chair and gestured for me to use Lindy's. I would have refused, but even improper contours are some relief to a tired body. "David, don't let him do it again. It's not just that." She gestured toward the iris. "I'm frightened with him in your body. While he was with me he knew exactly what to say and do to soothe my anxieties. As soon as he left, I knew it wasn't real and that it was wrong."

"He may not live through this," I told her bluntly. "His kidneys are failing. Even forty days may not be soon enough. In light of that, how can I refuse him?"

Jill was repelled. "Make his dying days as pleasant as possible?"

"Something like that."

She was almost vicious. "Lindy won't die; he's too strong! He has too much will power to let go."

"Maybe," I said. "Doc thinks that if I hadn't come, Lindy would have gone insane. I'm still worried about that. Ever thought about an insane telepath?"

I could tell she hadn't and she wasn't going to think about it now either. She was worried about something else.

"If you continue to let him possess you, he'll be convinced you're patronizing him. He'll find the same pity in you that he feared to see in me."

"I can't hide that from him. But he's been a telepath long enough to understand it's human for the mind to go off on tangents." Lindy's relation with me was disparate from the one between them. But Jill didn't quite understand; there was a bit of envy in her.

Jill shook her head. "As much as I want to be able to talk to him face to face—even if it's your face—I believe you're doing him a dis-service. It's not the best thing for *him.*"

She believed it. She didn't consider the disservice possession might do to me. "Jill, unless he agrees to respect my refusal to accommodate him, I'm not going to be able to stop him."

—What do you mean?— Her mental query formulated before she could even open her mouth to speak.

"Awake, I can refuse him." So far, that was true. "Asleep my conscious is open to invasion from him. Lindy is more powerful than I."

—You think he would use you against your will? No!— She hadn't the slightest doubt in him.

But I doubted. "I know the part that you have never seen and he's terrified of death. He's fighting it now, but later he'll become resentful and, eventually, accept it. It's the normal pattern. Using my body gives him a lot of power—at least in his mind—to fight death."

—He's not weak, David. Lindy has courage to spare for ten people.—

I nodded. "Perhaps you're right." The emotion casements around her words showed nothing could shake her belief. I didn't pursue the subject any further. Jill was remembering Lindy's keen perceptions of risk, which were always intelligently calculated, and she was interpreting his responses as bravery. I knew Lindy more intimately than his wife ever could, just as he knew me. We supplied strength where the other was weak, called on superiorities as if they were owned.

But years of trust were falling away. I feared Lindy was ruthlessly capable of using any means available to resist death. I understood his temptations just as he knew my suspicions. Lindy had laughed and I'd relaxed, but I couldn't deny what I saw. I feared my friend's superior strength.

He was sleeping. I decided the first step in resisting the man was to match sleep cycles. Awake, he could not take possession without my willingness. I left Jill and went to bed.

I outwitted Lindy for one sleep cycle. The next one, he was waiting and I awoke fighting from the place in my mind's corner. But there was no leverage for me to pry even one finger from his control and in minutes he was on his way to his cabin in my body.

"David?" Jill asked, when he entered. "I'm due on the bridge in a minute."

"Linden," he said quietly. I screamed my own name: It was heard only by Lindy, who didn't even flinch. But I did—just a shadow picture of Lindy performing a mutilation on my body before he returned to his own. Willful son of a bitch! I couldn't tell if he'd really do it, but I wasn't willing to take the chance. I cowered silently.

"I wish you'd tell me who's coming through that iris," Jill said, exasperated.

"David knocks . . . or doesn't he?"

"No. It seems you leave things like lock patterns in his head."

Lindy laughed.

"Lindy, this isn't wise. If for no other reason, consider my reputation. The crew is bound to see David coming in here and they won't think much of me allowing it while you're incapacitated."

"We three know the truth. Let them think what they wish."

"It's not like you to disregard crew opinion."

"It's only temporary."

"I still don't like it." Jill looked at him steadily. "Does David know you're in there?"

"Oh yes, he knows." Linden chuckled.

"And he was willing?"

Lindy frowned. "Does that matter?"

"Yes!"

Lindy didn't like the scathing thoughts he saw in her mind, nor did he understand them. "I should think you'd want me to spend my last days with you," he said.

—So that's it! I didn't believe David when he told me you were frightened. I can understand expediency because you are a self-centered man. But this! You say you don't want my pity yet you come sniffing around in another man's body and ask for pity. Sorry, I have none to give. Get out of my way, Lindy, I have work to do.—

Lindy let his wife pass. He could see she didn't accept the inevitability of his death for one minute and he thought her very unreasonable. Angrily, he stomped into the corridor, turned away from the direction of the bridge, and went to the nearest pole radiating up a shaft to the other levels. He took the grips one at a time instead of his usual two by two and then stepped off at the hydroponic level. He walked through a maze of crops suspended in clear nutrient sacks, their roots as twisted and tangled as the thoughts in his mind. He stopped when he reached his body, lying inert, breathing shallowly. It seemed little different from the tomato plants surrounding it with the sacks of sucrose and pumps supporting his life. The tomatoes at least had purpose. Lindy felt less certain of his own existence.

"There's no change, David." It was the doc's voice interrupting his maudlin musing.

Lindy nodded, then realized the doc was talking from a bed just beyond his own, where he'd taken up residency to tend his patient. Still nursing his abandonment by Jill, Lindy wondered if the doc's concern was only for the paper he wanted to write, but he couldn't tell, for the doc was not thinking along those lines.

"Is he asleep?" the doc said, swinging his feet over the bed and grabbing the rail to correct the overfast movement. He used more care to pull on his coveralls.

Lindy hesitated, then replied: "Yes."

"David, I'm concerned for you. If Captain Linden dies while your minds are linked, how will you be affected?"

"I've been with dying men before. It's a comfort to them. The hearing passes last . . . did you know that? Yes, well, I can answer their final questions."

"But this is different. You're *both* telepaths. You talk of Captain Linden's mind within your own. It seems the link between telepaths is different from the link you have with normals."

"That's true, it is different." It was all Lindy could say. He couldn't describe a process where vocabulary had never been developed. We'd devised symbols to close the gap, but they weren't anything you could draw or define for a normal.

"Could you be trapped in his mind at the moment of death?"

Lindy looked at the doc strangely, for dead minds could not be touched. Then he shook his head. "There is much about telepathy I don't know. Even . . . Captain Linden . . . does not know, though he's been telepathic since childhood." He looked up at the doctor. "Are you suggesting a mind transfer?" Fringe thoughts were being drawn in for consideration. Would there be a bit of himself in my mind after his death—leavings, like the lock pattern, in the mnemonics? It came to him quickly then: Or his whole awareness?

"Schizophrenia . . . or a dual personality."

"What?" Lindy said. The words shook him. Every telepath has flirted with insanity before learning to cope.

The doc sighed. "I pose questions, David. I have no answers and it seems you don't either."

Lindy grasped the rail of the bed where his body lay wasting. If he died, would it be a final death? Now he doubted it. He hadn't been distracted with near-death while he was in my body visiting Jill. Would he live on, in part? In entirety? In my body? What happened when a telepath who was half a love-bond died and the other half was near enough to possess? Suddenly, Lindy withdrew from my mind and I hastened to right the stagger it produced.

—Damn you, Linden!— I almost pummeled his body with my fists.

Lindy did not respond. His thoughts were spinning rapidly, seemingly shocked. I probed and he resisted.

I turned away from Lindy and the doc, traced a comma on the

comm-system and reached the bridge. "Send Jill to my cabin." She'd be wondering which telepath gave the order but she wouldn't refuse. I left without even saying good-by to the doc, slid down the nearest pole, and walked down the corridor. What I'd hoped were only fringe thoughts could no longer be ignored.

I gave him two feet in the brain. —Why does it scare you, Lindy? Did you think telepaths wink out like novas?—

He didn't answer, but was listening.

The implications were enough to have us both suspended between hope and fear. Skin prickling, I tried a solution on him. —We will share.—

—Ha! You think we won't fight over control? You think *I* would share? I am more powerful.—

While Jill walked the dish of the outer rim corridor toward me, I wondered what a battle of two minds within the same body would be like. When Jill and I met at my cabin, I barely had enough presence to hold the iris for her.

"David?" she asked.

"Yes, it's me."

"It's as you suspected," she said, beginning to explain Lindy's recent possession of my body. "He *is* frightened of death."

—David.— Lindy interrupted. —I want you to have the doctor sedate me.—

—Wouldn't work, Lindy. You can fight sedation. They can paralyze your muscles but nothing can stop your mind.—

—It would give me something to fight . . . besides you.—

I looked at Jill. "He's accepted death. In fact, he's making arrangements for it." Knowing he could live on in my body, suicide was a better word for it. Lindy wasn't capable of suicide.

—No! You must not accept dying. *I* don't!— Jill straight-lined to him.

—You heard?— I asked Lindy.

—She doesn't understand the danger. It's not Jill's place to decide, it's mine. I won't risk a schizophrenic captain at the head of Linden Fleet.—

—Yet you'd disregard Jill? Leave her alone?—

—I'm not worried about Jill, I'm worried about you . . . us and insanity. Send her out. We'll talk without her.—

I looked at Jill. She'd barely noticed the pause. "He wants to be sedated until it's all over."

—Linden, you can't just give up! I won't take that from you. I love you. You know that I do.— Jill blazed with fury, indignant in her half-comprehension. Her love was undeniable.

Lindy groaned. —I can't have her emotions distracting me now. Stop her. I've decided . . . David, please.—

There was a momentary silence.

Softly, his thoughts came to me. —When I'm dead you'll be the head of Linden Fleet. It's safe in your hands. Jill will get over it. Perhaps you and she . . .—

I blasted my reply, for I was angry with my temptation. —Don't try arranging my life for me!—

—If you don't do as I ask, I will spend the rest of your life doing just that!—

—No. I trust you, Lindy. If telepaths can live on after death, then there must be a way to cope with the dual existence. We'll take the risk and find a way.— I didn't believe myself, but I wanted to. Lindy, despite his pitiless mask, was my friend, closer to me than kin.

—You're a fool!—

—Only a fool would think you're dying.—

—Then we're both fools.—

And I knew it was true. But there was Jill with true emotional quality and steadfast belief, insisting: —Lindy, you can't die.— But *we* couldn't be sure, so we had to deal with the alternative. Shortly, she left my cabin, her faith still impervious to all influences. I felt a prevailing dread that she might be right, that Lindy couldn't die . . . at least, not his mind.

Lindy was outraged that I could think of sharing my body and of learning to cope with dual existence when all the while I was terrified. —You can't act on intellect,— he told me, angrily, —while every instinct shouts denial.—

—Our friendship precludes reservations.—

—Our friendship demands confidence and I have none left in you, David. You're groveling because I'm more powerful.—

There was no denying it. It hardly mattered that it occurred to him first; it fit in my head. —We both know I can't escape your superior strength, so why is it strange that I want to retain your good will?— He'd always been stronger. There were good friendship-preserving reasons for us working on two different ships, separated by light-years.

—I asked your help in preventing this fiasco. Instead, you're paving the way.—

—Drugs can't hold you for long. You *will* possess me when you feel death approaching. I don't think it will matter whether I'm awake or asleep when the times comes. Do you?—

—No, it won't matter. But if you let me do this, it will destroy us, and Jill too. Fight me!—

—No.—

I felt his resolve to stay in his body despite my invitation and we both knew such resolutions were useless. Then Lindy withdrew, but not before I felt his aversion and it nearly sickened me to know it.

I existed, hovering between somnolence and delirium; the drugs I'd denied Lindy I allowed for myself. Lindy saw it as escape from my torment. Perhaps it was. Or maybe I could not tolerate his growing disgust.

When the *Nightwine* returned with the specialist, I was barely lucid enough to comprehend. But while the surgeon and Doc Varner made preparations for surgery and Jill paced in the corridor, I . . . I fled to the *Nightwine*. Puzzled crew obeyed my orders to leave the parking orbit and put as much distance between the *Dandelion* and me as the thrusters could.

I stayed in my cabin. The last drugs I'd taken were amphetamines and I was as jittery as a loose strut on an airborne wing. Sixty times an hour, I searched my brain looking for him, suspecting my drug-clouded senses had overlooked him. I screamed his name but he wouldn't answer. Silently he lurked, waiting for an unguarded second in which to take control. Time passed. Had those first minutes of sedation been enough for me to escape without him?

There was a noise from my cabin iris. I froze, wondered where to hide from him. I glanced around. There was only the WC and he could break that down with his huge boots. The intercom blared my name: "Mr. Atkins? Mr. Atkins, are you all right?"

It was Greenberg's voice. Shaking, I traced the lock pattern and let him in. I saw his mental reflection of me and was startled to composure.

"The *Dandelion* has been trying to raise us for the last hour, but your orders not to respond . . ."

"The surgery must be over," I said. "I'll come to the bridge."

Greenberg looked at me suspiciously. "You all right, sir?"

"I'm fine." I wasn't exactly, but I was better; I knew I was alone. I followed him to the bridge, avoiding stares and quizzical thoughts. It was Jill's voice the speaker amplified. I motioned the comm-engineer out of the way and sat down.

"This is the *Nightwine,* Atkins here."

"David!"

I was glad I wasn't close enough to get the mental blast accompanying that single word. "How is he, Jill?"

Her voice was as cold as ice. "He's out of danger now. Where the hell did you go? Tell me what's going on!"

"Another time, okay?"

Jill hesitated. "All right, just hurry back."

"Back?" Right then I realized I had no intention of going back. I'd deserted my brother, severed his life line. I was sure he wouldn't want me near him.

"Of course, *back.* David, he's had surgery on his brain! His telepathic abilities might have been destroyed during surgery."

I still hedged. "Ask Lindy."

"He won't be able to talk for weeks."

"Jill, did you surmise this all along?"

"Yes."

And I thought she was hiding pity! Jill had strengths I'd not suspected. Lindy and I might learn something from a normal. Then I wondered how I'd dared to link his name to mine within the same thought. And I realized I had to know if our friendship had survived this ultimate test. "We're coming about, Jill."

Wake for a telepath or reunion with a friend? If reunion, what kind? Lindy might understand that my survival instinct was completely dependable, not something I could shut off, not even for him. But I wasn't sure: I was so damned filled with guilt that I didn't know how I'd have the gall to touch the man's mind.

Hand over hand, I pushed myself down the center pole. I'd do it for *Jill's* sake. Equivocating, of course, and poorly too. That rockhard woman was waiting for me when I touched the outer rim corridor in the *Dandelion,* her jaw as set as her thought pattern. I suspected an indignant barrage within her, one she wasn't going to let out until she didn't need me any more. I brushed past her.

"Is he . . . ?" I could hear her steps trailing me as I hurried toward the clinic. "David, is he receiving?" she said.

Maybe I was being unfair. Perhaps that privacy circle was for
Lindy's benefit. My defenses were hot-wired just then; I was half-
eager, half-anxious for this confrontation she'd forced on me. "He's
sleeping," I said. The iris dilated more quickly than I recalled, then
Jill and I were in the clinic. The doc was beaming at me, nodding at
his prize patient. "Out," I said, ignoring his desire for my expressed
gratitude. He thought he'd saved my closest friend, but for all I knew
Lindy might now be my enemy, the most powerful kind in the universe. If I didn't think I'd have to throw her bodily, I'd have ordered
Jill out of the room, too. Two angry telepaths are capable of quite a
lot of havoc, and angry we were. Lindy wasn't sleeping, he was ignoring me. Ha! Think again, David Atkins, disarming me!

I felt two feet in my brain, toes first, pointed and rigid. —You
should have kept running, David.— Then he realized Jill was present.
He delayed a second blow and sought her mind. I swayed, leaned
against the wall for support. My hands were at my temples and I was
blinking back tears. Pain tears and guilt tears. Lindy felt them and
hardened himself against them.

"Lindy?" Jill said. She'd moved to the bed and seemed a softer
woman than she had just a few moments ago. She looked at me ex-
pectantly.

—Tell her I'm all right,— Lindy said.

. . . And then he'd have at me. No, not word thoughts: Fringe
stuff leaking. So small only my hyper-fear sensed it. —Go to hell!— I
said. —You still need me.—

Lindy's denial flared, reflexively.

—If you won't recognize your need you can spend your conva-
lescence listening to Jill's lament. She'll pity you until you scream . . .
until you can scream again.—

He flung the vision I'd conjured from his mind. —What do you
want from me, David? A pat on the back? All right, well done. Your
deception was very clever.—

—I'm sorry,— I said. I meant it, but so what. I'd been willing to
sacrifice his existence for mine. Yet at least he was talking, not
striking.

—Jill's very anxious. Please tell her . . .—

—No, not yet,— I said. But I didn't know what to say next. I still
felt as if I'd attempted murder. Why was this guilt mine? I was nothing more than a circumstantial receptacle for his awareness.

—You didn't wait to see if I would attempt the transference.— Surrounded with a violent boiling over of feeling.

—It would have been too late.— But doubt nagged and Lindy seized it.

—You underestimated my restraint.—

Would he have died willingly to spare me? I deliberately used all my abilities to fathom the truth from his mind. —You *would* have possessed me had I been near enough. You'd have clung to me for life as a fetus clings to the womb. You would have left your body to the surgeon's mercy, left it without spirit, without will to live. *I* would be *we.*—

Then, for the first time, something he'd desperately been supressing surfaced. I'd seen the veils and thought hatred would come from that place, but it was his culpability. —I would have been a parasite in your body,— Lindy said. He hated admitting it.

I nodded. —I was the only human in the universe able to host you, but I was too cowardly to accept the obligation.— And I didn't like admitting that. Confession, it seemed, was also good for anger; our tempers subsided. Shaking my head, reaching out to him with my mind, I said, —Lindy, when the parasite is human, is it homicide to eliminate it?— Begging for exoneration.

I felt his mental sigh. —If only you could have hosted me willingly. Not by my forcing you, not through your fear of consequences . . .— He did not form the rest of his thought, but I understood. I'd repudiated a fraternal duty.

—Damn it, Lindy, I'm not a cow who doesn't understand the consequences of getting mounted!— I said, outraged. —It wasn't my duty. It was my *right!*— And when I said it, the words cut through my guilt and made mush of the fragments. —The choice was *mine*, not yours, not God's, and not mankind's.—

Lindy blinked. (A mind can do that.) —One day, it may be I who is faced with exercising my rights . . . or not, for you.— A warning implied? Perhaps, but his comprehension was complete and his wrath as shattered as my guilt.

—If you choose differently than I, my friend, it will be because you are prepared to accept the consequences.— I breathed deeply. More than ever I eagerly anticipated sharing a universe with my telepathic friend; now we appreciated that with rights go burdens and with honors go privileges. I turned to Jill. "He's all right. He's sending and receiving, loud and clear."

She looked at me sharply. "Truly all right?"

—Tell her that though the doctors don't know it yet, *I* know that I will walk again.—

And that the coma, already less deep, would pass, soon. I detected that he'd learned something about our bodies during the surgery, during that moment when he would have abandoned his but found he could not. Something he was willing to share with me, but not now. Not while he was eager to be with Jill. I was pleased, and I liked knowing I could be happy for him again. —Tell her yourself, Lindy,— I said.

He needed no second invitation; he quickly caught my body and went to Jill, explaining in my voice, brushing away her happy tears with my hands. Soon they/we left the clinic.

I really did work state vectors—after things calmed down, and I think I even went to sleep when they did. What the heck, I could spare a shift to sleep with my friends. But suddenly I was startled. Jill was nuzzling my cheek, blowing in my ear.

"Don't go to sleep on me now," she whispered. "You'll be in the cast for months and David won't be here."

—Lindy, what the hell is going on? Why'd you leave me here?—

—Damn doctor . . . sedative.—

I saw the lazy circle of sleep idly wandering in Lindy's satiated mind. —Fight it!— I said, and he said "sure" just before he snored.

I couldn't feign sleep and Lindy was content to nap, as was his habit. Damn, who'd have guessed Jill came around for seconds? She'd be mortified if I told her who she was lavishing her attentions on. She'd bolt upright in the bed and scream her fool head off. So, I thought, what the hell. He'd do it for me.

We're all artists in some sense, whether we paint pictures or plant gardens, cook meals or sing in the shower: every one of us has a natural urge to transform and create. Few are great artists, however, and those who aren't regard the talented with wonder. If you had the chance to see exactly how Vermeer painted his masterpieces, wouldn't you jump at it? What if you could become Vermeer?

The protagonist of this story had that opportunity, and he paid a great deal for it. He learned surprising things about art . . . especially about its ambiguities.

Gordon Eklund is the author of many science fiction stories and novels, including If the Stars Are Gods, *a collaboration with Gregory Benford based on their Nebula Award winning novelette from* Universe 4.

VERMEER'S WINDOW
Gordon Eklund

The painting emerges like a risen bird from the burnt substance of light alone. The artist draws no firm lines—either upon or beneath the painting. The colors—blue and gold predominate—flow automatically. As, over the course of many days, the face and shoulder of a wide-eyed young woman appear upon his easel, the artist reacts with excitement. This is the painting commonly identified as "Girl in a Turban," and it is, he believes, the most profound achievement of Vermeer's brief career—a painting as subtle, ambiguous, mysterious, and still as the play of sunlight through a half-open window. The swirl of a pearl earring is created in the sudden, swift motion of his brush. The artist is stricken with awe as the woman's cape, a green, magical garment, appears beneath his hand. He tries to paint with his eyes shut tightly, unable to bear the magnificent sight so near, but, only human, he soon must peek.

Jan Vermeer (1632–75) is the most enigmatic of great artists. Not only do his works defy precise interpretation, but little or nothing is known of his beliefs, influences, theories, or life. Born in Delph, Holland, Vermeer apparently achieved some degree of local fame, if not wealth, during his own lifetime, but it wasn't until the early years of the twentieth century that his fewer than forty works were rediscovered and hailed as the creations of fluent genius that they most undoubtedly are. With few exceptions, Vermeer's paintings depict a few figures—often only one—against the space of a single room. The faces of women predominate, and some critics have seen in these recurring individuals possibly autobiographical figures. Vermeer's work is further marked by a fascination with the shadings of natural sunlight. Some observers have asserted that the quality of the light in Delph must have been different from that found elsewhere in the world. More likely, the difference is in the painter, not his light.

The artist as a young boy is burdened by no ambition except to become a great painter. Born in New York City in 1988, he embarks upon his first pilgrimage to the Old World at the age of fourteen, only a few months subsequent to the untimely deaths of both parents. While in Europe, the artist does little but visit one museum after another, where he sits for hours and hours beneath the glorious creations of the old masters. It has been remarked that few individuals are capable of viewing a single painting for longer than it takes to peel and eat an orange. The artist, even as a youth, is one of these few individuals. At eighteen, his inherited fortune now secure, he revisits Europe to enroll as a student at the most famous of Paris's great art schools. Within two weeks he has left. According to his instructors, the young artist stands totally devoid of profound talent. His hands shake at the easel; he fails to control his brush stroke. His sense of color and paint are acknowledged to be masterful, but he has failed to indicate any ability to transform the gorgeous visions of his mind into a completed canvas. He is called a great critic, a poor painter.

Alone and despondent in twenty-first century Europe, the young artist falls in with a decadent crowd. Kapp, one of this group, tells the artist of a rare process which makes use of computer fine analyses and brain tapping facilities in order to transform selected people into individuals other than themselves. By means of this process, it is possible for anyone to become nearly anyone he wishes, as long as sufficient data exist concerning the projected new identity. Kapp wished to take advantage of the process himself but was coldly rejected for possible transformation by the corporation marketing the process because of a personal deficiency in funding. The young artist, who is incredibly rich, obtains the name of the corporation from Kapp and immediately books passage to the relevant Eastern European capital. There, a representative of the corporation explains the transformation process in somewhat more detail. "The philosophical foundation which makes our process work," says the representative, "is the concept of character determinism. In other words, given the facts concerning any man—and I mean *all* the facts, about his life, his friends, his family, his world—then that man must nearly always be what he will be. The matter of implanting preselected data within the brain is a simple one indeed—we've been doing it for years, beginning with computers and working up to flesh-and-blood people. Our corporation, through this transformation process, has taken this old technique and applied it to its fullest extent. All we ask you to do is give us a name. Who do you want to be? It may be any man or woman you wish, real and imaginary, though the former is generally preferred, both by us and our usual clientele. Once we have the name, then we set to work. The key factor here is our membership in the International Data Network, which as you probably know links up nearly all the world's largest and most sophisticated computers, including several whose very existence is a closely guarded state secret. What the Data Network is then able to provide us—at an immense cost, I can assure you—is a socio-historical collage of the individual chosen. This collage is put together—no human being or finite group of human beings could ever hope to duplicate the process—from all the data available from any conceivable source concerning the individual and his world. Once this collage is implanted within the memory circuits of your brain, you will then be, I can assure you, that very individual. What is more, as a bonus, because no memory erasure is required, you will be simultaneously aware of your past identity and thus fully able to appreciate the nuances of being two people at once. The process, I admit this candidly, does fail perhaps once in fifty tries. Should that happen in your case, a full refund will gladly be rendered." When the artist, after carefully considering all he has heard, tentatively suggests the name of Jan Vermeer, the representative is at first anxious. He agrees to consult with the corporate engineers, who are equally doubtful but also willing to try. So little is known of the life of the so-called Enigma of Delph that the challenge facing the Data Network is undoubtedly immense. Still, the engineers insist that the possibilities of success remain distinctly high. Vermeer was very much a product of a particular time and place—seventeenth-century Holland—a fact which may prove more consequential to his development as an artist than mere boyhood memories. The artist's own expectations of success do not run high and yet, returning to Western Europe after the completion of the operation, he is willing to accept that he is now Vermeer. His brain insists upon telling him this is so, and he does not choose, for the moment, to doubt it.

He settles in Amsterdam, a city that lies spiritually distant from the sleepy, silent Delph of Vermeer's one known cityscape but which is, the artist believes, as close as he might hope to come in twenty-first-century terms to that magical vista from the past. He retains, as guaranteed, all his old memories, but it is his identity as Vermeer which quickly comes to dominate his every conscious act. With his few remaining funds, he rents a small room in an old house and sets up his easel beside the single meshed window. He begins to paint, but the results are at first disastrous, as far from the art of Vermeer as the scribbled splashings of any talentless youth. Full of bitterness, he contemplates a demand for the immediate return of his own identity but then recalls that Vermeer's earliest accepted work, the Venetian-influenced "Diana and the Nymphs" was not produced until after Vermeer had turned twenty-two. The artist realizes that he must therefore wait for his own dawning moment of inspiration, and so each day until the last smog-bitten rays of the yellow sun vanish from view, he sits motionlessly in front of his barren easel. He sleeps long hours but eats only infrequently. At last, two months subsequent to his own twenty-second birthday, his fingers begin to move of their own accord. Soon enough, he is actually painting. At the bottom center of the canvas there appears quite magically a small white napkin which resembles in shape the image of a dove about to drink. The artist recognizes this as a crucial element in Vermeer's "Diana." He continues to paint, his fingers moving at a speed quite exclusive of his own free will. After many weeks, the finished work stands before him. Overcome by excitement, he rides his motorbike to The Hague, where he is able to view the original work by the first Vermeer. As far as his sharp eye can deduce, nothing—not even a single casual brush stroke—diverges in the slightest detail from his own recently completed work. Back in Amsterdam, he changes lodgings. With money borrowed from a family lawyer, he purchases a small store, which he opens as an art gallery. The first work that he hangs for sale is his own "Diana and the Nymphs." Soon, in his adjoining studio, his hands are at work creating "The Procuress."

In time the artist takes in marriage a wife, who will eventually bear him eleven children. The appearance neither of the wife nor the children surprises him, for he is aware that one of the few known biographical facts concerning Vermeer is that he was married and had nearly a dozen children. Like Catherina Vermeer, Bonnie, his new wife, is one year older than her husband. She explains how, at twelve, she left the home of her father, an accountant in America, and first came to Europe at the age of sixteen. She admits to two previous marriages and he often suspects that, prior to their marriage, Bonnie lived as a common street prostitute. Little in her manner or bearing has the least resemblance to the wealthy and respectable Catherina, but the artist bears in mind that it is he who is Vermeer and not Bonnie who is Catherina. She remains loyal to him and he feels an often fervent love and devotion toward her. His children, even though he remains uncertain of their actual names or identities, are equally dear to him. He can never be sure whether this love is being excited in his heart or in Vermeer's. Frequently, on quiet evenings, he sits beside Bonnie, who is experiencing tri-dee television, and studies the contours of her ripe, plump, cowish face. Before his staring eyes, her visage will then transform itself into an image far deeper and more ethereal than her own slack, pink flesh. He is convinced that what he is witnessing at these moments is nothing less than the true face of Vermeer's Catherina. Some of the features he glimpses seem similar to those he will eventually paint as "Girl with a Flute" and "Girl in a Red Hat," but the vision is never sufficiently specific for him to claim to have solved this particular biographical mystery.

The artist's studio consists of a single cramped cockroach-infested room adjacent to his gallery. In truth, the original purpose of the room was to serve as an automotive garage. There is only one window, which faces north and is heavily meshed against possible late night burglars, and little room for furnishings of any kind. In spite of this, he has no trouble at all from the time of "Young Woman Asleep" onward in painting the sun-bathed room, with its two-paneled window, that serves as a common setting for so much of Vermeer's mature art. It is neither his mind nor his eye which does the actual painting for him; it is his fingers alone that do the work. The muscles twitch ecstatically as the vision of the artist courses wildly through them. He could no more refuse to paint what they demand than he could willingly cease to make his heart pump blood.

His art dealership does not prosper. Because of his refusal to deal in works dated later than the seventeenth century, only art of modest quality comes into his hands. He stocks his own works too, of course, but the prices he chooses to ask for them are not severe. (Neither were those asked by the first Vermeer.) His patrons are often amused at discovering a work such as "Soldier and Smiling Girl" decorating a tiny corner of the gallery. A few, those most knowledgeable about painting, are more amazed than amused. They will stand staring for minutes at a time before finally turning away with a startled laugh. "Why, that replica is so good it might be the original." He replies honestly, "It is not the original." (It is, of course, *an* original.) In his spare time, while Bonnie or one of the children mind the gallery, he walks the streets of Amsterdam. The stark contrast between this exterior world of the twenty-first century and that interior seventeenth-century world which, as Vermeer, he paints constantly astonishes him. His favorite days are those in which the actual orb of the sun can be glimpsed past the dank yellow cloud which hovers continually above. Crime is, of course, rampant in Amsterdam as elsewhere and the artist is frequently robbed, mugged, and assaulted. On one occasion, he is stripped of his clothes by young thugs and forced to return home naked. Because of a severe pollution alert, only a few small children wander outside to observe his passage. These soon turn their heads aside in apparent shame and disgust. His dignity as an adult has been shattered in their eyes. Only the knowledge of his true identity—he is Vermeer, one of the half-dozen greatest painters in the history of the world—sustains him. Despite such agonies, the only parts of the city he takes special care to avoid are those housing the city's few remaining museums, even though four of Vermeer's most masterful paintings are hung there, including one, "Woman Pouring Milk," that he has only recently completed. At home in his studio, he keeps detailed notes on all his work. The exact chronology of Vermeer's career has long been a subject of critical dispute and he hopes to solve this mystery along with many others.

At times a painting will come to him that is a total surprise. These are, of course, the lost works of Vermeer and will in the end total thirteen. Most are similar in subject matter to other known works. He paints: "Woman Seated in Thought," "Two Soldiers and a Girl," "Woman with Pearls," and an unexpectedly religious work, "Christ and Two Apostles." The titles are necessarily of his own devising and sheer guesswork, for his fingers refuse to divulge their secret intentions, even while creating these previously unknown works. He hesitates to place any of the paintings in the gallery but finally relents from curiosity and hangs "Christ and Two Apostles." The sum he is spontaneously offered for the work far exceeds the most he has ever received for a single painting. This gesture pleases him deeply, yet he refuses and thereafter keeps the unknown paintings safely hidden in a dusty corner of his studio.

He is plagued at times by a certain confusion between his earlier self as a painter and his present identity as Vermeer. When he comes to paint "Street in Delph," he removes his easel from the studio for the first time and positions it and himself on a nearby avenue. His view here consists of ruined houses, broken windows, two seedy cheese shops, and three aging women who are most likely prostitutes. His fingers rush to interpret this vision as two adjoining brick houses and three faceless working women. The sky, presently saturated in a thick yellow-brown mist, becomes a lovely, cloud-flecked blue. Since he is Vermeer, he must paint what Vermeer has painted. Still, once the work at hand is complete and ready for sale, he returns to the spot and bravely, as an experiment, attempts to paint what he actually sees, wondering how Vermeer would interpret contemporary reality. In spite of his stern efforts, his fingers soon go stiff and refuse to move until he finally relents, stands, and returns to the studio. He makes a second attempt on a second day but once more fails. Some days after this incident, Bonnie, in bed beside him, says, "If you're such a great artist, how come you've never tried to do a picture of me?" Something makes him agree at once to her suggestion. (Perhaps Vermeer in his time had agreed to a similar request.) The following day, she sits for him, but the portrait soon turns stilted, ugly, and poorly colored; it lacks both unity and purpose. In despair because his fingers have produced such masterpieces, he takes a butcher knife and destroys the unfinished work. Bonnie, in a rage, refuses to speak to him for nine days. He wonders if a parallel might exist with some similar marital rift in Vermeer's own life. If so, this would tend to indicate that his wife's face did not appear among his works. But it is impossible to say for sure.

Soon after he has completed and hung "Two Gentlemen and a Lady with a Glass of Wine," a famous art critic from New York enters his shop. The critic's practiced eye immediately falls upon the recent work and he hastens to a corner to study it. After several minutes silent observation, he beckons the artist to join him. "This," the critic says breathlessly, "is simply amazing. Except for the faces, I'd swear it was the genuine Vermeer." (The artist neglects to point out that the faces visible in the so-called original painting were retouched at a later date by an artist far inferior to Vermeer. What appears on this canvas are Vermeer's original creations.) "Who painted it?" the critic demands. "It was I," the artist admits. The critic stares. "Thank God you're an honest man. I swear you could be greater than Van Meegeren if you wished."

Van Meegeren. Even the hint of such an accusation is enough to startle and then depress the artist. Hans van Meegeren was the great art forger of the middle twentieth century who fooled the art world for years with a succession of fake "Vermeers." The artist believes his own identity to lie far from that of a petty forger: he is as much Vermeer himself as the seventeenth-century Dutchman who first bore that name. Still, he cannot wholly rid his mind of the critic's foul innuendo. At last he boards a jettrain to Rotterdam, where "Meeting at Emmaeus," Van Meegeren's most successful fake "Vermeer," hangs in a secluded museum corner. For some hours, to the bemusement even of a guard, he studies the work. By the time he turns homeward, his heart and soul are much relieved. Van Meegeren, he now understands, was a forger strictly produced by his own limited time; his work, though curious, is utterly without value today. Van Meegeren's

brief success lay in his ability to paint works patterned in the mold
of how Vermeer was perceived in the 1930s. But Vermeer has since
changed, as all great artists must, and Van Meegeren has not. Studying his own works at home in the studio, the artist remains convinced
that he is Vermeer, not Van Meegeren. He does not paint in the
manner of Vermeer; he paints as Vermeer.

His primary responsibility in the creation of the paintings lies in
acquiring the proper tools: paints, canvas, brushes. Once such mechanical ends have been met, the paintings will then flow automatically from his finger tips. He may err in the application of a particular brush stroke but, when he does, his fingers immediately rise to
correct the mistake. There is no need for thought, consideration, or
decision. He recalls the considerable critical speculation over the possible use by Vermeer of a spectroscope. His own work can neither
deny nor affirm this possibility. He makes no use of such an instru-
ment and yet the odd perspective that led many critics to this theory
remains an integral part of the finished paintings. He is Vermeer, but
who was Vermeer? As the years pass, this unanswered question dis-
turbs him more and more. He realizes how little he has learned of the
man he has become. If he were to write a book on the subject, what
could he say that would be new? He could describe in detail the manner by which Vermeer produced a canvas such as "Woman Weighing
Pearls" (a work he has only recently completed), but that would be
all. He knows the *how* but not the *why*. Theories, principles, motiva-
tions, and beliefs continue to elude him. His fingers know but will not
speak.

The artist commences a passionate affair with a young bohemian
girl who lives next door. She is tall, with a long rectangular face, full
lips, and small brown eyes. She claims to work as a civil servant but
the clutter of articles in her rooms suggests a life of crime. He finds in
her figure and character the subject for his painting of "Woman with
a Flute." Bonnie, when informed of the affair by a neighborhood
warden, refuses to take legal remedies. The artist, deeply wounded by
this inaction, confronts his wife alone in the room they share.
Stricken by guilt as well as fury, he unburdens himself as never before. He confesses the fact of his dual identity and demands to know
which it is that Bonnie truly loves. She is amazed and shakes her
head. "Why, I love you, of course. Who else?" "But that is what I

am asking," says the artist. "Which of me is it that you love? Is it me
as I was born, or is it me as I have become—Vermeer?" Bonnie
remains puzzled. "Why, both of you, I guess. It's the only way I've
ever known you." He refuses to be so easily pacified and perseveres.
"But you can't love two people at once. It's got to be one or the
other." Bonnie laughs. "Are you sure?" She nods toward the adjoining house. "Did she make a choice?" Contrite, the artist breaks off
his affair with the young girl. He puzzles over the possibility of a similar act of passion in the life of the earlier Vermeer. Within a few
weeks, the young girl is conscripted into the army fighting in Yugo-
slavia. When the conflict is at last resolved, the girl fails to return. He
notices her name among a list of casualties but remains unmoved.
She was more Vermeer's lover than his own, and Vermeer refuses to
mourn.

A leading American astronomer announces the approach toward
the earth of a large comet, and this is immediately interpreted by
many as an indication of impending doom. As the comet draws
closer, the end of the world is generally proclaimed, and a series of
disturbances ensues. When the comet first appears in the sky, the turmoil becomes much worse. The artist decides to postpone his walks
through the city for the duration of the trouble. One evening, all of
the houses on the nearest two city blocks are burned to the ground.
His gallery is spared and, in the privacy of his studio, his fingers work
to complete two of Vermeer's most distinctive works, "The Geogra-
pher" and, ironically, "The Astronomer." The artist, who seldom attempts to interpret his own work, is unable not to see in these quest-
ing, probing figures all that was once most promising in human
science. It was the questions that these men dared to ask which for a
time forestalled the horror of existence, but once the questions were
answered and the answers found to be lacking, the dark undercurrent
of humanity's ocean again rose to the surface. Through the window,
the artist observes a black cloud hanging like a wreath above the
ruined city. Even the shining comet fails to penetrate this bleak veil,
and its disappearance serves to calm the general turmoil. Within a
few weeks, an army has appeared to restore order and begin the
process of reconstruction. The artist resumes his walks but continues
to paint in a furious manner. Inside of a week, he produces "Lady
Standing at the Virginals." The sight of it moves him to tears. He
attempts to explain the experience to Bonnie but fails. It is not the

sight of the painting, he decides, but the sound. In Vermeer's work, harmony can be heard to speak.

On a late summer's Sunday afternoon, while Bonnie is at church and the children at play, a small, withered, bald-headed man with broad eyes and large ears enters the shop. Going at once to the wall upon which such recent creations as "Lady Playing a Guitar" and "The Astronomer" are hanging, the small man laughs sharply. The gallery is empty, as it most usually is on a Sunday, and the two of them are quite alone. Turning away from the wall, the small man approaches the counter by a circuitous route that allows him to peep into every shadowed corner as a precaution against hidden intruders. "Vermeer," he says, extending a hand toward the artist, "I am Picasso." The artist is startled by this unanticipated revelation but subsequent conversation (conducted by both in harsh, furtive whispers) reveals that this small man has become the great twentieth-century Spanish artist by means similar to those used by the artist in becoming Vermeer. "Well," says the man who is now Picasso, "so what have you found out about the mysterious Vermeer?" The artist is forced to hang his head at this question and reveal his limited success. "I know that he was a very great painter and I know exactly how he applied his paint during the course of each work." "Yes, yes," Picasso says impatiently, "that is all well and good, but what of the man's motivation? What is the character that led him to produce such great works?" "I . . ." The artist feels shamed. "I do not know. The paintings flow automatically from my finger tips—my brain learns nothing." The small man expresses his shock and surprise. "Why, that is how it always must be. It is necessary for one to deduce the truth from, so to speak, the facts at hand. With Picasso, I must admit the task was not difficult." "Oh?" says the artist. "And what then was Picasso's character?" The small man grins (his teeth are unclean): "A charlatan. An absolute charlatan." Irritated by this facile slander, the artist demands a quick explanation. The small man says, "Pablo was no genius—I found that out right away. Do you know why he painted the way he did? Of course you don't, but I'm him, and I know. He painted exactly what the audience of his time demanded, but—and this is the crucial point—what the audience demanded were works of genius. So Pablo, to fill that need, became a genius, but is he the one who deserves the credit? I say no, never. The inspiration lay with the audience, not with the painter. Picasso was a whore with a few tubes of paint—his audience was a creature of true genius." Later the man who claims to be Picasso purchases two inexpensive seventeenth-century landscapes and departs. The artist is greatly disturbed by this visit and goes over and over what he has learned from the small man in hopes of uncovering a fallacy in his thinking. When Bonnie returns, she carries beneath an arm the two landscapes. She glares at the artist and says, "Damn it, what are you up to now? I found these things outside in the trash. We haven't enough money to go throwing such things away." On an impulse, the artist shakes his head sadly. "They are rank forgeries, I am afraid. While you were gone, a man came to me with absolute proof."

He believes he should be seeing the world with the eyes of Vermeer, and yet he finds almost no beauty at all outside his own cloistered studio. The contrast is too immense. The jettrains roar past his home, shaking the studio like a leaf caught in a wind; yet he can observe the stillness and silence of "Maid Holding Out a Letter to her Mistress." He discovers a child of nine starving in a secluded street and her eyes speak to him of lifetimes endured in the passing of a day; but he also knows the passive otherworldliness of "Girl in a Turban." The streets he walks are a mad cacophony of destruction and construction, falling concrete and rising steel; he views the mysterious orderliness of "View of Delph." The spirit of the artist is like a maddened pendulum, thrust wildly from one extreme to another. A great despair overwhelms him and in his studio one afternoon after completing Vermeer's masterwork, "An Artist in His Studio," he contemplates suicide and raises a knife to his chest, but before he can successfully plunge the sharp blade into his heart, too many questions rise to assail him. Did the first Vermeer suffer from despair? Did he once—perhaps at this very time in his life—attempt suicide? No, no, the artist realizes. He can become only what has already been lived. Vermeer did not kill himself and neither can he. Dropping the dagger, the artist rushes outside. He runs madly down the garbage-strewn streets of his neighborhood. The contrast remains: beauty and ugliness; order and chaos; pain and love. To survive, he must make his spirit blind to all that his fingers do not paint.

A wizened priest from a nearby cathedral visits the gallery one day and tells the artist, "My wife has told me of the excellence of your work. I would like to offer you a commission, if I may." Because of the nearby hovering presence of Bonnie, the artist agrees to accept the commission. Their poverty has increased with the passing years. The priest desires an allegorical painting on a New Testament theme. That same night, at Bonnie's urging, the artist sets to work in his studio. By the third day, he is aware that what his fingers are creating is the "Allegory of Faith," a work commonly accepted as Vermeer's very last. Surprised at the suddenness of this event, he takes time to calculate and determines that his present age is thirty-eight. Because Vermeer did not die until he was forty-three, that leaves him five full years in which to live without art. Almost deliberately, it takes him six months to complete the finished "Allegory." The wizened priest, angered at the delay, refuses to pay the artist more than half the agreed commission. The artist closes up his studio and never paints again.

During the final five years of his life, the artist finds that his love for his wife has grown stronger. He takes a new and powerful interest in his surviving children and even memorizes, for the first time, their complete names. Often now the entire family takes long walks through the closely guarded paths of the open city parks. At these times, alone with his wife while the children play, the artist reveals many of the concerns that have lately come to dominate his mind. He has spent many hours in the careful study of Vermeer's work; he has discovered little of value but now believes that this failure may be of significance in itself. He explains to Bonnie: "The greatness of an artist lies not in his mind, which may be a very ordinary one indeed, but rather in his finger tips or, to be less concrete, in his soul. Most people, if asked, will say that a great artist must also be a great man, but such is rarely, if ever, the case. When great artists fail to express great thoughts, we either blame ourselves or the limitations of the language, but a great artist must invariably express great thoughts—as they should, through their work. Take, for example, the seventeenth-century Dutch painter, Jan Vermeer. His paintings express the thought that our perception of reality really consists of nothing beyond the observable effects of sunlight. Is this a great thought, a truly profound one? I do not think so—not as I have expressed it—not in words. But the paintings Vermeer created in order to express this thought—now they are great works indeed." Bonnie seems puzzled by this outburst. Shaking her head tentatively, she says, "But I thought you were Vermeer. You told me that once." The artist says, "No, I was mistaken." "But you had an operation." "True, but it was a failure." "Then," says Bonnie, "you are not a great artist yourself." He pauses upon the path and speaks slowly: "No, I think I am. I am a great artist, yes, but I am not Vermeer. There can be only one Vermeer and he has been dead more than three hundred years. I am someone else—me. I speak to my own age, having seen and endured these times." "But aren't your paintings all the same?" asked Bonnie. "The same as this other man's—Vermeer's?" "They are the same," says the artist, "but I am different." In this, the artist is convinced that he has at last discovered Vermeer.

Wars of the future may be fought with strange weapons, especially if humanity comes into conflict with an alien race. Bombs, lasers, energy-swords . . . what are the dangers of these compared with a weapon that can cast spaceships into other universes where Teddy bears speak multiple languages, snakes have been bred as warriors, and tiny creatures arrange themselves to form hologram images?

Greg Bear, who's rapidly establishing twin careers as writer and artist in science fiction, tells a fast-moving, funny, frightening, and ultimately moving story of people and creatures thrown together in a strange universe.

SCATTERSHOT
Greg Bear

The Teddy bear spoke excellent Mandarin. It was about fifty centimeters tall, plump, with close-set eyes above a nose unusually long for the generally pug breed. It paced around me muttering to itself.

I rolled over and felt barbs down my back and sides. My arms were reluctant to move. There was something about my will to get up and the way my muscles reacted which was out of kilter; the nerves weren't conveying properly. So it was, I thought, with my eyes and the small black and white beast they claimed to see: a derangement of phosphene patterns, cross-tied with childhood memories and snatches of linguistics courses ten years past.

It began speaking Russian. I ignored it and focused on other things. The rear wall of my cabin was unrecognizable, covered with geometric patterns which shifted in and out of bas-relief and glowed faintly in the shadow cast by a skewed panel light. My fold-out desk had been torn from its hinges and now lay on the floor, not far from my head. The ceiling was cream-colored. Last I remembered it had been a pleasant shade of burnt orange. Thus totaled, half my cabin was still present. The other half had been ferried away in the—

Disruption. I groaned and the bear stepped back nervously. My body was gradually co-ordinating. Bits and pieces of disassembled vision integrated and stopped their random flights, and still the creature walked, and still it spoke, though getting deep into German.

It was not a minor vision. It was either real or a full-fledged hallucination.

"What's going on?" I asked.

It bent over me, sighed, and said, "Of all the fated arrangements. A speaking I know not the best of—Anglo." It held out its arms and shivered. "Pardon the distraught. My cords of psyche—nerves?—they have not decided which continuum to obey this moment."

"Mine, too," I said cautiously. "Who are you?"

"Psyche, we are all psyche. Take this care and be not content with illusion, this path, this merriment. Excuse. Some writers in English. All I know is from the read."

"Am I still on my ship?"

"So we are all, and *hors de combat*. We limp for the duration."

I was integrated enough to stand, and I did so, towering above the bear and rearranging my tunic. My left breast ached with a bruise. Because we had been riding at one G for five days, I was wearing a bra, and the bruise lay directly under a strap. Such, to quote, was the fated arrangement. As my wits gathered and held converse, I considered what might have happened and felt a touch of the "distraughts" myself. I began to shiver like a recruit in pressure-drop training.

We had survived. That is, at least I had survived, out of a crew of forty-three. How many others?

"Do you know . . . have you found out—"

"Worst," the bear said. "Some I do not catch, the deciphering of other things not so hard. Disrupted about seven, eight hours past. It was a force of many, for I have counted ten separate things not in my recognition." It grinned. "You are ten, and best yet. We are perhaps not so far in world-lines."

We'd been told survival after disruption was possible. Practical statistics indicated one out of a myriad ships, so struck, would remain integral. For a weapon which didn't actually kill in itself, the probability disrupter was very effective.

"Are we intact?" I asked.

"Fated," the Teddy bear said. "I cognize we can even move and seek a base. Depending."

"Depending," I echoed. The creature sounded masculine, despite size and a childlike voice. "Are you a he? Or—"

"He," the bear said quickly.

I touched the bulkhead above the door and ran my finger along a familiar, slightly crooked seam. Had the disruption kept me in my own universe—against incalculable odds—or exchanged me to some other? Was either of us in a universe we could call our own?

"Is it safe to look around?"

The bear hummed. "Cognize—know not. Last I saw, others had not reached a state of organizing."

It was best to start from the beginning. I looked down at the creature and rubbed a bruise on my forehead. "Wh-where are you from?"

"Same as you, possible," he said. "Earth. Was mascot to captain, for cuddle and advice."

That sounded bizarre enough. I walked to the hatchway and peered down the corridor. It was plain and utilitarian, but neither the right color nor configuration. The hatch at the end was round and had a manual sealing system, six black throw-bolts which no human engineer would ever have put on a spaceship. "What's your name?"

"Have got no official name. Mascot name known only to captain."

I was scared, so my brusque nature surfaced and I asked him sharply if his captain was in sight, or any other aspect of the world he'd known.

"Cognize not," he answered. "Call me Sonok."

"I'm Geneva," I said. "Francis Geneva."

"We are friends?"

"I don't see why not. I hope we're not the only ones who can be friendly. Is English difficult for you?"

"Mind not. I learn fast. Practice make perfection."

"Because I can speak some Russian, if you want."

"Good as I with Anglo?" Sonok asked. I detected a sense of humor—and self-esteem—in the bear.

"No, probably not. English it is. If you need to know anything, don't be embarrassed to ask."

"Sonok hardly embarrassed by anything. Was mascot."

The banter was providing a solid framework for my sanity to grab on to. I had an irrational desire to take the bear and hug him, just for want of something warm. His attraction was undeniable—tailored, I guessed, for that very purpose. But tailored from what? The color suggested panda; the shape did not.

"What do you think we should do?" I asked, sitting on my bunk.

"Sonok not known for quick decisions," he said, squatting on the floor in front of me. He was stubby-limbed, but far from clumsy.

"Nor am I," I said. "I'm a software and machinery language expert. I wasn't combat-trained."

"Not cognize 'software,' " Sonok said.

"Programming materials," I explained. The bear nodded and got up to peer around the door. He pulled back and scrabbled to the rear of the cabin.

"They're here!" he said. "Can port shut?"

"I wouldn't begin to know how—" But I retreated just as quickly and clung to my bunk. A stream of serpents flowed by the hatchway, metallic green and yellow, with spatulate heads and red ovals running dorsally. Observing so much at first glance was commendable.

The stream passed without even a hint of intent to molest, and Sonok climbed down from the bas-relief pattern. "What the hell are they doing here?" I asked.

"They are a crew member, I think," Sonok said.

"What else is out there?"

The bear straightened and looked at me steadily. "Have none other than to seek," he said solemnly. "Elsewise, we possess no rights to ask. No?" The bear walked to the hatch, stepped over the bottom seal, and stood in the corridor. "Come?"

I got up and followed.

A woman's mind is a strange pool to slip into at birth. It is set within parameters by the first few months of listening and seeing. Her infant mind is a vast blank template which absorbs all and stores it away. In those first few months comes role acceptance, a beginning to attitude, and a hint of future achievement. Listening to adults and observing their actions build a storehouse of preconceptions and warnings: *Do not see those ghosts on bedroom walls—they aren't there! None of the rest of us can see your imaginary companions, darling. . . . It's something you have to understand.*

And so, from some dim beginning, not *ex nihilo* but out of totality, the woman begins to pare her infinite self down. She whittles away at this unwanted piece, that undesired trait. She forgets in time that she was once part of all, and turns to the simple tune of life, rather than the endless and symphonic *before*. She forgets those companions who danced on the ceiling above her bed and called to her from the dark. Some of them were friendly; others, even in the dim time, were not pleasant. But they were all *her*. For the rest of her life, the woman seeks some echo of that preternatural menagerie; in the men she chooses to love, in the tasks she chooses to perform, in the way she tries to be. After thirty years of cutting, she becomes Francis Geneva.

When love dies, another piece is pared away, another universe is sheared off, and the split can never join again. With each winter and spring, spent on or off worlds with or without seasons, the woman's life grows more solid, and smaller.

But now the parts are coming together again, the companions out of the dark above the child's bed. Beware of them. They're all the things you once lost, or let go, and now they walk on their own, out of your control; reborn, as it were, and indecipherable.

"Do you have understanding?" the bear asked. I shook my head to break my steady stare at the six-bolted hatch.

"Understand what?" I asked.

"Of how we are here."

"Disrupted. By Aighors, I presume."

"Yes, they are the ones for us, too. But how?"

"I don't know," I said. No one did. We could only observe the results. When the remains of disrupted ships could be found, they always resembled floating garbage heaps—plucked from our universe, rearranged in some cosmic grab bag, and returned. What came back was of the same mass, made up of the same basic materials, and recombined with a tendency toward order and viability. But in deep space, even 90 per cent viability was tantamount to none at all. If the ship's separate elements didn't integrate perfectly—a one in a hundred thousand chance—there were no survivors. But oh, how interested we were in the corpses! Most were kept behind the Paper Curtain of secrecy, but word leaked out even so—word of ostriches with large heads, blobs with bits of crystalline sea water still adhering to them . . . and now my own additions, a living Teddy bear and a herd of parti-colored snakes. All had been snatched out of terrestrial ships from a maze of different universes.

Word also leaked, that out of five thousand such incidents, not once had a human body been returned to our continuum.

"Some things still work," Sonok said. "We are heavy the same."

The gravitation was unchanged—I hadn't paid attention to that. "We can still breathe, for that matter," I said. "We're all from one world. There's no reason to think the basics will change." And that meant there had to be standards for communication, no matter how diverse the forms. Communication was part of my expertise, but thinking about it made me shiver. A ship runs on computers, or their equivalent. How were at least ten different computer systems communicating? Had they integrated with working interfaces? If they hadn't, our time was limited. Soon all hell would join us; darkness, and cold, and vacuum.

I released the six throw-bolts and opened the hatch slowly.

"Say, Geneva," Sonok mused as we looked into the corridor beyond. "How did the snakes get through here?"

I shook my head. There were more important problems. "I want to find something like a ship's bridge, or at least a computer terminal. Did you see something before you found my cabin?"

Sonok nodded. "Other way in corridor. But there were . . . things there. Didn't enjoy the looks, so came this way."

"What were they?" I asked.

"One like trash can," he said. "With breasts."

"We'll keep looking this way," I said by way of agreement.

The next bulkhead was a dead end. A few round displays studded the wall, filled like bull's-eyes with concentric circles of varying thickness. A lot of information could be carried in such patterns, given a precise optical scanner to read them—which suggested a machine more than an organism, though not necessarily. The bear paced back and forth in front of the wall.

I reached out with one hand to touch the displays. Then I got down on my knees to feel the bulkhead, looking for a seam. "Can't see it, but I feel something here—like a ridge in the material."

The bulkhead, displays and all, peeled away like a heart's triplet valve and a rush of air shoved us into darkness. I instinctively rolled into a fetal curl. The bear bumped against me and grabbed my arm. Some throbbing force flung us this way and that, knocking us against squeaking wet things. I forced my eyes open and unfurled my arms and legs, trying to find a grip. One hand rapped against metal or hard plastic, and the other caught what felt like rope. With some fumbling,

I gripped the rope and braced myself against the hard surface. Then I had time to sort out what I was seeing.

The chamber seemed to be open to space, but we were breathing, so obviously a transparent membrane was keeping the atmosphere in. I could see the outer surface of the ship, and it appeared a hell of a lot larger than I'd allowed. Clinging to the membrane in a curve, as though queued on the inside of a bubble, were five or six round nebulosities which glowed dull orange like dying suns. I was hanging on to something resembling a ship's mast, a metal pylon which reached from one side of the valve to the center of the bubble. Ropes were rigged from the pylon to stanchions which seemed suspended in midair, though they had to be secured against the membrane. The ropes and pylon supported clusters of head-sized spheres covered with hairlike plastic tubing, or walrus' whiskers. They clucked like brood hens as they slid away from us. *"Gospodin!"* Sonok screeched.

The valve which had given us access was still open, pushing its flaps in and out. I kicked away from the pylon. The bear's grip was fierce. The flaps loomed, slapped against us, and closed with a final sucking throb. We were on the other side, lying on the floor. The bulkhead was impassively blank again.

The bear rolled away from my arm and stood up. "Best to try the other way!" he suggested. "More easily faced, I cognize."

I unshipped the six-bolted hatch and we crawled through. We doubled back and went past my cabin. The corridor, now that I thought of it, was strangely naked. In any similar region on my ship, there would have been pipes, access panels, printed instructions—and at least ten cabin doors.

The corridor curved a few yards past my cabin, and the scenery became more diverse. We found several small cubbyholes, all empty, and Sonok walked cautiously ahead. "Here," he said. "Can was here."

"Gone now," I said. We stepped through another six-bolt hatch into a chamber which had the vague look of a command center. In large details it resembled the bridge of my own ship, and I rejoiced for that small sense of security.

"Can you talk to it?" Sonok asked.

"I can try. But where's a terminal?"

The bear pointed to a curved bench in front of a square, flat surface, devoid of keyboard, speaker, or knobs. It didn't look much like a terminal—though the flat surface resembled a visual display screen—

but I wasn't ashamed to try speaking to it. Nor was I abashed when it didn't answer. "No go. Something else."

We looked around the chamber for several minutes, but found nothing more promising. "It's like a bridge," I said, "but nothing matches specifically. Maybe we're looking for the wrong thing."

"Machines run themselves, perhaps," Sonok suggested.

I sat on the bench, resting an elbow on the edge of the "screen." Nonhuman technologies frequently used other senses for information exchange than we did. Where we generally limit machine-human interactions to sight, sound, and occasionally touch, the Crocerians used odor, and the Aighors controlled their machines on occasion with microwave radiation from their nervous systems. I lay my hand across the screen. It was warm to the touch, but I couldn't detect any variation in the warmth. Infrared was an inefficient carrier of information for creatures with visual orientation. Snakes used infrared to seek their prey—

"Snakes," I said. "The screen is warm. Is this part of the snake ship?"

Sonok shrugged. I looked around the cabin to find other smooth surfaces. They were few. Most were crisscrossed with raised grills. Some were warm to the touch. There were any number of possibilities—but I doubted if I would hit on the right one very quickly. The best I could hope for was the survival of some other portion of my ship.

"Sonok, is there another way out of this room?"

"Several. One is around the gray pillar," he said. "Another hatch with six dogs."

"What?"

"Six . . ." He made a grabbing motion with one hand. "Like the others."

"Throw-bolts," I said.

"I thought my Anglo was improving," he said sulkily.

"It is. But it's bound to be different from mine, so we both have to adapt." We opened the hatch and looked into the next chamber. The lights flickered feebly and wrecked equipment gave off acrid smells. A haze of cloying smoke drifted out and immediately set ventilators to work. The bear held his nose and jumped over the seal for a quick walk through the room.

"Is something dead in here," he said when he returned. "Not like human, but not far. It is shot in head." He nodded for me to go with

him, and I reluctantly followed. The body was pinned between two
bolted seats. The head was a mess, and there was ample evidence
that it used red blood. The body was covered by gray overalls, and
though twisted into an awkward position, was obviously more canine
than human. The bear was correct in one respect—it was closer to me
than whiskered balls or rainbow snakes. The smoke was almost clear
when I stepped back from the corpse.

"Sonok, any possibility this could be another mascot?"

The bear shook his head and walked away, nose wrinkled. I wondered if I'd insulted him.

"I see nothing like terminal here," he said. "Looks like nothing
work now, anyway. Go on?"

We returned to the bridgelike chamber and Sonok picked out another corridor. By the changing floor curvature, I guessed that all my
previous estimates as to ship size were way off. There was no way of
telling either the shape or size of this collage of vessels. What I'd seen
from the bubble had appeared endless, but that might have been optical distortion.

The corridor dead-ended again, and we didn't press our luck as to
what lay beyond the blank bulkhead. As we turned back, I asked,
"What were the things you saw? You said there were ten of them, all
different."

The bear held up his paws and counted. His fingers were otter-like,
and quite supple. "Snakes, number one," he said. "Cans with breasts,
two; back wall of your cabin, three; blank bulkhead with circular
marks, four; and you, five. Other things not so different, I think now
—snakes and six-dog hatches might go together, since snakes know
how to use them. Other things—you and your cabin fixtures, so on, all
together. But you add dead thing in overalls, fuzzy balls, and who
can say where it ends?"

"I hope it ends someplace. I can only face so many variations before I give up. Is there anything left of your ship?"

"Where I was after disruption," the bear said. "On my stomach in
bathroom."

Ah, that blessed word! "Where?" I asked. "Is it working?" I'd
considered impolitely messing the corridors if there was no alternative.

"Works still, I think. Back through side corridor."

He showed me the way. A lot can be learned from a bathroom—
social attitudes, technological levels, even basic psychology, not to

mention anatomy. This one was lovely and utilitarian, with fixtures
for males and females of at least three sizes. I made do with the largest. The bear gave me privacy, which wasn't strictly necessary—
bathrooms on my ship being co-ed—but appreciated, nonetheless. Exposure to a Teddy bear takes getting used to.

When I was through, I joined Sonok in the hall and realized I'd
gotten myself turned around. "Where are we?"

"Is changing," Sonok said. "Where bulkhead was, is now hatch.
I'm not sure I cognize how—it's a different hatch."

And it was, in an alarming way. It was battle-armored, automatically controlled, and equipped with heavily shielded detection equipment. It was ugly and khaki-colored and had no business being inside
a ship, unless the occupants distrusted each other. "I was in an-
teroom, outside lavatory," Sonok said, "with door closed. I hear loud
sound and something like metal being cut, and I open door to see
this."

Vague sounds of machines were still audible, grinding and screaming. We stayed away from the hatch. Sonok motioned for me to follow him. "One more," he said. "Almost forgot." He pointed into a
cubbyhole, about a meter deep and two meters square. "Look like fish
tank, perhaps?"

It was a large, rectangular tank filled with murky fluid. It reached
from my knees to the top of my head, and fit the cubbyhole perfectly.
"Hasn't been cleaned, in any case," I said.

I touched the glass to feel how warm or cold it was. The tank
lighted up and I jumped back, knocking Sonok over. He rolled into a
backward flip and came upright wheezing.

The light in the tank flickered like a strobe, gradually speeding up
until the glow was steady. For a few seconds it made me dizzy. The
murk was gathering itself together. I bent over cautiously to get a close
look. The murk wasn't evenly distributed. It was made up of animals
no more than a centimeter long, with two black eyespots at one end,
a pinkish "spine," and a feathery fringe rippling between head and
tail. They were forming a dense mass at the center of the tank.

The bottom of the tank was crossed with ordered dots of lumines-
cence, which changed colors across a narrow spectrum: red, blue,
amber.

"It's doing something," Sonok said. The mass was defining a
shape. Shoulders and head appeared, then torso and arms, sculpted in
ghost-colored brine shrimp. When the living sculpture was finished, I

recognized myself from the waist up. I held out my arm, and the mass slowly followed suit.

I had an inspiration. In my pants pocket I had a marker for labeling tapas cube blanks. It used soft plastic wrapped in a metal jacket. I took it out and wrote three letters across the transparent front of the tank: WHO. Part of the mass dissolved and re-formed to mimic the letters, the rest filling in behind. WHO they spelled, then they added a question mark.

Sonok chirped and I came closer to see better. "They understand?" he asked. I shook my head. I had no idea what I was playing with. WHAT ARE YOU? I wrote.

The animals started to break up and return to the general murk. I shook my head in frustration. So near! The closest thing to communication yet.

"Wait," Sonok said. "They're group again."

TENZIONA, the shrimp coalesced. DYSFUNCTIO. GUARDATEO AB PEREGRINO PERAMBULA.

"I don't understand. Sounds like Italian—do you know any Italian?"

The bear shook his head.

"'*Dysfunctio,*'" I read aloud. "That seems plain enough. '*Ab peregrino*'? Something about a hawk?"

"*Peregrine,* it is foreigner," Sonok said.

"Guard against foreigners . . . 'perambula,' as in strolling? Watch for the foreigners who walk? Well, we don't have the grammar, but it seems to tell us something we already know. Christ! I wish I could remember all the languages they filled me with ten years ago."

The marks on the tank darkened and flaked off. The shrimp began to form something different. They grouped into branches and arranged themselves nose-to-tail, upright, to form a trunk, which rooted itself to the floor of the tank.

"Tree," Sonok said.

Again they dissolved, returning in a few seconds to the simulacrum of my body. The clothing seemed different, however—more like a robe. Each shrimp changed its individual color now, making the shape startlingly lifelike. As I watched, the image began to age. The outlines of the face sagged, wrinkles formed in the skin, and the limbs shrank perceptibly. My arms felt cold and I crossed them over my breasts; but the corridor was reasonably warm.

Of course the universe isn't really held in a little girl's mind. It's one small thread in a vast skein, separated from every other universe by a limitation of constants and qualities, just as death is separated from life by the eternal nonreturn of the dead. Well, now we know the universes are less inviolable than death, for there are ways of crossing from thread to thread. So these other beings, from similar Earths, are not part of my undifferentiated infancy. That's a weak fantasy for a rather unequipped young woman to indulge in. Still, the symbols of childhood lie all around—nightmares, and Teddy bears, and dreams held in a tank; dreams of old age and death. And a tree, gray and ghostly, without leaves. That's me. Full of winter, wood cracking into splinters. How do *they* know?

A rustling came from the corridor ahead. We turned from the tank and saw the floor covered with rainbow snakes, motionless, all heads aimed at us. Sonok began to tremble.

"Stop it," I said. "They haven't done anything to us."

"You are bigger," he said. "Not meal-sized."

"They'd have a rough time putting you away, too. Let's just sit it out calmly and see what this is all about." I kept my eyes on the snakes and away from the tank. I didn't want to see the shape age any more. For all the sanity of this place, it might have kept on going, through death and decay down to bones. Why did it choose me; why not Sonok?

"I cannot wait," Sonok said. "I have not the patience of a snake." He stepped forward. The snakes watched without a sound as the bear approached, one step every few seconds. "I want to know one solid thing," he called back. "Even if it is whether they eat small, furry mascots."

The snakes suddenly bundled backward and started to crawl over each other. Small sucking noises smacked between their bodies. As they crossed, the red ovals met and held firm. They assembled like a troop of acrobats and reared into a single mass, cobra-like, but flat as a planarian worm. A fringe of snakes weaved across the belly like a caterpillar's idea of Medusa.

Brave Sonok was undone. He swung around and ran past me. I was too shocked to do anything but face the snakes down, neck hairs crawling. I wanted to speak but couldn't. Then, behind me, I heard:

"Sinieux! A la discorpes!"

As I turned, I saw two things, one in the corner of each eye; the snakes fell into a pile, and a man dressed in red and black vanished into a side corridor. The snakes regrouped into a hydra with six tentacles and grasped the hatch's throw-bolts, springing it open and slithering through. The hatch closed, and I was alone.

There was nothing for it but to scream a moment, then cry. I lay back against the wall, getting the fit out of me as loudly and quickly as possible. When I was able to stop, I wiped my eyes with my palms and kept them covered, feeling ashamed. When I looked out again, Sonok was standing next to me.

"We've an Indian on board," he said. "Big, with black hair in three ribbons"—he motioned from crown to neck between his ears—"and a snappy dresser."

"Where is he?" I asked hoarsely.

"Back in place like bridge, I think. He controls snakes?"

I hesitated, then nodded.

"Go look?"

I got up and followed the bear. The man in red and black watched us as we entered the chamber, sitting on a bench pulled from the wall. He was big—at least two meters tall—and hefty, dressed in a black silk shirt with red cuffs. His cape was black with a red eagle embroidered across the shoulders. He certainly looked Indian—ruddy skin, aristocratic nose, full lips held tight as if against pain.

"Quis la?" he queried.

"I don't speak that," I said. "Do you know English?"

The Indian didn't break his stolid expression. He nodded and turned on the bench to put his hand against a grill. "I was taught in the British school at Nova Loudon," he said, his accent distinctly Oxfordian. "I was educated in Indonesia, and so I speak Dutch, High and Middle German, and some Asian tongues, specifically Nippon and Tagalog. But at English I am fluent."

"Thank God," I said. "Do you know this room?"

"Yes," he replied. "I designed it. It's for the Sinieux."

"Do you know what's happened to us?"

"We have fallen into hell," he said. "My Jesuit professors warned me of it."

"Not far wrong," I said. "Do you know why?"

"I do not question my punishments."

"We're not being punished—at least, not by God or devils."

He shrugged. It was a moot point.

"I'm from Earth, too," I said. "From *Terre.*"

"I know the words for Earth," the Indian said sharply.

"But I don't think it's the same Earth. What year are you from?" Since he'd mentioned Jesuits, he almost had to use the standard Christian Era dating.

"Year of Our Lord 2345," he said.

Sonok crossed himself elegantly. "For me 2290," he added. The Indian examined the bear dubiously.

I was sixty years after the bear, five after the Indian. The limits of the grab bag were less hazy now. "What country?"

"Alliance of Tribal Columbia," he answered, "District Quebec, East Shore."

"I'm from the Moon," I said. "But my parents were born on Earth, in the United States of America."

The Indian shook his head slowly; he wasn't familiar with it.

"Was there—" But I held back the question. Where to begin? Where did the world-lines part? "I think we'd better consider finding out how well this ship is put together. We'll get into our comparative histories later. Obviously, you have star drive."

The Indian didn't agree or disagree. "My parents had ancestors from the West Shore, Vancouver," he said. "They were Kwakiutl and Kodikin. The animal, does it have a Russian accent?"

"Some," I said. "It's better than it was a few hours ago."

"I have blood debts against Russians."

"Okay," I said, "but I doubt if you have anything against this one, considering the distances involved. We've got to learn if this ship can take us someplace."

"I have asked," he said.

"Where?" Sonok asked. "A terminal?"

"The ship says it is surrounded by foreign parts, and can barely understand them. But it can get along."

"You really don't know what happened, do you?"

"I went to look for worlds for my people, and took the Sinieux with me. When I reached a certain co-ordinate in the sky, far along the arrow line established by my extrasolar pierce, this happened." He lifted his hand. "Now there is one creature, a devil, which tried to attack me. It is dead. There are others, huge black men who wear golden armor and carry gold guns like cannon, and they have gone away behind armored hatches. There are walls like rubber which open onto more demons. And now you—and it." He pointed at the bear.

"I'm not an 'it,'" Sonok said. "I'm an *ours*."

"Small *ours*," the Indian retorted.

Sonok bristled and turned away. "Enough," I said. "You haven't fallen into hell, not literally. We've been hit by something called a disrupter. It snatched us from different universes and reassembled us according to our world-lines, our . . . affinities."

The Indian smiled faintly, very superior.

"Listen, do you understand how crazy this is?" I demanded, exasperated. "I've got to get things straight before we all lose our calm. The beings who did this—in my universe they're called 'Aighors.' Do you know about them?"

He shook his head. "I know of no other beings but those of Earth. I went to look for worlds."

"Is your ship a warper ship—does it travel across a geodesic in higher spaces?"

"Yes," he said. "It is not in phase with the crest of the Stellar Sea, but slips between the foamy length, where we must struggle to obey all laws."

That was a fair description of translating from status geometry—our universe—to higher geometries. It was more poetic than scientific, but he was here, so it worked well enough. "How long have your people been able to travel this way?"

"Ten years. And yours?"

"Three centuries."

He nodded in appreciation. "You know then what you speak of, and perhaps there aren't any devils, and we are not in hell. Not this time."

"How do you use your instruments in here?"

"I do not, generally. The Sinieux use them. If you will not get upset, I'll demonstrate."

I glanced at Sonok, who was still sulking. "Are you afraid of the snakes?"

The bear shook his head.

"Bring them in," I said. "And perhaps we should know each other's name?"

"Jean Frobish," the Indian said. And I told him mine.

The snakes entered at his whistled command and assembled in the middle of the cabin. There were two sets, each made up of about fifty. When meshed they made two formidable meta-serpents. Frobish instructed them with spoken commands and a language which sounded like birdcalls. They obeyed faultlessly and without hesitation, perfect servants. They went to the controls at his command and made a few manipulations, then turned to him and delivered, one group at a time, a report in consonantal hisses and claps. The exchange was uncanny and chilling. Jean nodded and the serpents disassembled.

"Are they specially bred?" I asked.

"Techtonogenetic farming," he said. "They are excellent workers, and have no will of their own, since they have no cerebrums. They can remember, and en masse can think, but not for themselves, if you see what I mean." He showed another glimmer of a smile. He was proud of his servants.

"I think I understand. Sonok, were you specially bred?"

"Was mascot," Sonok said. "Could breed for myself, given chance."

The subject was touchy, I could see. I could also see that Frobish and Sonok wouldn't get along without friction. If Sonok had been a big bear—and not a Russian—instead of an ursine dwarf, the Indian might have had more respect for him.

"Jean, can you command the whole ship from here?"

"Those parts that answer."

"Can your computers tell you how much of the ship will respond?"

"What is left of my vessel responds very well. The rest is balky, or blank entirely. I was trying to discover the limits when I encountered you."

"You met the people who've been putting in the armored hatches?"

He nodded. "Bigger than Masai," he said.

I now had explanations for some of the things we'd seen, and could link them with terrestrial origins. Jean and his Sinieux weren't beyond the stretch of reason, nor was Sonok. The armored hatches weren't quite as mysterious now. But what about the canine? I swallowed. That must have been the demon Frobish killed. And beyond the triplet valves?

"We've got a lot to find out," I said.

"You and the animal, are you together, from the same world?" Frobish asked. I shook my head. "Did you come alone?"

I nodded. "Why?"

"No men, no soldiers?"

I was apprehensive now. "No."

"Good." He stood and approached a blank wall near the gray pillar. "Then we will not have too many to support, unless the ones in golden armor want our food." He put his hand against the wall and a round opening appeared. In the shadow of the hole, two faces watched with eyes glittering.

"These are my wives," Frobish said. One was dark-haired and slender, no more than fifteen or sixteen. She stepped out first and looked at me warily. The second, stockier and flatter of face, was brown-haired and about twenty. Frobish pointed to the younger first. "This is Alouette," he said. "And this is Mouse. Wives, acquaint with Francis Geneva." They stood one on each side of Frobish, holding his elbows, and nodded at me in unison.

That made four humans, more if the blacks in golden armor were men. Our collage had hit the jackpot.

"Jean, you say your machines can get along with the rest of the ship. Can they control it? If they can, I think we should try to return to Earth."

"To what?" Sonok asked. "Which Earth waits?"

"What's the bear talking about?" Frobish asked.

I explained the situation as best I could. Frobish was a sophisticated engineer and astrogator, but his experience with other continua—theoretical or actual—was small. He tightened his lips and listened grimly, unwilling to admit his ignorance. I sighed and looked to Alouette and Mouse for support. They were meek, quiet, giving all to the stolid authority of Frobish.

"What woman says is we decide where to go," Sonok said. "Depends, so the die is tossed, on whether we like the Earth we would meet."

"You would like my Earth," Frobish said.

"There's no guarantee it'll be your Earth. You have to take that into account."

"You aren't making sense." Frobish shook his head. "My decision is made, nonetheless. We will try to return."

I shrugged and said no more about the matter. "Try as best you can." We would face the truth later.

"I'll have the Sinieux watch over the machines after I initiate instructions," Frobish said. "Then I would like Francis to come with me to look at the animal I killed." I agreed without thinking about his motives. He gave the meta-serpents their orders and pulled down a panel cover to reveal a small board designed for human hands.

When he was through programming the computers, he continued his instructions to the Sinieux. His rapport with the animals was perfect—the interaction of an engineer with his tool. There was no thought of discord or second opinions. The snakes, to all intents and purposes, were machines keyed only to his voice. I wondered how far the obedience of his wives extended.

"Mouse will find food for the bear, and Alouette will stand guard with the *fusil. Comprens-la?*" The women nodded and Alouette plucked a rifle from the hideaway. "When we return, we will all eat."

"I will wait to eat with you," Sonok said, standing near me.

Frobish looked the bear over coldly. "We do not eat with tectoes," he said, haughty as a British officer addressing his servant. "But you will eat the same food we do."

Sonok stretched out his arms and made two shivers of anger. "I have never been treated less than a man," he said. "I will eat with all, or not eat." He looked up at me with his small golden eyes and asked in Russian, "Will you go along with him?"

"We don't have much choice," I answered in kind.

"What do you recommend?"

"Play along for the moment. I understand." I was unable to read his expression behind the black mask and white markings; but if I'd been him, I'd have questioned the understanding. This was no time to instruct the bear in assertion, however.

Frobish opened the hatch to the wrecked room and let me step in first. He then closed the hatch and sealed it. "I've seen the body already," I said. "What do you want to know?"

"I want your advice on this room," he said. I didn't believe that for an instant. I bent down to examine the creature between the chairs more carefully.

"What did it try to do to you?" I asked.

"It came at me. I thought it was a demon. I shot at it, and it died."

"What caused the rest of this damage?"

"I fired a good many rounds," he said. "I was more frightened then. I'm calm now."

"Thank God for that," I said. "This—he or she—might have been able to help us."

"Looks like a dog," Frobish said. "Dogs cannot help."

For me, that crossed the line. "Listen," I said tightly, standing away from the body. "I don't think you're in touch with what's going on here. If you don't get in touch soon, you might get us all killed. I'm not about to let myself die because of one man's stupidity."

Frobish's eyes widened. "Women do not address men thus," he said.

"This woman does, friend! I don't know what kind of screwy social order you have in your world, but you had damn well better get used to interacting with different sexes, not to mention different species! If you don't, you're asking to end up like this poor thing. It didn't have a chance to say friend or foe, yea or nay! You shot it out of panic, and we can't have any more of that!" I was trembling.

Frobish smiled over grinding teeth and turned to walk away. He was fighting to control himself. I wondered if my own brains were in the right place. The few aspects of this man which were familiar to me couldn't begin to give complete understanding. I was clearly out of my depth, and kicking to stay afloat might hasten death, not slow it.

Frobish stood by the hatch, breathing deeply. "What is the dog-creature? What is this room?"

I turned back to the body and pulled it by one leg from between the chairs. "It was probably intelligent," I said. "That's about all I can tell. It doesn't have any personal effects." The gore was getting to me, and I turned away for a moment. I was tired—oh, so tired I could feel the weary rivers dredging through my limbs. My head hurt abominably. "I'm not an engineer," I said. "I can't tell if any of this equipment is useful to us, or even if it's salvageable. Care to make an opinion?"

Frobish looked over the room with a slight inclination of one eyebrow. "Nothing of use here."

"Are you sure?"

"I am sure." He looked across the room and sniffed the air. "Too much burned and shorted. You know, there is much that is dangerous here."

"Yes," I said, leaning against the back of a seat.

"You will need protection."

"Oh."

"There is no protection like the bonds of family. You are argumentative, but my wives can teach you our ways. With bonds of family, there will be no uncertainty. We will return and all will be well."

He caught me by surprise and I wasn't fast on the uptake. "What do you mean, bonds of family?"

"I will take you to wife, and protect you as husband."

"I think I can protect myself, thank you."

"It doesn't seem wise to refuse. Left alone, you will probably be killed by such as this." He pointed at the canine.

"We'll have to get along whether we're family or not. That shouldn't be too hard to understand. And I don't have any inclination to sell myself for security."

"I do not pay money for women!" Frobish said. "Again you ridicule me."

He sounded like a disappointed little boy. I wondered what his wives would think, seeing him butt his head against a wall without sense or sensibility.

"We've got to dispose of the body before it decays," I said. "Help me carry it out of here."

"It isn't fit to touch."

My tiredness took over and my rationality departed. "You goddamned idiot! Pull your nose down and look at what's going on around you! We're in serious trouble—"

"It isn't the place of a woman to speak thus, I've told you," he said. He approached and raised his hand palm-high to strike. I instinctively lowered my head and pushed a fist into his abdomen. The slap fell like a kitten's paw and he went over, glancing off my shoulder and twisting my arm into a painful muscle kink. I cursed and rubbed the spot, then sat down on the deck to consider what had happened.

I'd never had much experience with sexism in human cultures. It was disgusting and hard to accept, but some small voice in the back of my mind told me it was no more blameworthy than any other social attitude. His wives appeared to go along with it. At any rate, the situation was now completely shot to hell. There was little I could do except drag him back to his wives and try to straighten things out when he came to. I took him by both hands and pulled him up to the hatch. I unsealed it, then swung him around to take him by the shoulders. I almost retched when one of his shoulders broke the crust on a drying pool of blood and smeared red along the deck.

I miss Jaghit Singh more than I can admit. I think about him, and wonder what he'd do in this situation. He is a short, dark man with perfect features and eyes like those in the pictures of Krishna. We formally broke off our relationship three weeks ago, at my behest, for

I couldn't see any future in it. He would probably know how to handle Frobish, with a smile and even a spirit of comradeship, but without contradicting his own beliefs. He could make a girl's childhood splinters go back to form the whole log again. He could make these beasts and distortions come together again. Jaghit! Are you anywhere that has seasons? Is it still winter for you? You never did understand the little girl who wanted to play in the snow. Your blood is far too hot and regular to stand up to my moments of indecisive coldness, and you could not—would not—force me to change. I was caught between child and my thirty-year-old form, between spring and winter. Is it spring for you now?

Alouette and Mouse took their husband away from me fiercely, spitting with rage. They weren't talking clearly, but what they shouted in quasi-French made it clear who was to blame. I told Sonok what had happened and he looked very somber indeed. "Maybe he'll shoot us when he wakes up," he suggested.

To avoid that circumstance, I appropriated the rifle and took it back to my half-room. There was a cabinet intact, and I still had the key. I didn't lock the rifle in, however; better simply to hide it and have easy access to it when needed. It was time to be diplomatic, though all I really wanted for the moment was blessed sleep. My shoulder stung like hell and the muscles refused to get themselves straight.

When I returned, with Sonok walking point a few steps ahead, Frobish was conscious and sitting in a cot pulled from a panel near the hole. His wives squatted nearby, somber as they ate from metal dishes.

Frobish refused to look me in the eye. Alouette and Mouse weren't in the least reluctant, however, and their gazes threw sparks. They'd be good in a fight, if it ever came down to that. I hoped I wasn't their opposite.

"I think it's time we behaved reasonably," I said.

"There is no reason on this ship," Frobish shot back.

"Aye on that," Sonok said, sitting down to a plate left on the floor. He picked at it, then reluctantly ate, his fingers handling the implements with agility.

"If we're at odds, we won't get anything done," I said.

"That is the only thing which stops me from killing you," Frobish said. Mouse bent over to whisper in his ear. "My wife reminds me you must have time to see the logic of our ways." Were the women lucid despite their anger, or was he maneuvering on his own? "There is also the possibility you are a leader. I'm a leader, and it's difficult for me to face another leader at times. That is why I alone control this ship."

"I'm not a—" I bit my lip. Not too far, too fast. "We've got to work together and forget about being leaders for the moment."

Sonok sighed and put down the plate. "I have no leader," he said. "That part of me did not follow into this scattershot." He leaned on my leg. "Mascots live best when made whole. So I choose Geneva as my other part. I think my English is good enough now for us to understand."

Frobish looked at the bear curiously. "My stomach hurts," he said after a moment. He turned to me. "You do not hit like a woman. A woman strikes for the soft parts, masculine weaknesses. You go for direct points with knowledge. I cannot accept you as the bear does, but if you will reconsider, we should be able to work together."

"Reconsider the family bond?"

He nodded. To me, he was almost as alien as his snakes. I gave up the fight and decided to play for time.

"I'll have to think about it. My upbringing . . . is hard to overcome," I said.

"We will rest," Frobish said.

"And Sonok will guard," I suggested. The bear straightened perceptibly and went to stand by the hatch. For the moment, it looked like a truce had been made, but as cots were pulled out of the walls, I picked up a metal bar and hid it in my trousers.

The Sinieux went to their multilevel cages and lay quiet and still as stone. I slipped into the cot and pulled a thin sheet over myself. Sleep came immediately, and delicious lassitude finally unkinked my arm.

I don't know how long the nap lasted, but it was broken sharply by a screech from Sonok. "They're here! They're here!"

I stumbled out of the cot, tangling one leg in a sheet, and came to a stand only after the Indian family was alert and armed. So much, I thought, for hiding the rifle. "What's here?" I asked, still dopey.

Frobish thrust Sonok away from the hatch with a leg and brought the cover around with a quick arm to slam it shut, but not before a black cable was tossed into the room. The hatch jammed on it and sparks flew. Frobish stood clear and brought his rifle to his shoulder.

Sonok ran to me and clung to my knee. Mouse opened the cages and let the Sinieux flow onto the deck. Frobish retreated from the hatch as it shuddered. The Sinieux advanced. I heard voices from the other side. They sounded human—like children, in fact.

"Wait a moment," I said. Mouse brought her pistol up and aimed it at me. I shut up.

The hatch flung open and hundreds of fine cables flew into the room, twisting and seeking, wrapping and binding. Frobish's rifle was plucked from his hands and surrounded like a bacterium with antibodies. Mouse fired her pistol wildly and stumbled, falling into a nest of cables, which jerked and seized. Alouette was almost to the hole, but her ankles were caught and she teetered.

Cables ricocheted from the ceiling and grabbed at the bundles of Sinieux. The snakes fell apart, some clinging to the cables like insects on a frog's tongue. More cables shot out to hold them all, except for a solitary snake which retreated past me. I was bound rigid and tight, with Sonok strapped to my knee. The barrage stopped, and a small, shadowed figure stood in the hatch, carrying a machete. It cleared the entrance of the sticky strands and stepped into the cabin light, looking around cautiously. Then it waved to companions behind and five more entered.

They were identical, each just under half a meter in height—a little shorter than Sonok—and bald and pink as infants. Their features were delicate and fetal, with large gray-green eyes and thin, translucent limbs. Their hands were stubby-fingered and plump as those on a Rubens baby. They walked into the cabin with long strides, self-assured, nimbly avoiding the cables.

Sonok jerked at a sound in the corridor—a hesitant, high-pitched mewing. "With breasts," he mumbled through the cords.

One of the infantoids arranged a ramp over the bottom seal of the hatch. He then stepped aside and clapped to get attention. The others formed a line, pink fannies jutting, and held their hands over their heads as if surrendering. The mewing grew louder. Sonok's trash can with breasts entered the cabin, twisting this way and that like a crazy, obscene toy. It was cylindrical, with sides tapering to a fringed skirt at the base. Three levels of pink and nippled paps ringed it at equal intervals from top to bottom. A low, flat head surmounted the body, tiny black eyes examining the cabin with quick, nervous jerks. It looked like nothing so much as the Diana of Ephesus, *Magna Mater* to the Romans.

One of the infantoids announced something in a piping voice, and the Diana shivered to acknowledge. With a glance around, the same infantoid nodded and all six stood up to the breasts to nurse.

Feeding over, they took positions around the cabin and examined us carefully. The leader spoke to each of us in turn, trying several languages. None matched our own. I strained to loosen the cords around my neck and jaw and asked Sonok to speak a few of the languages he knew. He did as well as he could through his bonds. The leader listened to him with interest, then echoed a few words and turned to the other five. One nodded and advanced. He spoke to the bear in what sounded like Greek. Sonok stuttered for a moment, then replied in halting fragments.

They moved to loosen the bear's cords, looking up at me apprehensively. The combination of Sonok and six children still at breast hit me deep and I had to suppress a hysteric urge to laugh.

"I think he is saying he knows what has happened," Sonok said. "They've been prepared for it; they knew what to expect. I think that's what they say."

The leader touched palms with his Greek-speaking colleague, then spoke to Sonok in the same tongue. He held out his plump hands and motioned for the bear to do likewise. A third stepped over rows of crystallized cable to loosen Sonok's arms.

Sonok reluctantly held up his hands and the two touched. The infantoid broke into shrill laughter and rolled on the floor. His mood returned to utmost gravity in a blink, and he stood as tall as he could, looking us over with an angry expression.

"We are in command," he said in Russian. Frobish and his wives cried out in French, complaining about their bonds. "They speak different?" the infantoid asked Sonok. The bear nodded. "Then my brothers will learn their tongues. What does the other big one speak?"

"English," Sonok said.

The infantoid sighed. "Such diversities. I will learn from her." My cords were cut and I held out my palms. The leader's hands were cold and clammy, making my arm-hairs crawl.

"All right," he said in perfect English. "Let us tell you what's happened, and what we're going to do."

His explanation of the disruption matched mine closely. "The Alternates have done this to us." He pointed to me. "This big one calls them Aighors. We do not dignify them with a name—we're not even sure they're the same. They don't have to be, you know. Whoever has the secret of disruption, in all universes, is our enemy. We are companions now, chosen from a common pool of those who have been disrupted across a century or so. The choosing has been done so that our natures match closely—we are all from one planet. Do you understand this idea of being companions?"

Sonok and I nodded. The Indians made no response at all.

"But we, members of the Nemi, whose mother is Noctilux, we were prepared. We will take control of the aggregate ship and pilot it to a suitable point, from which we can take a perspective and see what universe we're in. Can we expect your co-operation?"

Again, the bear and I agreed and the others were silent.

"Release them all," the infantoid said with a magnanimous sweep of his hands. "Be warned, however—we can restrain you in an instant, and we are not likely to enjoy being attacked again."

The cords went limp and vaporized with some heat discharge and a slight sweet odor. The Diana rolled over the ramp and left the cabin, with the leader and another infantoid following. The others watched us closely, not nervous but intent on our every move. Where the guns had been, pools of slag lay on the floor.

"Looks like we've been overruled," I said to Frobish. He didn't seem to hear me.

In a few hours, we were told where we would be allowed to go. The area extended to my cabin and the bathroom, which apparently was the only such facility in our reach. The Nemi didn't seem to need bathrooms, but their recognition of our own requirements was heartening. Within an hour after the take-over, the infantoids had swarmed over the controls in the chamber. They brought in bits and pieces of salvaged equipment, which they altered and fitted with extraordinary speed and skill. Before our next meal, taken from stores in the hole, they understood and controlled all the machinery in the cabin.

The leader then explained to us that the aggregate, or "scattershot," as Sonok had called it, was still far from integrated. At least two groups had yet to be brought into the fold. These were the giant blacks in golden armor, and the beings which inhabited the transparent bubble outside the ship. We were warned that leaving the established boundaries would put us in danger.

The sleep period came. The Nemi made certain we were slumbering before they slept, if they slept at all. Sonok lay beside me on the bunk in my room, snukking faint snores and twitching over distant dreams. I stared up into the dark, thinking of the message tank. That was my unrevealed ace. I wanted to get back to it and see what it was capable of telling me. Did it belong to one of the groups we were familiar with, or was it different, perhaps a party in itself?

I tried to bury my private thoughts—disturbing, intricate thoughts—and sleep, but I couldn't. I was dead weight now, and I'd never liked the idea of being useless. Useless things tended to get thrown out. Since joining the various academies and working my way up the line, I'd always assumed I could play some role in any system I was thrust into.

But the infantoids, though tolerant and even understanding, were self-contained. As they said, they'd been prepared and they knew what to do. Uncertainty seemed to cheer them, or at least draw them together. Of course, they were never more than a few meters away from a very impressive symbol of security—a walking breast-bank.

The Nemi had their Diana, Frobish had his wives, and Sonok had me. I had no one. My mind went out, imagined blackness and fields of stars, and perhaps nowhere the worlds I knew, and quickly snapped back. My head hurt and my back muscles were starting to cramp. I had no access to hormone stabilizers, so I was starting my period. I rolled over, nudging Sonok into grumbly half-waking, and shut my eyes and mind to everything, trying to find a peaceful glade and perhaps Jaghit Singh. But even in sleep all I found was snow and broken gray trees.

The lights came up slowly and I was awakened by Sonok's movements. I rubbed my eyes and got up from the bunk, standing unsteadily.

In the bathroom, Frobish and his wives were going about their morning ablutions. They looked at me but said nothing. I could feel a tension, but tried to ignore it. I was irritable, and if I let any part of my feelings out, they might all pour forth—and then where would I be?

I returned to my cabin with Sonok and didn't see Frobish following until he stepped up to the hatchway and looked inside.

"We will not accept the rule of children," he said evenly. "We'll need your help to overcome them."

"Who will replace them?" I asked.

"I will. They've made adjustments to my machines which I and the Sinieux can handle."

"The Sinieux cages are welded shut," I said.

"Will you join us?"

"What could I do? I'm only a woman."

"I will fight, my wives and you will back me up. I need the rifle you took away."

"I don't have it." But he must have seen my eyes go involuntarily to the locker.

"Will you join us?"

"I'm not sure it's wise. In fact, I'm sure it isn't. You just aren't equipped to handle this kind of thing. You're too limited."

"I have endured all sorts of indignities from you. You are a sickness of the first degree. Either you will work with us, or I will cure you now." Sonok bristled, and I noticed the bear's teeth were quite sharp.

I stood and faced him. "You're not a man," I said. "You're a little boy. You haven't got hair on your chest or anything between your legs—just a bluff and a brag."

He pushed me back on the cot with one arm and squeezed up against the locker, opening it quickly. Sonok sank his teeth into the man's calf and brought forth cloth and blood, but before I could get into action the rifle was out and his hand was on the trigger. I fended the barrel away from me and the first shot went into the corridor. It caught a Nemi and removed the top of his head. The blood and sound seemed to drive Frobish into a frenzy. He brought the butt down, trying to hammer Sonok, but the bear leaped aside and the rifle went into the bunk mattress, sending Frobish off balance. I hit his throat with the side of my hand and caved in his windpipe.

Then I took the rifle and watched him choking against the cabin wall. He was unconscious and turning blue before I gritted my teeth and relented. I took him by the neck and found his pipe with my thumbs, then pushed from both sides to flex the blockage outward. He took a breath and slumped.

I looked at the body in the corridor. "This is it," I said quietly. "We've got to get out of here." I slung the rifle and peered around the hatch seal. The noise hadn't brought anyone yet. I motioned to Sonok and we ran down the corridor, away from the Indian's control room and the infantoids.

"Geneva," Sonok said as we passed an armored hatch. "Where do we go?" I heard a whirring sound and looked up. The shielded camera above the hatch was watching us, moving behind its thick gray glass like an eye. "I don't know," I said.

A seal had been placed over the flexible valve in the corridor which led to the bubble. We turned at that point and went past the nook where the message tank had been. It was gone, leaving a few anonymous fixtures behind.

An armored hatch had been punched into the wall several yards beyond the alcove, and it was unsealed. That was almost too blatant an invitation, but I had few other choices. They'd mined the ship like termites. The hatch led into a straight corridor without gravitation. I took Sonok by the arm and we drifted dreamily down. I saw pieces of equipment studding the walls which reminded me of my own ship, and I wondered if people from my world were around. It was an idle wonder. The way I felt now, I doubted I could make friends with anyone. I wasn't the type to establish camaraderie under stress. I was the wintry one.

At the end of the corridor, perhaps a hundred meters down, gravitation slowly returned. The hatch there was armored and open. I brought the rifle up and looked around the seal. No one. We stepped through and I saw the black in his golden suit, fresh as a ghost. I was surprised; he wasn't. My rifle was up and pointed, but his weapon was down. He smiled faintly.

"We are looking for a woman known as Geneva," he said. "Are you she?"

I nodded. He bowed stiffly, armor crinkling, and motioned for me to follow. The room around the corner was unlighted. A port several meters wide, ribbed with steel beams, opened onto starry dark. The stars were moving and I guessed the ship was rolling in space. I saw other forms in the shadows, large and bulky, some human, some apparently not. Their breathing made them sound like waiting predators.

A hand took mine and a shadow towered over me. "This way."

Sonok clung to my calf, and I carried him with each step I took. He didn't make a sound. As I passed from the viewing room, I saw a blue and white curve begin at the top of the port, and caught an outline of continent. Asia, perhaps. We were already near Earth. The shapes of the continents could remain the same in countless universes, immobile grounds beneath the thin and pliable paint of living things. What was life like in the distant world-lines where even the shapes of the continents had changed?

The next room was also dark, but a candle flame flickered behind curtains. The shadow which had guided me returned to the viewing room and shut the hatch. I heard the breathing of only one besides myself.

I was shaking. Would they do this to us one at a time? Yes, of course; there was too little food. Too little air. Not enough of anything on this tiny scattershot. Poor Sonok, by his attachment, would go before his proper moment.

The breathing came from a woman, somewhere to my right. I turned to face in her general direction. She sighed. She sounded very old, with labored breath and a kind of pant after each intake.

I heard a dry crack of adhered skin separating, dry lips parting to speak, then the tiny *click* of eyelids blinking. The candle flame wobbled in a current of air. As my eyes adjusted, I could see that the curtains formed a translucent cubicle in the dark.

"Hello," the woman said. I answered weakly. "Is your name Francis Geneva?"

I nodded, then, in case she couldn't see me, said, "I am."

"I am Junipero," she said, aspirating the *j* as in Spanish. "I was commander of the High-space ship *Callimachus*. Were you a commander on your ship?"

"No," I replied. "I was part of the crew."

"What did you do?"

I told her in a spare sentence or two, pausing to cough. My throat was like parchment.

"Do you mind stepping closer? I can't see you very well."

I walked forward a few steps.

"There is not much from your ship in the way of computers or stored memory," she said. I could barely make out her face as she bent forward, squinting to examine me. "But we have learned to speak your language from those parts which accompanied the Indian. It is not too different from a language in our past, but none of us spoke it until now. The rest of you did well. A surprising number of you could communicate, which was fortunate. And the little children who suckle—the Nemi—they always know how to get along. We've had several groups of them on our voyages."

"May I ask what you want?"

"You might not understand until I explain. I have been through the *mutata* several hundred times. You call it disruption. But we haven't found our home yet, I and my crew. The crew must keep trying, but I won't last much longer. I'm at least two thousand years old, and I can't search forever."

"Why aren't the others old?"

"My crew? They don't lead. Only the top must crumble away to keep the group flexible, only those who lead. You'll grow old, too. But not the crew. They'll keep searching."

"What do you mean, me?"

"Do you know what 'Geneva' means, dear sister?"

I shook my head, no.

"It means the same thing as my name, Junipero. It's a tree which gives berries. The one who came before me, her name was Jenevrboom, and she lived twice as long as I, four thousand years. When she came, the ship was much smaller than it is now."

"And your men—the ones in armor—"

"They are part of my crew, and there are women, too."

"They've been doing this for six thousand years?"

"Longer," she said. "It's much easier to be a leader and die, I think. But their wills are strong. Look in the tank, Geneva."

A light came on behind the cubicle and I saw the message tank. The murky fluid moved with a continuous, swirling flow. The old woman stepped from the cubicle and stood beside me in front of the tank. She held out her finger and wrote something on the glass, which I couldn't make out.

The tank's creatures formed two images, one of me and one of her. She was dressed in a simple brown robe, her peppery black hair cropped into short curls. She touched the glass again and her image changed. The hair lengthened, forming a broad globe around her head. The wrinkles smoothed. The body became slimmer and more muscular, and a smile came to the lips. Then the image was stable.

Except for the hair, it was me.

I took a deep breath. "Every time you've gone through a disruption, has the ship picked up more passengers?"

"Sometimes," she said. "We always lose a few, and every now and then we gain a large number. For the last few centuries our size has been stable, but in time we'll probably start to grow. We aren't anywhere near the total yet. When that comes, we might be twice as big as we are now. Then we'll have had, at one time or another, every scrap of ship, and every person that ever went through a disruption."

"How big is the ship now?"

"Four hundred kilometers across. Built rather like a Volvox, if you know what that is."

"How do you keep from going back yourself?"

"We have special equipment to keep us from separating. When we started out, we thought it would shield us from a *mutata,* but it didn't. This is all it can do for us now—it can keep us in one piece each time we jump. But not the entire ship."

I began to understand. The huge bulk of ship I had seen from the window was real. I had never left the grab bag. I was in it now, riding the aggregate, a tiny particle attracted out of solution to the colloidal mass.

Junipero touched the tank and it returned to its random flow. "It's a constant shuttle run. Each time, we return to the Earth to see who if any can find their home there. Then we seek out the ones who have the disrupters, and they attack us—send us away again."

"Out there—is that my world?"

The old woman shook her head. "No, but it's home to one group—three of them. The three creatures in the bubble."

I giggled. "I thought there were a lot more than that."

"Only three. You'll learn to see things more accurately as time passes. Maybe you'll be the one to bring us all home."

"What if I find my home first?"

"Then you'll go, and if there's no one to replace you, one of the crew will command until another comes along. But someone always comes along, eventually. I sometimes think we're being played with, never finding our home, but always having a Juniper to command us." She smiled wistfully. "The game isn't all bitter and bad tosses, though. You'll see more things, and do more, and be more, than any normal woman."

"I've never been normal," I said.

"All the better."

"If I accept."

"You have that choice."

" 'Junipero,' " I breathed. "Geneva." Then I laughed.

"How do you choose?"

The small child, seeing the destruction of its thousand companions with each morning light, and the skepticism of the older ones, becomes frightened and wonders if she will go the same way. Someone will raise the shutters and a sunbeam will impale her and she'll phantomize. Or they'll tell her they don't believe *she's* real. So she sits in the dark, shaking. The dark becomes fearful. But soon each day becomes a triumph. The ghosts vanish, but she doesn't, so she forgets the shadows and thinks only of the day. Then she grows older, and the companions are left only in whims and background thoughts. Soon she is whittled away to nothing; her husbands are past, her loves are firm and not potential, and her history stretches away behind her like carvings in crystal. She becomes wrinkled, and soon the daylight haunts her again. Not every day will be a triumph. Soon there will be a final beam of light, slowly piercing her jellied eye, and she'll join the phantoms.

But not now. Somewhere, far away, but not here. All around, the ghosts have been resurrected for her to see and lead. And she'll be resurrected, too, always under the shadow of the tree name.

"I think," I said, "that it will be marvelous."

So it was, thirty centuries ago. Sonok is gone, two hundred years past; some of the others have died, too, or gone to their own Earths. The ship is five hundred kilometers across and growing. You haven't come to replace me yet, but I'm dying, and I leave this behind to guide you, along with the instructions handed down by those before me.

Your name might be Jennifer, or Ginepra, or something else, but you will always be me. Be happy for all of us, darling. We will be forever whole.

The ecological problems of the late twentieth century have made us all aware of the need for living more in rhythm with nature—"walking lightly on the earth," as an American Indian saying puts it. In architecture, this ideal combines function with aesthetics: houses should blend into their surroundings and leave the native wildlife undisturbed. But are we sure we know all the forms of life around us?

Charles Ott is a talented new writer who has contributed stories to Analog, Vertex, *and other publications. "The Ecologically Correct House" marks his first appearance in* Universe.

THE ECOLOGICALLY CORRECT HOUSE
Charles Ott

He was trying to wave his arms in a whisper, gesticulating dramatically for the benefit of his wife without attracting the attention of the rest of the party. He was not entirely successful.

"It's an ugly house!" he hissed comically, sloshing his highball. "How can I say it's not ugly when it's ugly? Look around you—ugliness as far as the eye can see, right? It's just plain ugly!"

"Keep your voice down and your arms in, Hugh!" his wife hissed in return. "It's not your house and it's not your party so you just hush up. Anyway, George doesn't talk about *your* designs that way, does he?"

"I'll bet he does, when I'm not around," Hugh said moodily. "Fundamentally, we're two different kinds of architect—he's an idiot

and I'm not. Leah, you saw the way this house looks from the outside. Like it was shipwrecked here, am I right? He made a big deal
about the landscaping, working around the trees that were here, lots
of sodding and bushes and planting and borders and God knows
what-all and then he sticks in this horrible hamburger stand made out
of concrete and sheet glass. I need another drink."

"A lot of people like it," Leah said primly. "Hatterson in the *Sunday Press* said it had very clean lines. George is a big name architect.
I think you're just jealous."

Hugh began, "George is a big name . . ." He was interrupted by a
hearty voice from the stairwell. "Hugh! Leah! Good to see you! Can
I get you a drink? Do you need anything? Sorry not to meet you before, but this party is driving me up the wall. How do you like the
house?"

Leah got as far as, "George, it's *just* beauti—"

"Sure is ugly, George," said Hugh cordially. "Whatever possessed
you to build such a God-awful gas station? I can see it real clearly,
'cause I'm drunk. You get drunk, too. You'll see. Place looks like a
post office, or worse."

"Hugh, old buddy, you and I are old professional colleagues,
right?" George said. "Belong to the club together, refer business to
each other, all that, right? Nothing you could say could possibly
offend me, because I know you mean it as professional criticism." He
sipped at his drink. "However, just a friendly word of advice, old
buddy. Someday, somebody is going to cut your loudmouthed heart
out."

"Ha, ha, you're a great kidder there, George. Too bad you're not
as good an architect as you are a comedian."

"Oh, but I am! I built this house just as a gag. Boffo, don't you
think?"

Leah stepped anxiously between the two men. "George, do you
suppose you could show us around? I'd love to see what kind of a
house you designed for yourself. I'll bet it's got all sorts of clever personal touches."

"Oh, I guess so," he said. "Try to curb your spouse. In fact, let's
go into the kitchen and get some black coffee for him. I could use
some myself."

They filed down a free-standing spiral stairway and through the
living room, Hugh shambling behind. George played the genial host

with everyone they passed. Low beach sounds came through the sliding glass wall.

"Some kitchen, eh?" George said. "Everything in that row of metal panels is a different appliance—I had the uniform facings put on myself. The coffee's in the cupboard and you'll find hot water in the pot there. Leah, I believe there's sugar and cream behind you." The coffee mugs were a complicated stainless steel pattern covered with a decorative shell. Hugh looked at his sullenly, sipped cautiously. The kitchen also had sliding panels facing the beach; they walked out and sat at a table on the balcony deck. Small wavelets rolled in from the lake to make a low rushing noise.

George excused himself shortly to go back to hosting his party. After some time the noise began to fade as the gathering broke up. Hugh was on his third mug of coffee when George returned and sat heavily, puffing and making a show of exhaustion.

"Whew! What a mob! Leah, don't get up, I'll fetch myself something in a minute. That lake breeze sure does feel good. I'm glad I don't have to get up tomorrow." Leah stood anyway and went back into the kitchen. George asked softly, "Coming down yet, Hugh?"

"I guess," Hugh nodded. "Um . . . I owe you an apology."

"No problem. If you're still feeling all right I'll show you around after I've cooled down. I've been planning this house for years and I love to show it off."

"Actually, Leah and I went through it early this evening," Hugh said, a little formal with lingering tipsiness. "I'm afraid Leah was just trying to calm us down. You should get married again, George. I don't know what I'd do without Leah to get me out of trouble."

George smiled distantly, leaned back in his chair to watch the lake. The moon was just rising. Leah returned with a tray of rolls and mugs of bouillon and at the same time a big-eyed face appeared over the balcony rail, bearing a toothy grin. "George! Did you let everybody go home without telling me? What a bummer."

"Hello, Susie," George said without turning. "Been walking along the lake shore?"

"Yeah. Pretty out there tonight." The girl crossed to the steps and came up on the deck. She was twenty or so, dressed in ostentatious overalls and affected a tomboyish manner to match.

"Susie, this is Hugh and that's Leah. Hugh's a colleague of mine. Susie used to be one of my students," George explained, "when I was teaching Design." There were polite murmurs all around and Susie went into the kitchen.

"So what do you think of the house, Hugh?" George said, still without turning. "I really would like to know."

"Well . . . well, hell, George, the fact is that I really don't care for it. I mean, I've got to be honest. Listen, did I tell you I've finished building my own place?"

"Why, no," George said. "I hadn't heard anything about it. The last I heard it was just a plan."

Hugh looked abashed. "I haven't said much about it. I really hate parties and I'd have to give one if people heard. But look, I want you to come around some evening. Tomorrow, if you want. That house is everything I believe about architecture and it's everything this place isn't." Leah looked alarmed.

"Such as?" George asked placidly.

"Well, this promenade deck, for instance. The style is pure Kalifornia Koastline, but that beach is Lake Michigan, not the Pacific, and this is Illinois. It'll be too cold to use this more than two months out of the year. The whole house is like that: it doesn't fit in, doesn't even try. A house ought to blend in, be a part of its surroundings. This thing stands out like an appendectomy scar."

"But if a building's beautiful by itself," Leah said, in a devil's-advocate sort of voice, "isn't that enough?"

"No! Everything ought to be beautiful together, because everything *is* together. You have to consider the whole environment, the world-system. It's all a part of one thing. Do you see what I'm talking about?"

"Bravo!" cried Susie, emerging from the kitchen. "Are you a Libra, Hugh? Libras think in terms of harmony and wholeness."

"No, I'm a Capricorn. Sorry 'bout that."

"Oh." She dimpled. "Did you ever used to be a Libra?" They shared a companionable grin.

"Seriously, George," Hugh went on, "nature's bigger than you are —you ought to try to get along, be part of your natural community. There is a biocommunity even on a suburban lake shore, trees and ground cover and animals and waterfront insects and so forth, and I think you'd be happier if you lived with it instead of against it."

"I'll go along with that," Susie said. "You lead an unnatural life, George. I just looked in your cupboard and freezer. TV dinners, mixes, imitations, instants—why don't you eat some real organic *food* for a change? No wonder you're so crabby."

"You're ganging up on me," George protested.

"George, why don't you come to dinner tomorrow night?" Leah said. "Hugh is just being coy. We just raised the roof tree on the place two weeks ago and we're dying to show it off. Susie, you're invited too if you want."

"Thanks," Susie said.

George leaned forward. "You used that phrase 'raised the roof tree.' I'll bet you literally did just that, didn't you?"

"Um, yes, we did. Hugh thought it was a nice gesture."

"What's all this about?" Susie asked.

Hugh explained, "Oh, it's an old custom to hang a small tree or wreath from the highest point of a new house. Sort of a good luck charm."

"More than that," George said. "It attracts the attention of beneficent spirits. Am I right?"

"Okay. If you say so."

"Wow," said Susie. "This is something I've got to know more about."

At sunset the next day Hugh sat on a stump not far from his door placidly whittling, jacketed against a summer evening chill. The area around was a scrubby hilltop forest of pin oaks and hickorys, surrounded by farm lands and pastures on all sides. He was overlooking the dirt road that served the house: half a mile away George was gingerly easing his white Cadillac past the ruts. The scraping noises from the tail were clearly audible.

He arrived red-faced and exasperated, Susie sitting meekly quiet in the passenger seat. The bulky Cadillac looked anachronistic against the rustic background.

"Hugh, I thought you said you had your house built. Did you bring me all the way up here to look at your *lot?*"

"No, of course not. Hullo, Susie. Come on, I'll show you around." The three left the road by a lightly worn trail. Hugh pointed to a knoll covered with closely grown vetch. "That's the garage." They twisted and ducked around trees, coming shortly to the downward side of a woody overhang. Hugh gestured at the hollowed-out pocket thus formed. "Home sweet home, folks."

"Mr. Badger's house!" cried Susie delightedly, clapping her hands. "Is it all warm and snug inside?"

"Absolutely! The door's around the side," Hugh said. George squatted down and peered into the hollow, then reached out and rapped his knuckles on an invisible pane a foot or so in. "The window plastic is reflective-treated," Hugh told him. "Come on in and see how it looks from the other side."

The door was round-cornered, hidden in a tangle of roots but easily accessible by a flagstone path. There was a short stair that gave onto a broad, pleasant living room accented by a stone fireplace on one side and the wide, curving window on the other. It was obvious that the seemingly random forest had been groomed in the path of the window; the view soared magnificently through the tree-framed copse and across the fields and distant farmhouses all the way to the unsullied horizon, now gilded with the sunset. In that kindly light the rest of the furnishings seemed to glow, simple chairs and cushions, bright rugs and sturdy hanging kitchenware. The walls appeared to be quarried limestone, rough and friendly-looking.

Leah appeared, bearing a tray with coffee and biscuits. "George, there's room in the garage for your car," Hugh said. "Let's go bring it in. We'll be back in just a moment." Hugh led the way down a passageway that ended in an underground carport. Its entrance faced away from the road. "I need my car to get to work," he explained, a little apologetic, "but I'm going to get an electric just as soon as possible." They brought in the Cadillac and returned to the living room just as the sun finally vanished.

"Leah, do you really cook with those pots and pans hanging on the wall?" Susie was asking.

"Sure," Leah said. "I didn't want a lot of phony decorations around. We have a couple of paintings—real ones, I mean—and I tried to make everything else both beautiful and functional. Like the coffee?"

"It's wonderful."

"I've got this mellow old coffeepot downstairs that everybody thinks is just an antique for atmosphere. I got it from my mother. But I use it every day, with real ground beans and I break an egg in the coffee so it settles clear, and that's why it's good. You can't do that in an electric coffeemaker."

"On the other hand," Hugh put in, "the range downstairs is brand-new and fancy. That's the way we built the whole house; nothing's new or mechanical for its own sake but everything that ought to be new, is. It's a modern comfortable house, and yet you could walk by on the road and not know it's here. We tried to make everything fit in, inside and out."

"Very impressive," George said mildly. "How many rooms are there?"

"Just six. I'll show you the lower floor in a few minutes—it's a little larger than this and has the bedrooms, bath, kitchen, and library. Below that there's just a little utilities deck. The place is small because we don't expect the family to grow very much larger."

"What are the walls?" Susie asked. "Concrete?"

"Nope. That isn't facing, the walls are stone all the way through. We thought first of putting in paneling, but I decided that honest open walls were more in keeping with the spirit of the place. I like the texture, don't you?"

"I've got to look after supper," Leah said. "Hugh, why don't you start the Cook's tour? I'll be ready in just a few minutes."

There was a staircase at the far end of the living room, leading down into the library, which also contained Hugh's drafting table. "All the other rooms open from this hall here . . ." Hugh began, then trailed off. He was staring at a patch of dampness glistening on the wall, about the size of a place mat and irregular in shape. He was surprised, then disgusted, then decided to accept the situation with good grace. "That's sure embarrassing," he grinned. "I supervised the laying of those blocks myself. Shucks and damn."

"Hugh," Susie said, "is it just my eyes or is that patch shrinking?" Hugh considered for a moment. The dampness was vanishing, contracting to the size of a napkin, a saucer, a dime . . . it was gone, and the stone was dry and unmarked. The whole process had taken less than a minute.

"Must be dry in here," Hugh said feebly. "Although it smells a little wetter now—no, it doesn't either. Maybe it wasn't water, maybe it was a cleaning fluid stain or something?"

"Hugh, I don't know what it is and I don't think you do, either," George said. "Let's have a look."

They rubbed their finger tips on the wall, peered at it closely, sniffed foolishly, all without results. Finally Leah called them to dinner.

Sitting around the fire afterward with brandy, George excused himself to use the washroom. He returned a few minutes later, saying,

"Hugh, I like the rustic décor in the john, but I can't say I care much for the room deodorant. What's it supposed to be, damp leaf mold or something? It's woodsy, but phew!"

"That's odd," said Hugh. "We've also smelled something like that around here occasionally. I don't know where the smell comes from—it's certainly not supposed to be there."

"I thought I smelled pine awhile back," Susie said.

"I don't see how. I don't like to use artificial smells and there are no evergreens around. Some kind of scented soap or something, maybe." Hugh looked eager. "But that's all little stuff. Susie, George, how do you like the house? You've seen enough to have an opinion."

George looked pensive, staring into the fire. Susie hesitated a moment, watching him, then said, "Well, I think it's great. It's everything you said it would be, in touch with the biosphere, a real natural sort of dwelling. I'm not sure I'd go this far in designing a house, but I've already picked up a lot of ideas I can use."

"'I think I could turn and live with animals,'" George quoted dreamily, "'they are so placid and self-contained.'" His face grew harder. "Hugh, you've got yourself a real 'organic' burrow here. Like Susie said, it's Mr. Badger's house, and I don't doubt you fit into your ecological niche here the way a badger fits into his.

"But, Hugh, whose side are you on? You're not a badger, you're a man. Man doesn't *get along* with nature, he conquers it. That's what makes us human, sets us above the rest of evolution. Animals adapt to their environment, while we adapt the environment to ourselves. Remember what you said about my house, that it doesn't blend in? It doesn't. When I bought that lot there was nothing on it but sand dunes and grass, but I've made it into a comfortable place to live. That's what architecture is about, imposing man's will on this planet. We're supposed to be pushing back the wild places, not compromising with them." He became conscious that he was orating, fell guiltily silent. Hugh quietly poked up the fire.

Susie said accusingly, "George, I was in your class not more than six months ago when you lectured on 'Harmony in Design.'"

He grinned, said, "Well, maybe I overreacted. Still and all, I stick by my guns."

They were silent a few moments. Finally Hugh said, "George, I don't have to tell you how I feel about that—you can see what I think by looking around you. Does it really give you any joy to draw up those concrete and metal things you do?"

"Don't push me into a corner. I know there's a lot of faceless, in-human buildings around and hell, maybe I helped make some of them. But, Hugh, even when we fail, we *try!* We assert ourselves, take a stand. You've given up here, chosen to live with formlessness. I've heard you talk about farming as a way to get back to nature, but even a farmer contours the land to his own purposes. You've gone too far with this house, you've lost sight of the essentials."

"I wonder if you've gone far enough, rather," Susie said. "This isn't a natural house in the way some of the places I've read about are. You still get your electricity from that stinky plant in the city, you have lots of appliances and artificial lights, and you've got flush plumbing and all that. It's not really a man-dwelling, the way George means, but I wonder if the earth spirits will have you either?"

"Earth spirits? You believe in that?" Hugh asked, and Leah and Susie grinned at each other.

"I think I know what's she's talking about," Leah explained. "I think we read it in the same *Cosmo,* right?"

"Yeah. It was a screwy little article about how we're all getting neurotic in the cities because the earth spirits don't come near us any more."

"I'd tend to think it was the other way around," George said amia-bly. "I don't see why earth spirits should like us very well anyway, so if they avoid the cities, the better for us."

"Look," said Hugh impatiently, "let's bring this back to reality—"

"Wait a moment." George held his hand up regally. "Sure, this earth spirits thing is silly, but let's look at it as a symbol. Suppose there were . . . well, beings that live *in* the earth as naturally and eas-ily as you and I live *on* it, OK? Now, I've never seen them, and why is that? Maybe it's because they really don't come near the cities, be-cause those are man-territory and we've got our man-smell or some-thing all over them. Maybe animals see these beings and don't care, because they're quote natural unquote and have a sort of under-standing. So where does that leave you? Do you see what I'm getting at?" George looked thoughtfully at the fire and remarked offhand-edly, "Maybe you should move those grills closer to the fireplace, Hugh. I believe they're starting to rust."

"Damn!" Hugh turned. "Those are brand-new, too. Oh, well. Yeah, I see what you're saying—you're calling me a fence straddler. I'd rather think of it as walking a middle road between extremes, that's all. I built this place to suit myself and nobody else. I can't say

I worry much about the opinions of earth spirits, or earth worms for that matter."

"Well, it wouldn't be *opinions,* exactly," Susie said, musing. "Maybe they just wouldn't notice you one way or the other, since you weren't friend or foe. They'd turn away from the cities, but they'd just go in one side of this house and out the other, going on whatever sort of errands earth spirits do." She looked startled. "That wet patch . . ."

"Was the mark of a water spirit going past," Hugh finished for her. He laughed. "A right planar section of an undine on my wall! Come on, give me a break."

"Some earth spirits would smell earthy," George said slyly, "and you said yourself you get odd smells here."

"And that rust on the fireplace screen could be the Great Essence of Oxidation on his way to the office," Susie giggled. She yawned and added, "By the way, excuse me, but I think we ought to be getting home. OK with you, George?"

"I guess. Hate to run out on you so early, Hugh, but you know it's a long drive back to my place."

"Sure, I understand. I'll fetch your jackets." Hugh went to the closet by the door, then stopped and peered up into the short stairwell. "George, Leah, Susie," he said presently, his voice strained, "could you come over here a moment?" They joined him silently.

"You ever hear those old stories about fence posts sprouting?" Hugh asked. "Look here." The once smooth boards of the door were twisted and showing gaps. Roots trailed from the bottom of each of them, anchoring them solidly into the ground. Fresh twigs and pale leaves grew near the tops.

"I don't . . ." Susie began, then checked herself. "No, I *do* believe it. But I think it's a trick."

"It's not," Hugh said dully. No word passed among the four, but they turned and walked with deliberate slowness down the passage to the garage. Before they turned the last corner they were greeted with a smell of rust and dampness. The cars were both spotted with patches of rust, incongruously dark against the slick new paint. The bumper of the Cadillac dangled from one brace, the other having corroded through. As they watched, a large wet patch on the wall grew to umbrella size, then slowly vanished.

George strode to the end of the garage and yanked sharply at the sliding door. It refused to move, the latch and frame welded together by rust. He swore softly.

"Look, let's all go back to the living room," Hugh said with disingenuous brightness. "I'll call the police and have them bring something to open the doors. I don't know what this is but I'd rather sit down with a brandy to figure it out. Hell, if any gnomes come out of the walls maybe we could offer them a snifter full, right?" Leah gave him a sharp look but followed the others back.

Hugh spent a few minutes on the phone, then joined the others sitting near the fire. "The state cops cover this area," he said, "and I had to do a long song and dance to get them to come out here without saying what was wrong. But they said they'd get here in ten minutes."

"Do those windows open?" Susie asked.

"This is kind of embarrassing," Hugh said, "but no, they don't. I've got central air conditioning. They're hard to break, too; had 'em made out of Lexan plastic. Let's just be cool and wait for the cops." Comically uniform, all four looked down into their glasses. Leah swirled her liquor, quietly tense.

"Hugh, I just thought of something," she said presently. "Remember, about two nights ago, just after we went to bed . . . do you think that could have been the same sort of thing as . . . um . . ." Hugh turned slightly pink.

"You're such a puritan, you're fun to embarrass," Susie said kindly. "What's the story, Hugh?"

"Oh, it was just a funny thing that happened the other day. We were going to bed one night and we felt pretty good, so we decided to, you know, make love. The thing is, we've always had a lot of fun in bed. I mean, we really do enjoy sex, right?" Hugh sounded defensive. "But this particular night, we started off like usual and then all of a sudden, for no reason, we were both just *inflamed*. We were grunting and biting and rolling around in a way we never did before. And then just like that it was over and we were lying there looking at each other."

"You think it might have been sort of an elemental or something going by?" Susie asked. "I guess there would be spirits for sex if there were any at all." Leah nodded her head indecisively.

"But why should they all congregate here this particular night?" Hugh asked, not belligerently.

George raised his head. "Do you happen to know what the phase of the moon is tonight?" he asked.

"No," said Hugh. Leah busied herself for a few moments straightening her dress, then excused herself to go downstairs.

A few minutes later, there was a tapping at the window. Two state patrolmen in broad hats were standing outside peering into the living room. Hugh went to the window and began shouting and pantomiming to them while George and Susie sat quietly.

An odor drifted up from the stairwell, a gaggingly foul air of putrescence and rot, a spoiled-meat smell of palpable intensity. George, quickly pale and breathing shallowly, rushed to the head of the stairs but hesitated at stepping through the doorframe. "Leah?" he called, without much breath. "Leah, what is that? Are you all right?" He swallowed convulsively, then was helplessly sick.

The police had gone back to their car for tools. Hugh turned at the sound of George's cry and rushed to the stairs. The other man was already stumbling downward, heroically, but robbed of dignity by his tottering posture. Hugh followed pell-mell, ignoring a frightened cry from behind.

The air was somewhat clearer below but weighted with another scent, a fetid dank atmosphere. Hugh slipped and went sprawling on the wooden floor: patches of a slick cottony white mold clung to his shoes. The grain of the wood was raised in some places on the walls, as though by dry rot.

George ran into the bathroom, shouting. He reappeared immediately and headed for the bedroom. There was no sign of Leah.

Pulling himself up, Hugh went to the doorway of the guest room. He stepped into the darkness and groped along the wall for the light switch, then stopped uncertainly. There were faint shiftings of light in the room, currents of denser, moister darkness. He had the impression of an inkstain, yards high and wide, spreading and rippling in lazily moving water, a cohesive soft cloud of blackness pouring in from one solid wall and flowing out another. It traveled in slow sinuous waves and ribbons, graceful as an eel or a school of fish, turning and doubling in easy curves. As he watched a negligently gentle arch grew toward and above him, dreamy as a bubble in thick syrup, trailing a filmy veil. With a gasping cry he threw himself backward, slamming the door.

Above him he heard hollow booming sounds, as though the police might be battering in the windows. The rhythm was underlined by high hysterical sobbing from Susie. On the lower floor, though he strained for any sound from the others, there was no sound but his own irregular breath.

The light was on in the bedroom but flickering unsteadily as though from a corroded connection. In the uneven flashes Hugh leaned against a dresser and shouted hoarsely for Leah, then George. A smear of greasy carbon black on the tufted bedspread caught his eye. He walked slowly to the far side of the room. A body lay stiffly on the rug, so badly burned it was impossible to discern who it had been. It was charred to the bone marrow in some places, only enough to cook the flesh in others. With a sick horror Hugh realized that his idiot salivary glands were already reacting to the smell of meat.

A path had been burned across the floor and included the body, a straight-edged triangle dwindling away to smoke stains at the point.

The guttering bulb finally gave out. In the light from the hallway Hugh shrank back and pressed himself into the corner of the room as a new presence penetrated the walls. It was a bubbly, lumpish mound, stretched into a low frothy form like a wave top, cutting across the room at an angle. It moved with deliberate speed: surely it would intersect him.

It was an amalgam of all corrupt colors—rust and verdigris, bile and punkwood, green mold and gold fungus. It fermented like yeast, was acid as lichens, brown as insects, crisp as ergot, soft and wet as carrion flesh. It stank and seethed, implacable as the most delicate erosion of stream water, traveling on a steady chord. Abruptly the booming upstairs was rewarded with a rending crack as the plastic burst.

Hugh opened his mouth to scream, red-faced, incontinent, gasping, weeping so violently as to befoul his lips and chin with mucus: anticipating communion with nature.

Biological science has made such startling breakthroughs in recent years that government legislators are now trying to impose brakes on research until questions of morality and individual rights can be thoroughly debated. But research can't be halted forever, and if some discoveries alter the basic patterns of society then we'll simply have to learn to live differently. For instance, if a means is found to confer near-immortality on people who are treated at a young age, that will change the way tomorrow's youths regard life.

But perhaps it will force even greater changes in those people who are too old for the treatments.

"Hunting," a quietly told story that brings large questions into focus in the life of one man, was Michael Cassutt's first sale. He's sold several stories since, and once you've read this one you'll look forward to the others to come.

HUNTING
Michael Cassutt

He left California on a suborbital flight before dawn. Tom had made the reservation for him—Sara was too busy, for once—otherwise he might have been traveling at a saner time of day. At his age he had no liking for early hours, and no need of haste. But once airborne he began to enjoy the feeling of isolation, floating alone and untouched above the white world. It was an excellent place in which to brood. Fifty minutes later he was in Minneapolis, almost regretting the quickness of the flight. A robot shuttle waited to fly him to the lodge.

Now, three hours later, he had his fill of silent, frozen desolation. He no longer felt forced into the vacation; he decided he would enjoy it. He wanted to get out in the cold snow and walk. He wanted to hunt.

The shuttle's control panel beeped and a recorded voice said, "Please secure for landing, Mr. Seabury. We are approaching the lodge." Somewhere up front, Seabury knew, the computer's transponder had locked onto the lodge signal. He looked out but saw only the rough carpet of pines flowing past beneath him. Occasionally he glimpsed the ribbon of the lodge road—except for that, this might have been an ancient wilderness, as untouched as it had been four centuries ago.

He leaned back in his seat, the middle of three forward ones. His bags rested in the rear three instead of in the luggage compartment. It had seemed silly to bother with it when he had all this room inside. A couple of months ago, in mid-October, the shuttle would have been carrying five more passengers, five other rich, jaded businessmen out for a week of roughing it in the woods. But this was the off-season.

The shuttle dropped lower and began to hover. Seabury could see the lodge. It sat in a cluster of trees that hugged a low hill. It was a misshapen thing, what had probably once been a single large rectangular building with additions built on over many years by different people. The roof of the largest addition was flattened into a helipad, and the shuttle dropped toward it. For a brief moment Seabury thought the shuttle was going to overshoot, but he laughed: a man spends thirty-five years in a business and still doesn't trust what he makes. The shuttle bumped lightly and settled. "Welcome to the lodge, Mr. Seabury," the taped voice said.

A bearded young man ran up to the vehicle as Seabury opened the door. A light breeze sifted the loose snow that lay on the helipad. The air was warmer than Seabury had expected it to be. "Mr. Seabury?" the boy asked.

"Yes."

The boy extended his hand. "Hi; I'm Kevin Russell. Let's get this stuff inside." He reached into the back seats and pulled out the bags.

The interior of the lodge was modern rustic. It had no elevator. Seabury and Kevin walked down wide wooden stairs. Logs were used as railings, and the walls were rough boards—yet the place was warm and brightly lit.

A stout, balding man a few years younger than Seabury stood sorting file cards at the front desk. "David Seabury? I'm Ted Russell," he said. "Welcome to the lodge. We're very happy to have you here, sir. It's our slow season."

"My pleasure," Seabury said. "I hope it'll be a nice change of pace for me."

"I think it will be. Let's see. . . ." Russell punched keys on a tiny cathoderay terminal behind the desk. "Your reservation is confirmed. We're giving you our best room—with a view to the west. It's very nice."

"Thank you."

"I guess that's it for the moment. If you need anything, I'll be around. Or ask Kevin. We're a little shorthanded this time of year."

"I understand. I doubt I'll need much. When can I get outside? It's still early—"

Russell smiled. "Kevin will help you pick out your gear. Through that door, once you're settled upstairs."

They walked along the top of a ridge, and below them lay a sea of trees with a few small islands of white. The trees were a dead brown, except for the pines, and the snow was packed and wet—stale. It hadn't seemed like that from the air. Seabury slapped his hands together. He had been out all afternoon. He was cold, and his breathing was starting to quicken. "Kevin!" he called.

The young man ahead of him stopped and shifted the pack he carried. "Yes, Mr. Seabury?"

"Let's rest a bit."

"Fine with me." The boy unshouldered the pack, set it down, and leaned it against a tree. Seabury merely stood, one hand hiding in a pocket, the other hooking a thumb in the sling of the rifle on his back.

"You think we're going to find anything today?" he asked.

"I don't know," Kevin said. "With the early snow this year, the herd may have headed for different territory—or it may be hungry and careless. If they're hungry, we'll find something. Can't say more than that. See, if you'd chosen to do this the *modern* way we'd have had the herd spotted and tagged for you. All you'd have to do is walk out here to the right spot and pick your shot. You'd have a decent weapon instead of that old clunker." He looked out toward a small field nearby below them. "Well, the snow should help tracking."

Seabury nodded and fumbled in his pocket for the heater. He could afford to be patient, for a while. "It's not much of a challenge, is it? Hunting the new way?"

Kevin spat. "I have no idea." He got up and moved out to the edge of the ridge. "You ever been up this way before, Mr. Seabury?" he asked, hands on hips and back facing the older man.

"I grew up in this part of the country. I was born across the river a ways, in Minnesota, but my folks moved here when I was just a baby."

"Then this is nothing new for you."

"On the contrary: I don't think I ever went hunting in all the years I lived here. My father was no hunter—he hated guns. I just never got the . . . habit, I'm afraid. I did do a little shooting now and then— and, of course, later, in the Army." He had come out to where Kevin was standing. "But I never went hunting."

"That's funny—" Kevin said. He looked at Seabury and laughed. He wasn't much more than nineteen, Seabury guessed, in spite of the full beard and the long hair. He looked much younger when he laughed, but with the beard—who could tell? Tom had a beard like that, and Tom was older than nineteen. "I can't see how a person could live around here and not go out at least *once*."

"There were more people around here then; lots of people I knew didn't hunt. There was no pressure to—in fact, it had fallen a bit into disfavor when I was about your age. The deer population was in trouble then. Most animal populations were, in the last century."

"Back in the good old days?" Kevin asked, with a bare touch of sarcasm.

"Yes, the good old days," Seabury replied quickly. "But then, I'm prejudiced." He clapped Kevin on the shoulder and turned away from the ridge.

Keven hunched forward, down on his knees, watching silently. "Want to see something?" he whispered.

"What is it?"

"Sssh. Come here."

Seabury crawled back. Kevin pointed. "Out there, in the clearing." He followed the boy's hand where it pointed across the clearing below. Three deer stood cautiously at the edge of the snow-covered meadow. Two females and one buck—handsome, lean, proud-looking animals. They sniffed and looked, then one by one flew across the clearing and were gone.

"Beautiful," Seabury said.

"Part of our indigenous deer population, Mr. Seabury. That's what you're hunting."

"Are we going after them?"

"No," Kevin said. "They'll be too far away by the time we can work our way down there, and it's too late to start a long chase. Tomorrow. We better be getting back."

Ted Russell was working behind the front desk when Seabury came down from upstairs. "Evening, Mr. Seabury."

"Good evening, Mr. Russell."

Russell looked up from the paper he was writing on. It was covered with names and numbers in neat rows, all of them inscribed in a fine hand that could have passed for printing. "My boy tells me you managed to spot three beauties this afternoon."

"Yes. I guess we were pretty lucky."

Russell grunted. "I'll say. You get *anything* this time of year, you're lucky. Of course, Kevin's my best guide—been at it since he could walk—but even so: three of them. Stars must be in your favor. This really isn't the season."

"No, it isn't."

"Dinner'll be ready pretty quick. It's programmed and just waiting for someone to punch buttons. If you'll excuse me, I'll go do just that." He stood up.

"Certainly." Russell went out and Seabury was left standing alone at the desk. A fire cracked and popped in the stone fireplace across the room. He moved over to it, thinking of Sara and Tom out in California. They would probably be enjoying an early dinner. The sun would just be going down, casting a red glow over the sea and the hills below the house. Sara would be as she had been for years, as she always would be: the impeccably dressed red-haired beauty, quiet and laughing gently now and then at something Tom had said. And then there was Tom: with his young good looks and his leering and his . . . concern. Seabury wondered if they would be talking about him. Were they worried? Of course, Sara was. That was one thing he had always loved her for: she did not forget. There was always a reminder from her—a letter or a call when he was away, a gift or a hello at just the right time. Of all her virtues, that was the one that caused him to continue to forgive.

That made him feel guilty. Forgive what? Forgive her for being a

child of her times? He had no right to complain. Tom was more than
he had a right to get in a co-husband. It was supposed to be reassur-
ing to know that his business and his marriage could go on without
him, momentarily or permanently. They told him, someone somewhere had told him, that the most basic stable form is the triangle.
He tried to believe that, but he viewed love as a sort of mutual possession. And to know that the one person he wanted did not want
only him—

"Mr. Seabury?" Kevin was in the doorway to the dining room.
"Dinner's ready."

"I'll be in in a moment." He put his hands out to the fire. He felt
very tired.

"Kevin, your father tells me you're taking up, what is it, history?"

The boy nodded. "Yeah, I used to read so much of it when I was
younger that I just got hooked. I took some TV courses last year.
Maybe next year I'll go down to Madison and see what I can pick up
there. I don't know. I'm in no hurry."

"No need to be, at your age." They ate dinner in the lodge dining
room, a large place that with all its empty tables should have seemed
barnlike; the warmth and the quiet made it seem almost cozy. The
room had a large window that looked out from a balcony toward the
road which wound away into the trees. Dinner was brought in dis-
creetly by an old-fashioned cart—semiconscious, Seabury thought,
and having to be carefully programmed down to the last ac-
tion/decision. It was a reliable old piece of machinery, though.

"See, Mr. Seabury," Russell said, "this time of year none of the
help is around. I've got three more full-time guides, and a few part-
time ones. During the season all of us eat here together. The hunters
sort of like that—it's old-fashioned, frontier-style."

"Do you still get many hunters here?"

Russell stared at his plate. "That's a tricky question. Up until the
last year, why, I would have said yes without a doubt. But with this
new Methuselah treatment, I can't say. Most of my hunters are in the
young set, a little older than Kevin. Now most of them won't want to
take time off from their series—more of them won't want to risk a gun
accident when they can look forward to, well, a couple of hundred
years. The older ones'll come back, I hope. I'll have to see."

Seabury noticed for the first time that Kevin wasn't eating what he
and Russell were. "Kevin? You're taking the treatments?"

"Yeah," the boy said, "I'm taking them."

"How far along are you?"

"A little over halfway."

"Another year to go?"

The boy nodded. "Once a week. The day after tomorrow I go into town."

Seabury laughed. "Excuse me if I show my ignorance. The process never really interested me—since I was unable to take part in it myself." Tom had been interested, though. He *was* able.

"Well, I don't know much about it," Kevin said. "I just go down there, get some injections once a week, and watch what I eat. It's not so much—"

"—for the promise of 'eternal life'?"

"They don't promise that," the older Russell said.

"No, of course not."

They finished eating. The cart rolled in, asked in a halting, high-pitched voice if anyone wished anything else, then rolled out again with the dishes. Seabury stood up. "Well, I must be getting to bed. The fresh air tired me. Kevin? Early tomorrow."

"Fine, Mr. Seabury."

"I'll see you then. Good night." He went out and upstairs to his bedroom, wondering when Sara would call.

"Here we go," Kevin said, kneeling in the snow. "Tracks."

"Do you think they're from the ones we saw yesterday?" Seabury asked.

Kevin stood up and followed the tracks for a few meters to where they began to head up into the trees. "I think so. There are three sets, and they're well spaced. Those beauties must have been in a hurry. Let's see where they're hurrying to."

Seabury didn't reply, but fell in behind the boy. It was late morning. They had been outside since before sunrise—hours ago, but with the day warming nicely Seabury felt as if he could go all day. He hefted the rifle and hurried to catch up with Kevin.

They followed the tracks through a mixture of brush and trees, working their way slowly up into the hills. Kevin moved quickly, stepping lightly over fallen branches. He would stop occasionally, to kneel and check the tracks—and to wait for Seabury. Seabury found himself hurrying. Once he misstepped and went sprawling on his face in the snow. He picked himself up, panting, and brushed snow off the rifle. Kevin was waiting not far ahead.

"Like to rest a little?" the boy asked.

"No, no. Let's keep going."

"Well, *I'd* like to stop for a minute, okay?"

"If you want to."

"I want to. I don't think we're going to have too much luck today anyway."

Seabury unslung his rifle. "Why not? The tracks seem fresh to me." They were standing on the crest of a small hill, and the tracks—three pairs of them—wound clearly down the far slope.

Kevin pointed down the hill. "Sure they're fresh and clear now—and they may be for quite a ways yet. But it's warming up; the snow's melting. Besides, down in that valley—well, we just won't be able to follow these tracks much farther. I've been through here enough times to know that."

"If the snow's melting we should hurry."

Kevin took off a glove and brushed at his beard. "What is your goddamned hurry? You want a nice fourteen-point buck to take home, you should have come up earlier, in the fall. If you're out for the exercise, that's one thing. Relax and enjoy it. I've never seen anyone so itchy to kill a stupid animal. Going to mount the rack in your beach house or something?"

"I don't really care if it's a buck or not. I'll settle for any deer."

"Well, they'll still be here next year. I told you, it's just too late."

"I *know*," Seabury said. "When I was your age, this would have been out of season. It's just—I've never killed anything larger than an insect. An animal. I've always wondered . . . how it felt."

Kevin stared at him, then began laughing. "I thought I'd heard most of the justifications for hunting, but that's a new one. Just want to see a little blood and twitching, eh? I'll let you gut it, if you want. I've got a knife."

Seabury picked up the rifle. "Let's get one first, then we'll see." He started to follow the tracks down the hill toward the valley. He stopped and called back. "Are you coming along?"

Kevin waved. "I'll catch up."

Seabury was slow and clumsy on the trail. He did not have a trained eye and a rocky break would throw him off momentarily. He was in rougher country as well, and had to watch his footing.

He reached level ground and made better time. The tracks were easier to follow here. Kevin was still not in sight, but Seabury really didn't care. He could do this by himself—he would show Kevin, and Tom. He hurried on, almost running, until he came to the bank of a wide, shallow stream. Melting ice crawled out from the bank for a few meters, then gave way to open water. The tracks ended here; one print could be seen on the mushy ice, and that was all. Seabury searched the far bank, but saw only bushes and snow. There was no reason for the deer to have gone straight across anyway.

Something snapped behind him. Kevin stood in the path, laughing. "I guess that's *it* for today, Mr. Seabury," he said. He turned to go, and Seabury, after a moment, followed him.

They said nothing to each other all the way back.

A wind had come up on the way back to the lodge. It was a cold wind, whipping rain that promised snow. Inside his room Seabury shed his clothes, glad to be in out of it. He went downstairs to ask Russell if there had been any calls. "Nothing," Russell said. He had a small TV set up behind the desk and was watching a weather report. "Looks like we're in for a good snow."

"Yes, it got cold and wet pretty quickly."

Kevin came through the hallway and passed in silence. Russell looked after him, then said to Seabury, "You and Kevin getting along all right?"

"As well as can be expected."

"Well, I get worried. I haven't had much trouble with him; he's a good boy. Missed his mother when she moved out a few years ago, but that's natural. With this Methuselah business—I don't know, he seems different. Older, maybe. Doesn't really kid around any more. He's nineteen and he seems to be *watching* what he does like he was, oh hell, my age."

"Or mine."

Russell laughed. "Yeah, the two of us. I wonder what's ahead for him, though. He *might* live forever, but what kind of life's it gonna be? Population changes and all—this other stuff, how things change. Hell, I know *I* couldn't adapt to most of it. That's why I'm out here in the sticks."

"I don't think any of us can really adjust. We have to . . . deal with the situations we find ourselves in, the best we can." He excused himself and went into the living room, by the fireplace. A low fire burned. Seabury eased himself onto the couch. He hadn't noticed earlier how tired and sore he was. He thought about Sara and Tom—still no word from either of them. Perhaps they were only doing what he had asked them to do: Let me get away for a while. I just want to get away. As he said it he hadn't completely believed it—and he grew to disbelieve it. But he had come to this place. He sighed. His back hurt so much.

The wind shook the window. Seabury woke from sleep with a start. There was a blanket over him, and a huge fire roaring in the room. Russell was piling some logs in the woodbox. "You're awake."

"What time is it?"

"Around nine. I threw a blanket over you. You could catch a hell of a cold sleeping down here without a blanket."

Seabury laughed. "So my mother always said."

"Yeah, mine, too. If you want dinner, or a drink—"

"No, no thank you. I think I'll just . . . lie here, for a while."

Russell nodded silently and left.

He could remember how it started. He had seen it coming and that, perhaps most of all, was what tore at a small, fragile thing inside him. Perhaps he could have prevented it. You take a busy man and a younger wife, the wife works as a low-echelon executive for a textile company, the husband is in electronics and robotics. The wife meets a younger man and is attracted to him, and the brief affair that follows is nothing new, for either the husband or the wife. This is liberation, after all—but this time it isn't quite the same. This young man is special, someone different. But she still loves you: so she suggests, why not all three of us? It's a common thing, she says, knowing you've always prided yourself on your openness. The younger man seems nice, if unassuming and unambitious, and you've heard that such a relationship might be more stable, more mature. Casually (all the major events in your life happen casually), you agree. But there is something growing inside you, and something dying.

Snow still fell the next morning, but the wind had died. The lodge road could be seen only as an opening in the trees. Seabury ate breakfast alone. It was still early. He hadn't shaved or changed clothes since the day before. It was the breaking of two lifelong habits, and breaking them gave him an oddly thrilled feeling.

Kevin came into the kitchen and began to program breakfast. He didn't see Seabury. "Good morning," Seabury said.

The boy almost jumped. "What are you doing up?"

"Thought we'd get an early start."

Kevin shook his head. "Not today. I have to go into town. Besides, *look* out there! You know how much fun it would be to slog around in that. I'm going to have a tough enough time making it to the clinic as it is."

"Your treatments."

"Mmm-hmm."

"No hunting today, then."

"No, I told you. It wouldn't be any good."

"Tomorrow, then."

"If it stops snowing by afternoon, yes. We might have some tracks by tomorrow morning. If they're out there at all. If they didn't just take off."

"I think we'll find them. I feel it."

The boy stopped eating. "You *feel* it. Good." He stood up and took his plate to the disposal. "Well, then, practice your shooting today. Tomorrow you'll *really* be ready."

"I'll do that," Seabury said, returning the boy's mocking tone.

Kervin blushed. "Look," he said, "I'm sorry. It's just—I don't know, maybe the treatments are affecting me. I get rude."

Seabury smiled. "It's okay. Let's say I'm used to it. See you later."

The boy left, and from the window Seabury watched him go. The shuttle flew off toward the gap in the trees where the now invisible trail lay. Seabury followed it with his eyes until it disappeared, and thought about the deer, out there in the cold.

The snow stopped just after noon.

They started north from the lodge early the next morning. "The tracks were headed that way a couple of days ago," Kevin said. "There's also a lot better protection against a storm up that way— trees, ravines and things."

"Sounds good," Seabury said. He felt rested and ready. The rifle was light on his back and there was extra spring in his legs. He felt as if he could run, really run, for hours. He looked forward to the hills and the hunt.

The snowfall had not been as heavy as it had seemed to Seabury. Looking out the window at the whirling, wind-blown mess, he had expected snow up to his knees and heavy going. But he found that he sank only to his ankles until he hit tougher base snow.

They headed out between two hills, up a winding valley that took the lodge out of their sight. The trail sloped gently upward, and they followed it for what seemed to Seabury to be an hour, until it finally began to slope down, out of the trees, and widened. Kevin said nothing the entire time; he was only a hypnotic robot drone slogging steadily along in front of Seabury. They saw no tracks.

"Stop here for a while," Kevin said. "I'm going on ahead to see if I can pick something up. If they're in this area, they had to come through here at least once. I'm going to check back that way a bit. I can do it fastest alone. I'll only be gone about ten minutes. Wait." He handed Seabury his rifle and sprinted off.

Seabury stood alone in the clearing. He felt good—a little more tired than he had been, maybe, but a brief rest would take care of that. His feet and hands were cold, though. He jumped up and down a couple of times and clapped his hands. He wished Kevin would hurry up. He was anxious; the day was bright, yet he felt he had to do something quickly. In his mind he rehearsed what he would do. The rifle was an old one with a bolt action. It would need to be loaded. He did that now. Pull back, slap the shell into the chamber, close it. Set yourself. Safety off. Sight, then aim. Squeeeze. *Crack!* The deer jerked violently to its side and lay bleeding in the snow. That was all there was to it.

"Seabury!" Kevin called, and Seabury turned to see him waving from a hundred meters away. He shouldered the two rifles and hurried over to him.

"Look here," Kevin said. He knelt and took off his glove. Seabury shaded his eyes against the glare: he saw one set of deer tracks. "I'll bet it's one of your does. You may be in luck. She's headed toward the turnaround."

"Turnaround?"

"Valley with only one way out. It's a long way off, but if we get going we might catch her before she figures it out."

"Let's go then," Seabury said.

"Yes, *sir!*"

They walked for minutes, then for an hour, then for nearly two. The trail was easy to follow, but it suddenly began to get rugged. Trees had fallen across it in many places, some recently and some not so recently. Seabury had to climb, and he was getting tired. He stopped halfway over one, and leaned against the bank. Kevin stopped, too. "Let's go, Pops. You were the one who wanted to haul ass after this animal, so let's haul it." And Seabury climbed the rest of the way over.

The deer had apparently had troubles in one place: the tracks doubled back over each other many times, then went up and across a fallen tree on the side of the valley. Kevin began crawling up the same way, but he slipped and slid down in a heap. He rolled over. "Christ!" he said, brushing snow away from his neck.

He looked so comical sitting there in the snow that Seabury began to laugh. Kevin looked up. "What's so goddamn funny, you old wreck?" he snapped.

Seabury stopped laughing. "That's no way to talk, Kevin. So I'm old. It happens to everyone—" He paused. "It used to, anyway."

"*That's* the problem, isn't it? I've seen this coming. I've almost been able to *feel* your goddamn eyes on my back. Look, *sir,* I'm sorry I was born when I was. I'm sorry you were born when *you* were. What the hell can I do about it?"

"You can stop acting like a spoiled child. I don't resent your . . . good fortune to have been born at a time when you have a chance at immortality."

"The *hell* you don't resent it." Kevin stood up. "You resent it because there's nothing you can do about it. So you come out here to kill dumb animals, for fun!"

Tom could have said that. Seabury was silent for a moment, then he spat and snapped his rifle around and pointed it at Kevin's stomach. "Can't I do something about it? You young son of a bitch, you may not *think* I can use this thing, but at this distance even an old wreck like me could blow you and your immortality all over the hillside. Think about *that!*"

Kevin stared at the rifle. "I guess," he said, "you could."

"You're damned right I could." He lowered the rifle. "Now—let's forget it and go." He was trembling.

Kevin moved slowly, picking up his cap and rifle. "If it means anything, I'm sorry," he said quietly.

"You said that once already."

He looked at the ground. "I mean it this time."

"I said forget it." He was still shaking. He had almost pulled the trigger—how did it feel to kill?

The boy made the climb and held out his hand for Seabury. Seabury slung the rifle on his back and pulled himself over. They started walking again, Kevin keeping a good distance ahead.

It was all Sara's fault, Seabury thought. If *she* hadn't wanted the situation to develop, it never would have. He had only let it happen; she had made it happen. Maybe she was making something else happen. Maybe she and Tom were making plans that didn't include him. Maybe they had moved while he was gone—no, that was silly. The business. He was getting tired.

He fell into the rhythm of the tracking. Walk a bit, climb or go around, walk again. Kevin was silent ahead of him, and he went only as fast as he seemed to think Seabury wanted to go, no faster. It was early afternoon now. They had a quick lunch, then continued on. "It isn't far," Kevin said at last, "and these tracks look fresh."

Seabury only nodded.

The trail began to drop ever so slightly. Ahead lay a ring of hills. This was the turnaround. "Here," Kevin said. "She's down here. I know it."

"You *feel* it," Seabury said.

A brief laugh. "Yeah, I feel it. I'm going to go back up around and try to flush her. She'll have to come back this way. If you plant yourself down here somewhere, you'll get one shot. Don't bet on getting two. She'll probably be running like hell."

"Okay, where do you want me?"

Kevin led him down the trail a little further. Three logs lay across the trail here. Two of them had been there for a while; they were half-buried by the snow. The third sat higher, at waist height. "Get behind these," Kevin said. "You'll have a good field. She might not stand out against the trees, and the sun isn't too good here, but you'll see her because you're looking for her."

"She can't get out anywhere else?"

"I'd be very surprised. The place has steep sides. With the snow, I think a mountain cat might have trouble. No, she'll be through. Watch." He went back up the trail and disappeared, leaving Seabury alone.

This is it, he thought. He unslung the rifle and leaned it against one of the logs. He set himself in the snow, comfortably, but in such a way that he could move quickly. He snapped the safety off and pointed the rifle between the top and the bottom logs.

He could hear nothing except for his own sounds of breathing and shifting. There wasn't even the familiar rustling of branches as the wind brushed through them. The snow was cold against his backside. He heard a far-off yell—Kevin. Then nothing for a longer time, and then yelling again. He peered down the trail, but saw nothing. Where was she? She had to be here. Kevin had said so, unless he was getting some sort of revenge—

Yelling again; this time it was closer.

He heard a snap, and there she was. She stood less than twenty meters away, brown and white against the trees and the snow. She looked at him as she picked her way, twitching her tail once, then twice. Seabury was careful not to move. Slowly, he turned the rifle, sighting down the barrel. Please, he thought, and holding his breath, squeezed the trigger.

The gun kicked into his shoulder and the deer recoiled, then toppled. The echoes of the rifle report sang down the valley. Seabury was frozen: he could see that the deer was only wounded. She twisted and tried to crawl, staining the snow with blood. This wasn't right, this wasn't how he had expected it to be at all. You either missed or you killed—nothing halfway. He didn't know what to do.

He set the rifle aside and pulled himself out of the blind. His muscles ached from sitting so long, and he was out of breath. That surprised him. He hadn't been doing anything, had he? And the deer was still writhing on the ground near a fallen tree—more slowly now. The bullet had hit her in the flank above her left foreleg, and she kept stretching her neck toward it, as if she could fix whatever was wrong with her if only she could touch where it hurt. Seabury cursed himself for not having used a modern weapon, one that killed at a touch; there was nothing he could do now but watch.

There was thrashing in the distance behind the deer. Seabury picked up his rifle. Another deer? No: it was Kevin, struggling through the heavy brush. He appeared on the edge of the slope and crawled down. "I heard a shot."

He looked in the direction Seabury was looking. "Jesus," he said, "you got her." The deer twitched visibly. "Goddammit, she's not *dead!*"

"I know," Seabury said.

"What's the matter with you? She's suffering!" He thrust his rifle at Seabury. "Finish what you started!"

Seabury didn't move. "I can't."

"*Can't?* An hour ago you were ready to shoot *me* in the guts. Well, I'm telling you: finish what you started!"

The wind whipped suddenly, spraying snow over them. The deer was still alive, and the crimson stain was bigger and darker than ever. Seabury took the rifle and walked over to the deer. He cocked the weapon, disengaged the safety, and aimed the muzzle at the deer's head. Her eyes were open: terrified, Seabury thought. He closed his own eyes and gently squeezed the trigger. He heard the sharp crack and felt the rifle recoil. The deer's head jerked once, then became still. Seabury could see a tiny hole under her ear. He gripped the rifle with all his strength, as if he could break the weapon in half with his bare hands.

"Well," Kevin said after a while, "you've got your trophy now. I hope you like venison." He picked up Seabury's rifle and came over to retrieve his own. "It's too late to walk back. I'll call the shuttle. But we're going to have to drag her to a clearing with us."

"Drag what?"

"The deer. Your deer." He broke out a communicator. "You better sit down and rest for a few minutes."

He didn't want to rest now. "No. Let's just"—he gestured with his hands—"move her."

"As soon as I call." Kevin started off toward the top of the ridge, pulling out the radio's antenna as he walked.

The sun was down behind the hills by the time the shuttle arrived. They had dragged the carcass to a clearing and waited as Kevin talked the shuttle to a landing. They lashed the deer to the rear rack, winding it with Kevin's finger-thick rope. "Hate to lose her, wouldn't you," the boy said.

"Yes," Seabury replied, "I'd definitely hate to lose her."

They climbed inside the shuttle. Kevin took it into the air on manual control, then set the autopilot to bring them back to the lodge.

They didn't speak on the trip back, sitting side by side in the shuttle cabin. It was well after sunset when the lodge crept into view. Kevin reacquired control and set the shuttle easily on the roof. Both men sat still inside the craft as the whine of the engines died.

Seabury looked out toward the darkening trees, and at the ribbons of powder drifting across the landing pad. Throughout the entire trip back he had been aware that he wanted to say something to Kevin, or that Kevin wanted to say something to him—but what? He was about to speak when the pad was flooded with light. Kevin's father, well-bundled, appeared at Seabury's door. "God, you got one."

Seabury nodded.

"A nice one, too. You can be proud of yourself. This isn't the season, not at all." He turned to his son. "Kevin, ain't this something?"

But Kevin was walking away. "What the hell?" Russell looked pleadingly at Seabury. It only lasted a second; the man began untying the deer, as if nothing had happened, then gave up. "It's cold," he said.

Kevin was standing out at the edge of the pad, in darkness. Seabury came up behind him. The boy didn't turn around, but only stared at the eastern sky, where a bright Venus hung above the hills.

"Kevin." Seabury cleared his throat. He was just beginning to realize how utterly cold and tired he was. "I just wanted to . . . thank you. I never did anything quite like this before."

"You're very welcome, sir." Kevin's voice was overly polite. His back remained toward Seabury.

"Maybe we could go out again sometime. Tomorrow—"

Suddenly Kevin faced him and Seabury saw the boy's face was wet with tears. "No, I don't think we'll go out again, Mr. Seabury. I don't think *I'll* go out there again. This whole thing is wrong for me. It's immoral, for me. Maybe it's all right for you—you face the same sentence that deer faced. But I don't. Lots of us don't, now, and it isn't fair."

He looked at Kevin and had a feeling he'd thought as lost to him as sexual innocence, a feeling of having all time left to him—more years left to go than he had gone. He wanted to start work, to make ridiculously ambitious plans and believe that they might come true.

"Mr. Seabury!" Russell was calling from the door. "There's a phone call for you. If you—"

The spell was broken. "Excuse me," he said to Kevin, and went inside.

He reached the front desk and realized that he was actually sick with exhaustion and fear. He didn't want to talk to Sara now, he didn't want the reality of that . . . world back there intruding on this. Besides, he had always distrusted telephones. It seemed they always brought bad news.

"David! Hello, love. How's the north country?" She wore a white robe and looked sunburned and sleepy.

"Colder than your favorite metaphor. And I'm paying for years of indolence."

She laughed. "You can afford to. Are you *relaxing,* though? That's what you deserted us for—"

"*Deserted?*" He was too tired to appreciate her bantering. "I don't recall even *wanting* to take a vacation alone."

"David!" She seemed surprised and hurt. "Don't, please. I just called to see how you were. Don't you think I care any more?"

He sighed. "How's Tom?"

"Fine. A little under it today. He's been so busy."

"He started taking the treatments."

She tossed her head, brushing long red hair away from her face. "Bitter, David?"

"Bitter?" Shouldn't I be, he thought? And what about you, Sara my one true love—just a bit too old for treatments to do you any good, though you'll *take* them, God knows it's the fashionable thing to do. "Sometimes, I guess." Aren't you? Or don't you think about it. "It's not like I've got one foot in the grave, you know. I'll be around for a few more years."

"When do you think you'll be back? Tom does miss you. And it's been *so* lovely here." She tilted the pickup so he could see out toward the patio, toward the ocean.

He didn't want to go back. He shrugged.

"Having that much fun?" she asked.

"I'll give you and Tom a little time to yourselves."

"Oh, David, we've been through this—"

"I'm fine, hon. Thanks for calling."

She hesitated, then flashed a relaxed smile. Poor Sara, he thought, Tom will never get older, but *you* will. *I* can afford to wait for you. "Enjoy yourself," she said. "And stay in touch."

He hung up the phone and rubbed his eyes. Russell appeared with a drink and handed it to him. "Traditional," the man said. "After a kill. We can have the head mounted for you in a couple of days, and the meat dressed, if that's what you want. Were you planning to stick around?"

"No," he answered, surprising himself. "Ah—I'll give you my home address; you can ship it."

"No problem," Russell said. "You'll be leaving when?"

"Tomorrow. Could you book me on a flight to, oh, Zurich?" He laughed. "I always wanted to try mountain climbing."

Russell nodded and walked away.

Seabury paused on his way upstairs. He could see Kevin, in the living room, sitting before a low fire, seeming lost in thought. He started to say something, but didn't. Time is my ally too, boy.

Short-short stories are exceptionally difficult to write in science fiction. It's necessary to evoke a new world in every story, and once the background is explained there isn't much space left for plot, characterization, and the other requirements of fiction. But if background, plot, and character are so closely interconnected that writing about one tells us about the rest, a great deal can be said in few words.

Greg Benford has written impressively in all lengths—his most recent novel is In the Ocean of Night—*but he says he's intrigued by the challenges of short fiction. "Nooncoming" could serve as a textbook example of how to meet those challenges.*

NOONCOMING
Gregory Benford

Saturday night, and they straggled into the cramped bar on Eucalyptus Boulevard. They nudged through the crowd and found friends, these aging people, ordered drinks, watched the crystal clouds at the ceiling form lurid, fleshy stories. But the best tales were the ones they told each other: *Janek's got a newsy flapping needs a big cast, senso and all, the works, I—so I go back and there are people living in my goddamn office for Christ's sakes hanging out washing and the desks gone, just gone, the file cases made into a bureau— programmers? who needs programmers? this guy says to the crowd and Jeff, he throws a—could still maneuver one of those three-piecer rigs, ten gears an' all, if some bastards hadn't broken 'em all down into little skimpy ratass haulers with—asked why an' I guess I just wanna stay close to the old centers, hopin' some big Brazilian money*

will come in like in '72 an' a good derrick man can get on—queen she
was from hunger and not gonna bust her head for any factory that
traded her off—

Only one woman in the bar was eating alone and she was tucked
back in a shadowed corner, far from the oily light. She was big-boned
and deeply tanned, her denim pants and shirt cut in a manner that
meant she had deliberately chosen them that way; they seemed to
bracket her body rather than enfolding it. She wore only eyeshadow
and her widely spaced eyes seemed to make her face broader than it
was, more open, just as the backward sweep of her hair bared her
face more than necessary. The long strands of it were held back by a
clip and had occasional flecks of blond, enough to hint that with a little treatment she could have been a striking beauty. She ate steadily,
no becoming hesitations, winding up neat cylinders of artichoke spa-
ghetti and rolling them through the red sauce before taking precise
bites out of them. Somehow the strands of green didn't break free
and hang down as she did this. She ignored the buzz of talk around
her and drank regularly from a tumbler of dark red wine. Every few
moments she would look up, not at the swirling lattice above that
featured tangled bodies, nor at the Saturday night crowd in their
flossy clothing, but toward the doorway.

The man she was waiting for appeared there, shouldering his way
by a giggling clump of aging heavy drinkers, just after 1800 hours,
thirty minutes late. He wore a frayed synthetic jacket, antique, like
several others she had seen in the bar.

"Joanna, frange it, sorry I'm late."

"I started without you," she said simply, still chewing.

"Yes. A good house wine, isn't it? Petite Sirah."

"Right."

He sat down and hunched forward, elbows on the burnished pine
table. "I've already had something."

"Oh?" She raised an eyebrow. He seemed fidgety and pale to her,
but maybe that was because she was so used to seeing tanned people;
everybody in town today had looked rather sickly, now that she
thought about it.

"Yes. I, ah, I was celebrating. With some friends."

"Celebrating returning to High Hopes?" She smiled. "That doesn't
sound like the Brian I—"

"No. I'm going back."

"*What?*"

"Back . . . on vacation."

"Getting vacated, you mean. Renting space."

She grimaced and put down her fork.

"However you want to describe it," he said precisely.

"You tappers have your little words," she murmured scornfully. "*Going on vacation.* Sounds like a free ride somewhere."

"It is."

"Stealing your *life* is—"

"Joanna." He paused. "We've had this discussion before."

"Look. You know High Hopes doesn't like you selling yourself off this way—"

"They agreed to let me do it."

"On an occasional basis."

"Okay, it's just getting *less* occasional. Let's put it that way."

"*Skrag* that."

"I don't owe you—"

"The hell you don't. High Hopes has put up with your renting your lobes for—what?—three years, off and on. We let you run off to San Francisco and tap in, and then take off and squander the bills on—"

"High living," he said sarcastically. His face wrinkled up into a thin smile.

"Right. Your fatcat amusements."

"Travel. Good food. Too rich for your tastes, I know, but good nonetheless. But the rest of it—Joanna, it's the *work.* I'm doing some damned interesting physics these days."

"Useless," she said decisively.

"Probably. Nonlinear dynamics—not much use in digging potatoes."

"You never did that. You were a pod cutter."

"Grunt labor is all the same."

Her eyes flashed. "Group work is *never*—"

"I know, I know." Brian waved a hand listlessly and looked around. "Think I'll have some of that red ink."

He got up and squeezed through the packed room, toward the wine barrel and glasses. There were no waiters here, to keep costs down. Joanna watched him move and suddenly it struck her that Brian was getting older, at least forty-five now. He had a certain heavy way of moving she wasn't used to seeing at High Hopes.

"Good stuff," he said, sitting back down. He sipped at the glass and studied the layered air around them. There was a musty, sour scent.

"Did we have to meet here?" Joanna said, resuming eating.

"Why not?"

"All these old—well, some of them look pretty seamy."

"They *are* seamy. We're getting that way."

"If they'd pitch in, get some exercise—"

"Ha! Look, my sturdy girl of the soil, these people are artists, engineers, scientists, administrators, men and women with education. They like living in town, even if it's this little dimple of a burg, two hundred klicks down from the city they all want to live in, San Francisco."

"A bunch of rattle-headed sophies," she said, chewing.

"Sophies?"

"Sophisticates, isn't that what you call yourselves?"

"Oh, you've got a name for us."

"Why not? You're the biggest trouble back at High Hopes. Always wanting what you can't have any more."

He licked his lips. "We want the old days. Good jobs. To own something worth a damn."

"Possessions," she said wryly. "Only *they* possess *you*—that's what you people forgot."

"We still remember the dignity of it."

She snorted and took a long drink. "Ego feeding."

"No!" he said earnestly. "There were people, ideas, things happening."

"*We're* making things happen, if that's what you want," she said. She finished the last green strand and dropped her fork into the plate with a rattle. The thick crockery was filmed with grease.

"Surviving, that's all," he murmured.

"There are good problems. We're not just a bunch of simple-minded farmers, you know. You seem to've forgotten—"

"No, I haven't. Tapping doesn't blur the memory."

"Well, it must. Otherwise you'd come back to the one group of people who care about you."

"Really? Or do you want me to patch up the chem and bio systems?"

"There's that," she said grudgingly.

"And sit around evenings, pinned to the communal 3D, or bored to death."

"We do more than that," Joanna said mildly.

"I know. And you have wondrous thighs, Joanna, but they can't encompass all my troubles."

She smiled and brushed at her severely tied-back hair. "You're still possessive about the sex thing, too, aren't you?"

"Terribly old style of me, I know."

"Ummm," she said. Brian tipped his glass at her in mock salute and went to refill it. Joanna leaned back in her chair, reflecting moodily. She remembered the old English woman who had died last year, working with a kind of resigned energy right up until her last day. The woman had said to Joanna, as she went inside the dormitory to lie down for what proved to be the last time, "You know, my dear, you're wrong that suffering ennobles people." She'd stopped to massage her hip, wincing. "It simply makes one cross." So was that it —Brian and the rest of the older ones looked on the honest labor in the pod rows as petty, degrading?

Joanna watched Brian standing patiently in line by the wine barrel. She remembered that Brian had talked to the English woman a lot, while most of High Hopes was watching the 3D in the evenings. They'd talked of what they'd once had, and Brian even spoke of it when he and Joanna lay together occasionally. The dry dead past, gaudy and stupid. She remembered Brian frowning in displeasure as the sounds of the next couple came through the thin walls. He had disapproved of them strongly, and it was all Joanna could do to stop him leaping out of bed and going next door to stop Dominic—it was usually Julie and Dominic—beating her. He had the idea that things people did together for sex were public somehow, that there were rules High Hopes should maintain. Standards, he called them. And even when they were at it themselves, pumping with a steady rhythm as though propelling each other over the same steepening slope of a familiar hill, when the sound came of Julie's high, wavering cry— which then slid into something almost like a laugh, a chuckle at some recognizable delight that lay ahead and would come upon her—then Brian would freeze against her loins and seethe, his mood broken. And she, mystified at first, would try to rock him gently back into reality and out of his dusty obsessions. She would wrap herself around him and draw him back down; once, she misunderstood and offered to do those things for him, perform whatever he liked, and the look on his face told her more about Brian than all the conversations.

Odd, she thought, that she should remember that now. Her sexual interest in him was no greater than for any of the others at High Hopes. A recreation, a kind of warming exercise that bound them all together and eased the days of labor into sleep.

He returned, smiling in the wan lamplight. "Can you stay in town tonight?"

"Why?" she said.

"Not so I can hear more lectures on High Hopes, I assure you of that. No, I want to sleep with you again."

"Oh," she said, and realized she was saying it stiffly, formally, that something in her was drawing away from Brian and the memories of Brian.

"Come on."

"It isn't that *way,* Brian. You don't *own* somebody—"

"I know, I've heard it. These flesh shows"—he gestured at the tangled bodies on the ceiling above—"are very much a cultural remnant. Like everybody in here."

Joanna looked around, grimacing. "Unsatisfied people. They can't stand being frogs in a small pond."

"No, it's not that," Brian said wearily. "They remember when they could *do* more, *be* more. Make sound sculptures, explore new things, use their *minds* for once—"

"Loaf around in a university."

He smiled wanly. "I'm surprised you remember the word. The regime has just ruled that only the Davis Agriworks is legal now—crop studies, that's it. I don't—"

"*Look,* Brian," she said abruptly. "I came into town to get some supplies and pick you up. The bus doesn't run into mid-Sur any more, so you'd have had to hike in. We've got a lot of new people drifting in, refugees from southern California, starving, most of them. Don't know a damn thing about work. That's why we need you— you're our best, y'know. We have to—"

"I told you," he said, stony-faced. "I'm going on vacation."

"Those damned franging computers don't need you! We *do.* They could get *animals*—"

"I've told you before. Animals don't have enough holographic data-storing capability. They lose too much detail."

"Then the hell with the whole skrag!"

"That's right," he said savagely, "tear it down. You don't understand it so you want to sacrifice the whole biosystems inventory, the ecological index, everything that's holding this poor battered world together—"

"Don't come on noble with *me*. You like the pay, getting to live back in the rotten city again—"

Her voice rose to a shrill edge and several people turned their heads, frowning. She was suddenly aware of how old and strange and distant all these people were, with their broken dreams and memories. And she glanced at the only window in the room to see a yellowish fog pressing against the pane. Beaded moisture glinted in the wan light. She would have to get started soon, before it thickened.

"You're right," Brian said, and his voice was oddly quiet. "I like to be among my own kind. I don't mind the price I pay. They hook me up during peak periods and the computers, which don't have enough solid state electronics banks left to do the calculations, push into my lobes and use the space there. I know what you think of it and I don't care. I know it looks grotesque to you, on the outside. I lie there still as a stone and the data flits through me, the machines using my neural capacity to do their work, and it's like dreaming and drifting and dreaming again, only when you wake up you can't remember what it was all about. You're vacated—every memory you had in those spaces is wiped, gone. But it's usually unimportant stuff and, Joanna, that doesn't matter, that isn't *it*. That's merely the price —what I get is freedom, time to talk to other people who're working in my field and still care about those things, some feeling of the old days."

"So you're going to stay there."

"Right."

"Instead of working for a better world, *here*—"

"I'm going to clutch after the only way I can stay in the old one. And I'm needed there, too, Joanna. The cost of making new computer elements is enormous. How much better, to link into the best, most compact neural net ever made—our brains—and use the few educated people left to work with the computer systems, *guide* them, be both storage space and programmers—"

Her face barely repressed the rage she felt. "*We* need you. You're a resource, trained people are scarce who'll work in the communes, and—"

"No," he said, shaking his head. With an abrupt gesture he tossed back the glass of wine. "I want the old way. I'm not going to bust my tail."

They looked at each other and she suddenly felt alien and alone in this strange place, this room of people who had washed up like refuse in the towns, refusing to go out into the forgiving countryside any more, clinging to the dear dead past, and felt the abyss that opened between them and her. They were living in some place that the world had once been, and would never be again. So in an odd way she and her kind were parents to their elders now, and must shelter them against the world. It was at that moment that she realized that the revolution she had been a part of was over, the morning was finished, and the long day of the human race was beginning.

"Have some more wine, Brian," she said softly after a while. "I've got to head on back pretty soon now."

There are no secrets in science, but history is a somewhat different field of knowledge: facts are continually lost in the deepening silt of time. Trust R. A. Lafferty to dig them out, however, for he approaches reality without preconceptions. (One of his characters in the novel Past Master *escaped from prison by walking through walls. "It isn't difficult," he said. "I believe that it has been insufficiently tried.")*

Consider this history of the first great series of television dramas, produced in 1873 by Aurelian Bentley and starring the remarkably resourceful actress Clarinda Calliope. Till recently these dramas have been lost, but Lafferty has gone to great expense (one hundred and thirty-five dollars) to resurrect them. Due to the peculiar nature of their recording, he may also have discovered some darker secrets behind the making of those dramas. . . .

SELENIUM GHOSTS OF THE EIGHTEEN SEVENTIES
R. A. Lafferty

Even today, the "invention" of television is usually ascribed to Paul Nipkow of Germany, and the year is given as 1884. Nipkow used the principle of the variation in the electrical conductivity of selenium when exposed to light, and he used scanning discs as mechanical effectors. What else was there for him to use before the development of the phototube and the current-amplifying electron tube? The resolution of Nipkow's television was very poor due to the "slow light" characteristics of selenium response and the lack of amplification. There were, however, several men in the United States who transmitted a sort of television before Nipkow did so in Germany.

Resolution of the images of these even earlier experimenters in the field (Aurelian Bentley, Jessy Polk, Samuel J. Perry, Gifford Hudgeons) was even poorer than was the case with Nipkow. Indeed, none of these pre-Nipkow inventors in the television field is worthy of much attention, except Bentley. And the interest in Bentley is in the content of his transmissions and not in his technical ineptitude.

It is not our object to enter into the argument of who really did first "invent" television (it was not Paul Nipkow, and it probably was not Aurelian Bentley or Jessy Polk either); our object is to examine some of the earliest true television dramas in their own queer "slow light" context. And the first of those "slow light" or selenium ("moonshine") dramas were put together by Aurelian Bentley in the year 1873.

The earliest art in a new field is always the freshest and is often the best. Homer composed the first and freshest, and probably the best, epic poetry. Whatever cave man did the first painting, it remains among the freshest as well as the best paintings ever done. Aeschylus composed the first and best tragic dramas, Euclid invented the first and best of the artful mathematics (we speak here of mathematics as an *art* without being concerned with its accuracy or practicality). And it may be that Aurelian Bentley produced the best of all television dramas in spite of their primitive aspect.

Bentley's television enterprise was not very successful despite his fee of one thousand dollars per day for each subscriber. In his heyday (or his hey-month, November of 1873), Bentley had fifty-nine subscribers in New York City, seventeen in Boston, fourteen in Philadelphia, and one in Hoboken. This gave him an income of ninety-one thousand dollars a day (which would be the equivalent of about a million dollars a day in today's terms), but Bentley was extravagant and prodigal, and he always insisted that he had expenses that the world wotted not of. In any case, Bentley was broke and out of business by the beginning of the year 1874. He was also dead by that time.

The only things surviving from *The Wonderful World of Aurelian Bentley* are thirteen of the "slow light" dramas, the master projector, and nineteen of the old television receivers. There are probably others of the receivers around somewhere, and persons coming onto them might not know what they are for. They do not look much like the television sets of later years.

The one we use for playing the old dramas is a good kerosene-powered model which we found and bought for eighteen dollars two years ago. If the old sets are ever properly identified and become collectors' items, the price on them may double or even triple. We told the owner of the antique that it was a chestnut roaster, and with a proper rack installed it could likely be made to serve as that.

We bought the master projector for twenty-six dollars. We told the owner of that monster that it was a chicken incubator. The thirteen dramas in their canisters we had for thirty-nine dollars total. We had to add formaldehyde to activate the dramas, however, and we had to add it to both the projector and the receiver; the formaldehyde itself came to fifty-two dollars. I discovered soon that the canisters with their dramas were not really needed, nor was the master projector. The receiver itself would repeat everything that it had ever received. Still and all, it was money well spent.

The kerosene burner activated a small dynamo that imposed an electrical grid on the selenium matrix and awakened the memories of the dramas.

There was, however, an oddity in all the playbacks. The film-fix of the receiver continued to receive impressions so that every time a "slow light" drama is presented it is different, because of the feedback. The resolution of the pictures *improves* with use and is now much clearer and more enjoyable than originally.

The librettos of the first twelve of the thirteen Bentley dramas are not good, not nearly as good as the librettos of the Jessy Polk and the Samuel J. Perry dramas later in the decade. Aurelian Bentley was not a literary man; he was not even a completely literate man. His genius had many gaping holes in it. But he was a passionately dramatic man, and these dramas which he himself devised and directed have a great sweep and action to them. And even the librettos from which he worked are valuable for one reason. They tell us, though sometimes rather ineptly and vaguely, what the dramas themselves are all about. Without these outlines, we would have no idea in the world of the meaning of the powerful dramas.

There was an unreality, a "ghostliness," about all the dramas, as though they were made by sewer light underground: or as if they were made by poor quality moonlight. Remember that the element *selenium* (the metal that is not a metal), the chemical basis of the dramas, is named from *Selene,* the moon.

Bentley did not use "moving pictures" of quickly succeeding frames to capture and transmit his live presentation dramas. Although Muybridge was in fact working on the zoopraxiscope (the first "moving picture" device) at that very time, his still incomplete work was not known to Aurelian Bentley. Samuel J. Perry and Gifford Hudgeons did use "moving picture" techniques for their primitive television dramas later in the decade; but Bentley, fortunately perhaps, did not. Each of Bentley's thirty-minute live dramas, however it appeared for the first time in the first television receiver, was recorded in one single matrix or frame: and, thereafter, that picture took on a life and growth of its own. It was to some extent independent of sequence (an effect that has been attempted and failed of in several of the other arts); and it had a free way with time and space generally. This is part of the "ghostliness" of the dramas, and it is a large part of their power and charm. Each drama was one evolving moment outside of time and space (though mostly the scenes were in New York City and in the Barrens of New Jersey).

Of course there was no sound in these early Bentley dramas, but let us not go too far astray with that particular "of course." "Slow sound" as well as "slow light" is a characteristic of selenium response, and we will soon see that sound did in fact creep into some of the dramas after much replaying. Whether their total effects were accidental or by design, these early television dramas were absolutely unique.

The thirteen "slow light" dramas produced by Aurelian Bentley in the year 1873 (the thirteenth of them, the mysterious *Pettifogers of Philadelphia,* lacks Bentley's "Seal of Production," and indeed it was done after his death: and yet he appears as a major character in it) the thirteen were these:

1. *The Perils of Patience, a Damnable Chase.* In this, Clarinda Calliope, who was possibly one of the greatest actresses of American or world drama, played the part of Patience Palmer in the title role. Leslie Whitemansion played the role of Simon Legree. Kirbac Fouet played the part of "the Whip," a sinister character. X. Paul McCoffin played the role of "the Embalmer." Jaime del Diablo played "the Jesuit," one of the most menacing roles in all drama. Torres Malgre played "the Slaver," who carried the forged certificate showing that

Patience had a shadow of black blood and so might be returned to slavery on San Croix. Inspiro Spectralski played "the Panther" (Is he a Man? Is he a Ghost?), who is the embodiment of an evil that is perhaps from beyond the world. Hubert Saint Nicholas played the part of "the Guardian," who is really a false guardian.

This *Damnable Chase* is really a galloping allegory. It is the allegory of good against evil, of light against darkness, of inventiveness against crude obtuseness, of life against death, of openness against intrigue, of love against hatred, of courage against hellish fear. For excitement and intensity, this drama has hardly an equal. Time and again, it seemed that the Embalmer, striking out of the dark, would stab Patience with his needle full of the dread embalming fluid and so trap her in the rigidity of living death. Time and again, it seemed that the Whip would cut the flesh of Patience Palmer with his long lash with viper poison on its iron tip that would bring instant death. At every eventuality, it seemed as though Simon Legree or the Slaver would enslave her body, or the Jesuit or the Panther would enslave her soul. And her mysterious Guardian seems always about to save her, but his every attempt to save her has such reverse and disastrous effects as to cast doubt on the honesty and sincerity of the Guardian.

A high point of the drama is the duel of the locomotives that takes place during a tempestuous night in the West Orange Switching Yards. Again and again, Patience Palmer is all but trapped on railroad trestles by thundering locomotives driven by her adversaries (the West Orange Switching Yards seem to consist almost entirely of very high railroad trestles). Patience finally gets control of a locomotive of her own on which to escape, but the locomotives of her enemies thunder at her from every direction so that she is able to switch out of their way only at the last brink of every moment.

The Embalmer attempts to stab her with his needleful of embalming fluid every time their locomotives pass each other with double thunder and only inches to spare. The Whip tries to lash her with his cruel lash with its poisoned tip; and the Slaver threatens her with the outreached forged certificate of color, and only by fantastic cringing can she cringe back far enough to keep from being touched by it as their locomotives roar past each other in opposite directions.

It seems impossible that the racing locomotives can come so close and not hit each other, with their dazzling switching from track to track. And then (Oh, God save us all!) the Panther (Is he a Man? Is he a Devil?) has leapt from his own locomotive to that of Patience

Palmer: he is behind her on her own locomotive, and *she does not see him.* He comes closer—

But the climax of *The Perils of Patience* is not there in the West Orange Switching Yards. It is at a secret town and castle in the Barrens of New Jersey, a castle of evil repute. In this place the enemies of Patience were assembling a gang of beaters (slack-faced fellows with their tongues cut out), and they were readying bloodhounds to hunt Patience down to her death. She somehow obtains a large wagon piled high with hay and pulled by six large and high-spirited horses. With this, she boldly drives, on a stormy night, into the secret town of her enemies and down that jagged road (there was a lightning storm going on that made everything seem jagged) at the end of which was the castle itself. The bloodhounds leap high at her as she passes, but they cannot pull her from the wagon.

But the Panther (Is he a Man? Is he a Beast?) has leapt onto her hay wagon behind her, and *she does not see him.* He comes closer behind her—

But Patience Palmer is already making her move. Driving unswervingly, carrying out her own intrepid plan, at that very moment she raises a key in her hand very high into the air. This draws the lightning down with a stunning flash, and the hay wagon is set ablaze. Patience leaps clear of the flaming hay wagon at the last possible moment, and the blazing, hurtling inferno crashes into the tall and evil castle to set it and its outbuildings and its whole town ablaze.

This is the flaming climax to one of the greatest chase dramas ever.

This final scene of *The Perils* will be met with often later. Due to the character of the "slow light" or selenium scenes, this vivid scene leaks out of its own framework and is superimposed, sometimes faintly, sometimes powerfully, as a ghost scene on all twelve of the subsequent dramas.

2. *Thirsty Daggers, a Murder Mystery.* This is the second of the Aurelian Bentley television dramas of 1873. Clarinda Calliope, one of the most talented actresses of her time, played the part of Maud Trenchant, the Girl Detective. The actors Leslie Whitemansion, Kirbac Fouet, X. Paul McCoffin, Jaime del Diablo, Torres Malgre, Inspiro Spectralski, and Hubert Saint Nicholas played powerful and menacing roles, but their identities and purposes cannot be set exactly. One must enter into the bloody and thrilling spirit of the drama without knowing the details.

More even than *The Perils of Patience* does *Thirsty Daggers* seem to be freed from the bonds of time and sequence. It is all one unfolding moment, growing always in intensity and intricacy, but not following a straight line of action. And this, accompanied by a deficiency of the libretto, leads to confusion.

The libretto cannot be read. It is darkened and stained. Chemical analysis has revealed that it is stained with human blood. It is our belief that Bentley sent the librettos to his clients decorated with fresh human blood to set a mood. But time has spread the stains, and almost nothing can be read. This is, however, a highly interesting drama, the earliest murder mystery ever done for television.

It is nearly certain that Maud Trenchant, the Girl Detective, overcomes all the menaces and solves all the crimes, but the finer details of this are forever lost.

3. *The Great Bicycle Race,* the third of the Bentley television dramas, has that versatile actress Clarinda Calliope playing the lead role of July Meadowbloom in this joyful and allegorical "journey into summertime." It is in *The Great Bicycle Race* that sound makes its first appearance in the Bentley dramas. It is the sounds of all outdoors that are heard in this drama, faintly at first, and more and more as time goes on. These are country and village sounds; they are county-fair sounds. Though the sounds seem to be an accidental intrusion (another ghostly side-play of the selenium response magic), yet their quality lends belief to the evidence that the full and original title of this drama was *The Great Bicycle Race, a Pastoral*.

But there are other sounds, sometimes angry, sometimes imploring, sometimes arrogant and menacing—more about them in a bit.

Sheep and cattle sounds are all through the play; goat and horse and swine sounds; the rattle of ducks and geese; all the wonderful noises of the countryside. There are birds and grasshoppers, windmills and wagons, people calling and singing. There are the sounds of carnival barkers and the chants of gamblers and shills. There are the shrieks and giggles of young people.

And then there are those intrusive sounds of another sort, the separate overlay. These seem to be mostly indoor sounds, but sometimes they are outdoor grandstand sounds also, bristling talk in the reserved shadows of crowd noise and roaring.

"No, no, no. I'll not be had. What sort of a girl do you think I am?"

"All these things I will give you, Clarie. No one else would give you so much. No one else would ever care so much. But now is the time for it. Now is the summer of our lives. Now we cut hay."

"Let's just see the price of a good hay barn first, Aurie. Let's just get some things down on paper right now. We are talking about a summertime check that is as big as all summer. And we are talking about a much larger settlement to back up the other seasons and years."

"Don't you trust me, Clarie?"

"Of course I trust you, Bentie babe. I trust that you will get that trust fund that we are talking about down on paper today. I am a very trusting woman. I believe that we should have a trust fund to cover every condition and circumstance."

Odd talk that, to be mixed in with the sounds of *The Great Bicycle Race.*

The race was in conjunction with the Tri-county Fair, which counties were Camden, Gloucester, and Atlantic. The bicycle racers rode their twenty-mile course every afternoon for five afternoons, and careful time was kept. There was betting on each day's race, but there was bigger betting on the final winner with the lowest total time for the five days, and the kitty grew and grew. From the great fairground grandstand, one could see almost all of the twenty-mile course that the riders rode, or could follow it by the plumes of dust. The grandstand was on high ground and the whole countryside was spread out before it. Cattle and mules were paraded and judged in front of that grandstand, before and during and after that daily race; then the race (for the approximate hour that it took to run it) was the big thing. There were seven drivers in the race, and all of them were world famous:

1. Leslie Whitemansion drove on a Von Sauerbronn "Special" of fine German craftsmanship. This machine, popularly known as the "whizzer," would get you there and it would bring you back. It was very road-worthy and surprisingly fast.

2. Kirbac Fouet was on an Ernest Michaux Magicien, a splendid machine. It had a socket into which a small sail might be fitted to give greater speed in a favorable wind.

3. X. Paul McCoffin was on a British Royal Velocipede. There are two things that may be remarked about the British Royal: it had solid rubber tires (the first rubber-tired bicycle ever), and it had

class. It had that cluttered austerity of line that only the best of British products have.

4. Jaime del Diablo was on a Pierre Lallement "Boneshaker" with its iron-tired wooden wheels, the front one much larger than the rear.

5. Torres Malgre was on an American-built Richard Warren Sears Roadrunner, the first all-iron machine. "The only wood is in the heads of its detractors" was an advertising slogan used for the Roadrunner.

6. Inspiro Spectralski (Is he a Man? Is he a Cannon Ball?) was riding a McCracken's Comet. This comet had won races at several other county fairs around the state.

7. Hubert Saint Nicholas had a machine such as no one in the state had ever seen before. It was a French *bicyclette* named the Supreme. The bicyclette had the pedals fixed to drive the *back* wheel by the ingenious use of a chain and sprocket wheel, and so was not, strictly speaking, a bicycle at all. The true bicycles of the other six racers had the pedals attached directly to the *front* wheels. There was one syndicate of bettors who said the bicyclette had a mechanical advantage, and that Hubert would win on it. But other persons made jokes about this rig whose back wheel would arrive before its front wheel and whose driver would not arrive before the next day.

It was on these great riders that all the six-shot gamblers around were wagering breath-taking sums. It was for them that sports came from as far away as New York City.

Clarinda Calliope played the role of Gloria Goldenfield, the beauty queen of the Tri-county Fair in this drama. But she also played the role of the "Masked Alternate Rider of Number Seven." (All the racing riders had their alternates to ride in their places in case of emergency.) And Clarinda also played a third role, that of Rakesly Rivertown, the splurging gambler. Who would ever guess that the raffish Rakesly was being played by a woman? The author and director of *The Great Bicycle Race* did not know anything about Clarinda playing these latter two roles.

The grandstand, the bandstand, the pleasures of a country carnival in the summertime! And the "slow smells" of the selenium-directed matrix just becoming ripe and evocative now! Smell of sweet clover and timothy hay, or hot horses pulling buggies or working in the fields, smells of candy and sausage and summer squash at the eating places at the fair, smells of dusty roads and of green money being counted out and thumped down on betting tables for the bicycle race!

And then again there was the override of intrusive voices breaking in on the real summer drama by accident.

"Clarie, I will do handsomely by you in just a day or so. I have placed very, very heavy bets on the bicycle race, and I will win. I am betting against the wildest gambler in this part of the country, Rakesly Rivertown, and we will have the bet up to a cool million with one more raise. He is betting the field against number seven. And number seven will win."

"I have heard that this Rakesly Rivertown is about the sharpest gambler anywhere, and that he has a fine figure and makes an extraordinary appearance."

"A fine figure! Why, the fraud is shaped like a girl! Yes, he is a sharp gambler, but he doesn't understand mechanics. Number seven, the Supreme, has a rear-wheel drive with a gear-ratio advantage. Hubert Saint Nicholas, who is riding number seven, is just toying with the other riders so far to get the bets higher, and he can win whenever he wants to. I will win a million dollars on the race, my love. And I will give it to you, if you act a little bit more like my love."

"Surely your love for me should transcend any results of a bicycle race, Aurie. If you really loved me, and if you contemplated making such a gift to me, you would make it today. That would show that your appreciation and affection are above mere fortune. And, if you can't lose, as you say that you cannot, you will have your money in the same amount won back in two days' time, and you will have made me happy two days longer."

"All right, I guess so then, Clarie. Yes, I'll give it to you today. Right now. I'll write you a check right now."

"Oh, you are a treasure, Aurie. You are a double treasure. You can't guess how double a treasure you are!"

The wonderful Tri-county Fair was near its end, and its Great Bicycle Race with it. It was the last day of the race. Hubert Saint Nicholas on number seven, the Supreme, the French bicyclette with the mechanical advantage, was leading the field by only one minute in total elapsed time going into that last day's racing. There were those who said that Hubert could win any time he wanted to, and that he stayed so close only to keep the bets a-growing.

And the bets did grow. The mysterious gambler with the fine figure and the extraordinary appearance, Rakesly Rivertown, was still betting the field to win against number seven. And a still more mysterious gambler, working through agents, was betting on number seven to *place,* but not to win. These latter bets were quickly covered. Number seven would *win,* unless some terrible calamity overtook that entry; and, in the case of such terrible calamity, number seven would not finish second, would not finish at all most likely.

The seven intrepid racers were off on their final, mad, twenty-mile circuit. Interest was high, especially with the moneyed gamblers who followed the riders from the grandstand with their binoculars. At no place was the winding, circuit course more than four miles from the grandstand; and there were only three or four places, not more than three hundred yards in all, where the racers were out of sight of the higher tiers of the grandstand. One of those places was where Little Egg Creek went through Little Egg Meadow. Something mysterious happened near Little Egg Creek Crossing that neither the libretto nor the enacted drama itself makes clear.

Hubert Saint Nicholas, riding the French bicyclette, number seven, the Supreme, with the rear-wheel drive and the mechanical advantage, was unsaddled from his mount and knocked unconscious. The race master later and officially entered this incident as "A careless rider knocked off his bicycle by a tree branch," though Hubert swore that there wasn't a tree branch within a hundred yards of that place.

"I was slugged by a lurker in the weeds," Hubert said. "It was a criminal and fraudulent assault and I know who did it." Then he cried, "Oh, the perfidy of women!" This latter seemed to be an unconnected outcry; perhaps Hubert had suffered a concussion.

Fortunately (for whom?) the alternate rider for number seven, the Mysterious (though duly certified) Masked Rider, was in the vicinity of the accident and took control of the bicyclette, the Supreme, and continued the race. But number seven, though having a one-minute lead ere the race began, did not win. Number seven did come in second though in total elapsed time.

The Great Bicycle Race is a quaint little drama, with not much plot, but with a pleasant and bucolic atmosphere that grows more pleasant every time the drama is played back. It is a thoroughly enjoyable "Journey into Summertime."

And there were a few more seconds of those intrusive "ghost" voices breaking into the closing moments of the pastoral drama.

"Clarie, I have been took bad, for a big wad, and I don't know how it happened. There is something funny about it all. There was something funny and familiar about that Masked Alternate Rider for number seven. (I swear that I know him from somewhere!) And there has always been something double funny and familiar about that gambler Rakesly Rivertown. [I swear and be damned if I don't know *him* from somewhere!]"

"Don't worry about it, Aurie. You are so smart that you will have all that money made back in no time at all."

"Yes, that's true, I will. But how can I write and produce and direct a drama and then get taken in it and not know what happened?"

"Don't worry about it, Aurie."

I myself doubt very much whether Aurelian Bentley knew about the "slow sounds" from nowhere-town that sometimes broke into the playing of his dramas, much less the "slow smells" which now began to give the dramas a character all their own.

4. *The Voyages of Captain Cook* was the fourth of the Bentley-produced television dramas of the year 1873. In this, Clarinda Calliope played the role of Maria Masina, the Queen of Polynesia. If *The Great Bicycle Race* was a journey into summertime, *The Voyages of Captain Cook* was a journey into tropical paradise.

Hubert Saint Nicholas played Captain Cook. Inspiro Spectralski (Is he a Man? Is he a Fish?) played the Shark God. Leslie Whitemansion played the Missionary. X. Paul McCoffin played the Volcano God. Torres Malgre played the God of the Walking Dead. Jaime del Diablo played Kokomoko, the bronzed surf boy and lover boy who was always holding a huge red hibiscus bloom between his white teeth.

The people of the South Sea Islands of the Captain Cook drama were always eating possum and sweet potatoes and fried chicken (a misconception) and twanging on little banjoes (another misconception) and talking southern U. S. Darky Dialect (but these ghost voices were not intended to be heard on the television presentation).

The complete libretto for *The Voyages of Captain Cook* has survived, which makes us grateful for those that have not survived for several of the dramas. The story is replete. It is better to disregard the libretto with its simultaneous curses invoked by the Shark God, the Volcano God, and the God of the Walking Dead, and to give oneself over to the charm of the scenery, which is remarkable, considering that it was all "filmed," or "selenium-matrixed," in the salt swamps of New Jersey.

The anomalous intrusive voices are in this drama again, as they will be in all the subsequent dramas.

"A 'South Sea bubble,' yes, that's what I want, Aurie, one that can't burst. Use your imagination [you have so much of it] and your finances [you have so very much of those] and come up with something that will delight me."

"I swear to you, Clarie, as soon as my finances are in a little better order, I will buy any island or group of islands in the Pacific Ocean for you. Do you hear me, Clarie? I will give you any island or group you wish, Hawaii, Samoa, Fiji. Name it and it is yours."

"So many things you promise! But you don't promise them on paper, only on air. Maybe I will find a way to make the air retain the promises you make."

"Not on paper, not on air, Clarie, but in real life. I will make you the real and living Queen of Polynesia."

The essence of the South Sea appeal is just plain charm. It may be that this Bentley drama, *The Voyages of Captain Cook*, was the original charm bush whence so many things bloomed. No, in things of this sort, it is not necessary that a scion ever be in contact with its source or even know its source. Without the *Voyages* would there ever have been a Sadie Thompson, would there have been a Nellie Forbush? Would there have been a Nina, daughter of Almayer? Well, they wouldn't have been as they were if Clarinda Calliope hadn't, in a way, played them first. Would there have been a *White Shadows of the South Seas* if there hadn't first been *The Voyages of Captain Cook*? No, of course there wouldn't have been.

5. *Crimean Days* was the fifth of the Aurelian Bentley television dramas. In this, the multitalented Clarinda Calliope played the role of Florence Nightingale, of Ekmek Kaya, a Turkish lady of doubtful virtue who was the number-four wife and current favorite of the Turkish admiral, of Chiara Maldonado, a young lady camp follower with the army of Savoy, of Katya Petrova, who was a Russian princess as well as a triple spy, and of Claudette Boudin, a French lady journalist. Clarinda also masqueraded as Claudette's twin brother Claude, a colonel with the French forces, and as such she led the French to a surprising victory over the Russians at Eupatoria. The unmasqueraded Claude himself was played by Apollo Mont-de-Marsan, a young actor making his first appearance in the Bentley dramas.

The Crimean War was the last war in which the field officers of all
sides (Leslie Whitemansion was a British field officer, Kirbac Fouet
was a French, Jaime del Diablo was an officer of the forces of Savoy,
Torres Malgre was the Turkish admiral, Inspiro Spectralski was a
general of the Czar, X. Paul McCoffin was a special observer of the
Pope), after their days of tactical maneuver and sometimes bloody
conflict, would dress for dinner and have formal dinner together. And
it was at these dinners that Clarinda Calliope, in her various guises,
shone.

There was a wonderful and many-leveled table intrigue, and I believe that more and more of it will come through every time the
drama is replayed. And it was here in this drama that one of the most
strange of the Bentley-effect phenomena first appeared. There is un-
mistakable evidence that some of the subvocalizations (thoughts) of
the people were now to be heard as "slow sound," which was really
selenium-triggered "slow thought." Some of these manifestations
were the role thoughts of the actors so strangely vocalized (Clarinda
Calliope, for instance, could not speak or think in any tongues except
English and her own Pennsylvania Dutch in normal circumstances:
but in her triple spy roles we find her thinking out loud in Turkish
and Greek and Russian); and other of the vocalizations are the real
thoughts of the actors (the amazingly frank intentions of Leslie Whitemansion and of the new Apollo Mont-de-Marsan as to their lady
loves of the evening after they should have received their two-dollar
actors' fee for the day).

It was a wonderful play and too intricate to be described. This one,
above all, has to be seen. But again there was the anomalous intrusion of voices that were not a part of the scenes of the play:

"Get rid of that Greek Wop kid, Clarie. I told him he was fired,
and he said that he would stick around and work for nothing. He said
he loved the fringe benefits. What are fringe benefits? I told him I'd
run him off, and he said that this was the free state of New Jersey and
that no one would run him off. I won't have him around."

"Oh, Aurie, there isn't any Greek Wop kid. That was me playing
that role too. Am I not talented to play so many roles? And you *will
not* fire me from this role. I will continue to play it, and I will be paid
for it. It isn't the principle of the thing either: it's the two dollars."

"Yes, I understand that much about you. But you say that was you
playing the part of that smart-mouth Apollo Dago Greek? That

couldn't be. I've seen you both at the same time. I've seen you two together too many times. I've seen you smooching each other."

"Ah, Aurie, that was quite an advanced technique and illusion, not to mention double exposure, that I used there. What other actress could play both roles at once and get away with it?"

"Your techniques and illusions are becoming a little bit too advanced, Clarie. And do not be so sure that you *are* getting away with it."

All through *Crimean Days,* there was some tampering with history going on for dramatic effect. The Light Brigade, for instance, was successful in its famous charge and it won a great victory. But the final outcome of the war was left in doubt. Aurelian Bentley had somehow become a strong partisan of the Russians and he refused to show them being finally defeated by the allies.

6. *Ruddy Limbs and Flaming Hair* is the sixth of the Bentley television dramas. In this piece, the dramatic Clarinda Calliope plays the part of Muothu, the Maid of Mars, for the Ruddy Limbs and Flaming Hair are on the planet Mars itself. There are some fantastic elements in this piece, as well as amazing scientific accuracy. There is, in fact, a technical precocity that is really stunning. Aurelian Bentley has foreseen circumstances that even the scientific community did not then see, and he has dealt with those circumstances.

He posits, for instance, an atmosphere composed mostly of an eno-magnetized, digammated, attenuated form of oxygen. Being eno-magnetized, that atmosphere would naturally cling to its planet even though the gravity would not be strong enough to retain it otherwise. Being digammated, it would produce no line in the Martian spectrum, would have no corona or optical distortion effect, and could in no way be detected from Earth. And yet a human Earthling would be able to breathe it freely.

This was a good-natured utopian drama of total realization and happiness. The Ruddy Limbs and Flaming Hair apply both allegorically to the planet Mars and literally to the highly dramatic Clarinda Calliope as Muothu. Muothu displayed rather more of the ruddy limbs than were ordinarily shown on Earth, but it was explained that customs on Mars were different.

Ruddy Limbs and Flaming Hair was the last of the dramas in which the apparently tormented and disturbed Aurelian Bentley still showed the strong hand of the master as scenarist, dramaturgist, director, and producer generally. After this we come to the four "Trough of the Wave" dramas, and then the three bewildering and hectic displays on the end of the series.

7. *The Trenton Train Robbery* is the seventh of the Bentley television dramas, and the first of the four "Trough" plays where Aurelian Bentley and his effects are sunken in the slough of despond and have lost their brightness and liveliness and hope. We will pass through them quickly.

In the *Train Robbery,* the peerless Clarinda Calliope plays Roxana Roundhouse, the daughter of the slain locomotive engineer Timothy (Trainman) Roundhouse. Armed with a repeating rifle, a repeating shotgun, a repeating pistol, and a few pocket-sized bombs, Roxana rides the rods of the crack Trenton Express in the effort to catch or kill the murderers of her father. These murderers have sworn that they will rob that very Trenton Express again.

And Roxana Roundhouse does catch or kill all the murderers of her father. In spite of some good shots of landscapes rushing by, this is not one of Aurelian Bentley's best efforts.

And again the voices of unknown persons creep into the drama:

"You've already flayed me, Clarie, and scraped both sides of my pelt for whatever might cling to it. What more do you want from me? Go away with your lover and leave me alone." And then in a fuzzier voice (apparently the "thought voice" made vocal) the same person said or thought: "Oh, if only she *would* go away from me, then I might have a chance! For I will never be able to go away from her."

"Grow more skin, Aurie," the other voice said. "I'm not nearly finished fleecing you and flaying you. Oh, don't look so torn up, Aurie. You know I could never love anyone except you. But a little token of our love is required now and then, and especially now, today. Yes, I know you are going to use your old line, 'I gave you a million dollars last week,' but, Aurie, that *was* last week. Yes, I know that you have expenses that the world wots not of. So do I. Believe me, Aurie, I wouldn't ask for these tokens of affection if I didn't want them." And then in a fuzzier voice, a "thought voice," the same person said or thought: "I'll never get another fish like this one and I sure can't afford to lose him. But gentle handling doesn't get it all the time. When the hook in him shows signs of working loose a bit, it has to be set in again with a very hard jerk on the line."

8. *Six Guns on the Border* is the eighth of the Bentley television dramas. In this drama, Clarinda Calliope (is there no end to her versatility?) plays the part of Conchita Allegre, the half-breed Apache and Mexican girl, on the Arizona border during the Mexican War. Conchita hates the American soldiers who are invading that area. She has them come to her secretly, with promises of love, and then she has them ambushed and killed. She kills many of them herself with her own six gun, and she makes antimacassars out of their skins. The sort of gentlemen that Conchita really likes use a lot of oil on their hair so Conchita needs a lot of antimacassars at her house.

But there are a few of the American officers so awkward and oafish that Conchita simply can't stand to have much to do with them, not even long enough to seduce them and have them killed. These horrible specimens are:

Captain James Polk (played by Leslie Whitemansion).
General Zachary Taylor (played by Kirbac Fouet).
Captain Millard Fillmore (played by X. Paul McCoffin).
Captain Franklin Pierce (played by Jaime del Diablo).
Captain James Buchanan (played by Torres Malgre).
Captain Abraham Lincoln (played by Inspiro Spectralski).
Captain Andrew Johnson (played by Apollo Mont-de-Marsan).
Captain Sam Grant (played by Hubert Saint Nicholas).

There was a lot of historical irony in this play, but maybe it belonged somewhere else.

There was a lot of "Comedy of Manners" stuff in it but it falls a little flat, mostly because the eight oafish officers spared by Conchita were too unmannerly to be in a comedy of manners.

Aurelian Bentley came near the bottom of his form in this piece. But for the energy of Clarinda Calliope (she played five other parts besides that of Conchita) there would have been hardly any drama at all.

And, as always, there were those intrusive voices hovering over the playbacks.

"Clarie, believe me! Believe me! Believe me! I will do all these things for you. I promise it."

"Yes, you promise it to the earless walls and to the earless me. Promise it to the pen and ink and paper here."

"Get rid of that Apollo kid first, Clarie."

"You get rid of him. You have a lot of rough-looking men around."

9. *Clarence Greenback, Confidence Man* was the ninth of the Aurelian Bentley television dramas. Hubert Saint Nicholas played the role of Clarence Greenback, the casino owner. It was the first time that Clarinda Calliope had not played the lead role in a drama. Is it possible that Clarinda had somehow slipped? Or was this another instance of the left lobe of Aurelian Bentley having lost its cunning, and casting badly. The talented prestidigitator of drama did not have his sure touch nowadays. Oh sure, Clarinda played many other roles in the drama, but she did not have the lead role.

Clarinda played the role of Gretchen, the sweep-out girl at the casino. She played the role of Maria, the mounting-block girl in the street outside the casino. She played the role of Elsie, the chimney-sweep girl. She played the part of Hennchen, the scullery maid in the third and vilest kitchen of the casino. She played the part of Josephine, the retriever who had to gather up the shattered bodies of the suicides below Suicide Leap Window of the casino and take them to East Potters' Field and dig their graves and bury them. Elsie made a good thing out of her job, from the gold teeth of the late patrons of the casino, but the dramatist and producer did not know about the good thing she had here.

There were hazards in all these different roles.

"No, of course we can't put out the fires for you to clean the chimneys," said Leslie Whitemansion, who was in charge of fireplaces and chimneys at the casino. "Clean them hot." And it was very hot working inside those tall chimneys with the fires roaring below, and Elsie the chimney-sweep girl suffered.

For keeping a copper coin that she found while sweeping out the casino, the sadist Baron von Steichen (played by X. Paul McCoffin) had Gretchen hung up by her thumbs and flogged.

And Maria, the mounting-block girl, who had to stand in the muddy street outside the casino and bend her back for the gentlemen to step on her when they mounted or dismounted their horses, she had it worse on the muddy days. Oh, the great muddy boots of those men!

"Maybe they're trying to tell me something," Clarinda Calliope spoke or thought (by slow talk-thought). "I do like subtle people." But a good actress can play any role, and Clarinda has her revenge today. Hardly anyone remembers the plot of *Clarence Greenback, Confidence Man,* but everybody remembers the tribulations of those pretty little servant girls.

And then there were those other intrusive voices of the overlay. It was almost as if they belonged in another sort of drama.

"Clarie, this has to stop. Not counting the special gifts, and they're fantastic, I'm giving you ten times as much as the President of the United States is making."

"I'm ten times as good at acting as he is. And how about *my* special gifts?—and they're fantastic. Why do you have all the private detectives running around the last couple of days? To spy on me?"

"To spy on everything and everyone. To save my life. Frankly, Clarie, I am afraid of being murdered. I have premonitions of being killed, with a knife, always with a knife."

"Like in *Thirsty Daggers, a Murder Mystery?* That one wasn't really very well worked out, and I believe it's one of the things bothering you. Your undermind is looking for a better solution, I believe, for a neater murder. It is seeking to enact a more artistic murder. I believe it will do it. I believe you will come up with quite an artistic murder for yourself. There are good murders and bad murders, you see."

"Clarie, I don't intend to let myself be killed at all, not by either a good or a bad murder."

"Not even for art's sake? It seems it would be worth it, for the perfect murder, Aurie."

"Not when *I'm* the murdered one, Clarie."

Then, a moment later, the female person said or thought something further, in a "slow thought-voice."

"Sometimes persons have perfection thrust upon them in spite of themselves. An artful murder for Aurie would make up for a lot of the bad art that he's been guilty of lately."

10. *The Vampires of Varuma* was the tenth of the Aurelian Bentley television dramas. This is the fourth and last of the "Trough of the Wave" dramas, which show Bentley's dramatic powers in almost complete decline and himself mightily disoriented. Yet, in this bottoming-out, there is a curious resurrection of his powers in a slightly different form. His sense of plotting and story movement did not return yet, but his sense of dramatic horror as motive force was resurrected to its highest pitch.

Clarinda Calliope played Magda the peasant maid, Miss Cheryl Somerset, the governess from England, and the Princess Irene of Transylvania. All three of these had been traveling to Castle Khubav on rational errands by the regular coach of the road; and each of the three had seen all the other passengers dismount hastily, and had then experienced the coach horses being whipped ahead frantically by an invisible coachman, or by no coachman at all. And each of these ladies had arrived, on successive days, in the apparently driverless coach, not at Castle Khubav, but at the dread Castle Beden. And inside the Castle Beden were the seven ("no, not seven, eight" was written into the libretto in a weirdly different hand) insane counts in their castle of evil. These were:

Count Vladmel, played by Leslie Whitemansion.

Count Igork, played by Kirbac Fouet.

Count Lascar, played by X. Paul McCoffin.

Count Chort, played by Jaime del Diablo.

Count Sangressuga, played by Torres Malgre.

Count Letuchaya, played by Inspiro Spectralski (Is he a Man? Is he a Bat?).

Count Ulv, played by Hubert Saint Nicholas.

And then there is another one added in the libretto in that weirdly different hand:

Count Prividenne, played by Apollo Mont-de-Marsan. There is a slip-up here somewhere. Apollo is supposed to have been "gotten rid of," to have shuffled off the mortal coil, and the sheriff's report said that he died of indigestion. But if Apollo has not been "gotten rid of" then certain money was paid in vain.

The seven (or eight) evil counts are sometimes conventional counts in evening clothes and monocles. And sometimes they are huge bat-winged creatures flitting ponderously down the lightning-lit corridors of Castle Beden. The castle, in fact, is the main character in the drama. It does not have formal lighting, as it is lit by lightning all twenty-four hours of every night (there is no daylight at Castle Beden). The floors and walls howl and chains rattle constantly. The counts have sometimes conventional six-inch-long eyeteeth, and then suddenly they will have hollow fangs eighteen inches long and deadly. And there is a constant lot of howling and screaming for what is supposed to be a silent television drama.

A flying count will suddenly fold his bat wings and land on the broad bosom of one of the three maidens and have into her throat with his terrible blood-sucking fangs. And every time it happens, there is a horrible flopping and screeching.

The voice of Clarinda Calliope is heard loud and clear and real in a slow angry sound.

"Dammit, Aurelian, that's real blood they're taking out of my throat."

And came the suave voice of the master dramatist Aurelian Bentley (but the voices shouldn't be breaking in like this):

"Right, Clarie. It is on such verisimilitude that I have built my reputation as a master."

Clarinda, in her three roles, seemed to lose quite a bit of blood as the drama went on, and she fell down more and more often. And the drama was a howling and bloody success, no matter that the story line was shattered in a thousand pieces—for each piece of it was like a writhing blood snake that gluts and gloats.

And then, after the drama itself was ended in a spate of final blood, there came those intrusive voices that seemed to be out of some private drama.

"Aurie, if you are worrying about being killed, how about providing for me before it happens?"

"I leave you half of my kingdom, ah, estate, Clarie, right off the top of it. My word is good for this. And stop falling down."

"I'm weak. It took a lot out of me. Yes, your written word is good on this, Aurie, if it is written and attested to in all the right places. Let's take care of that little detail right now."

"Clarie, my spoken promise is enough, and it is all that I will give. I hereby attest that half of my estate, off the top, belongs to you. Let the eared walls of this room be witnesses to what I say, Clarie. If the walls of this room will swear to it, then surely they will be believed. Now don't bother me for a few days. I will be busy with something else. And stop falling down. It's annoying."

The female person then said or thought something in a fuzzy thought-voice:

"Yes, I believe I *can* make the walls of this room attest for me when the time comes. (I might have to put in another amplifying circuit to be sure.) And I believe that the attesting walls will be believed."

The male person then said or thought something in a fuzzy thought-voice:

"I have Miss Adeline Addams now. Why should I care about this Calliope clown? It's irritating the way she keeps turning chalk-white and falling down. I never saw anyone make such a fuss over nine

quarts of blood. But now I am on a new and more glorious dawn
road. Is it not peculiar how a man will fall in love with one woman
and out of love with another one at the same time?"

11. *The Ghost at the Opera* is the eleventh of the Aurelian Bentley
television dramas in the year 1873. *The Ghost* is based on Verdi's *Il
Trovatore,* but Bentley's production is quite original for all that. The
role of Leonora is played by Miss Adeline Addams. But the same
role is also played by Clarinda Calliope, who was originally selected
to play the role by herself. This business of having two different persons playing the same role creates a certain duality, one might almost
say a certain duplicity, in the drama.

The "Ghost" is the doubling: it is the inept and stumbling Clarinda trying again and again to sing parts of the Leonora role and
failing in it totally and being jerked off stage by the stage manager's
crook; and it is the beautiful and brimming genius Adeline Addams
coming on and performing the same role brilliantly. This provides the
"cruel comedy" that is usually lacking in Verdi; for, without cruelty,
only a limited success is ever possible in opera. But Clarinda took
some very bad falls from the stageman's crook jerking her off her
feet, and besides she was still weak and falling down from all the
blood she had lost in her roles in *The Vampires of Varuma.* She was
suffering.

"Why do you go through with it, Clarinda?" Hubert Saint Nicholas
asked her once in an outside-of-the-play-itself voice. "Why do you
allow yourself to be tortured and humiliated like that?"

"Only for the money," Clarinda was heard to say. "Only for the
actor's fee of four dollars a day. I am clear broke and I am hungry.
But if I can stick it out to the end of the opera, I will have four dollars tonight for my wages."

"Four dollars, Clarinda? The rest of us get only two dollars a day.
Are you playing another role that I don't know about?"

"Yes, I am also playing the role of Wilhelmia, the outhouse
cleaner."

"But I thought that you had millions from that old tyrant,
Clarinda."

"It's gone, Hubie, all gone. I had expenses that the world wotted
not of. I gave Apollo most of the money when I was in love with him.
And I gave the rest of it to him today to do a special favor for me."

"You gave the money to him today? But he was buried yesterday."

"Time seems to go faster as we get older, doesn't it?"

Meanwhile, back on the opera stage, a new Verdi was being hammered out. Leslie Whitemansion was playing Manrico. X. Paul McCoffin was playing Ferrando. Hubert Saint Nicholas was playing Count di Luni. Apollo Mont-de-Marsan was playing the ghost. But was there a ghost in the libretto besides the double ghost of the two females playing the same role? Yes there was; there was a real ghost in the libretto. It was written in there in a queer "other" hand, really a "ghostly" hand, and it wrote that Apollo was playing the role of the ghost.

So the merry comic opera went along almost to its end. It was just when Manrico was being led to the executioner's block and the evil Count di Luni was gloating in triumph, when everything was finally being shaped up in that drama that had some pleasure for everybody, that a horrible thing happened in one of the loges or boxes that overhung the stage.

Aurelian Bentley was knifed there in his box at the opera. Oh God, this was murder! "Your mind is looking for a better solution, I believe, for a neater murder." Oh, that had been the voice of another sort of ghost. But now, to be slain by the ghost of a man dead only a day or two, and in the presence of several thousands of persons here! (For it was, possibly, none other than Apollo Mont-de-Marsan, who had been "gotten rid of," who was getting rid of Aurelian Bentley.) And again: "There are good murders and bad murders, you see. . . . It seems it would be worth it, for art's sake, for the perfect murder." Aurelian Bentley was stabbed to death in his box at the opera there, but even he had to admit, with some appreciation, as he went, that it was done with art.

And immediately, as the opera on stage came to its great conclusion, there welled up cries of "Author, Author, Bentley, Bentley!"

Then the dying (or more likely dead) man rose for the last time, bowed formally, and tumbled out of his box and onto his face on the stage, stark dead, and with the thirsty (now slaked) dagger twinkling between the blades of his shoulders.

What other man had ever made such an exit from or on life's stage! That was Theater! That was Drama!

12. *An Evening in Newport* was intended to be the twelfth of the Bentley television dramas. But it was never produced; possibly because of the death of its producer. It exists only as libretto.

This was a high society "drama of manners," as Miss Adeline Addams knew it, as Aurelian Bentley with his quick mind and quick mimicry knew it from his brief brushes with it. But does not a drama or comedy of manners depend largely on the quip and the arch aphorism? How could it be done in silent presentation?

By art, that's how it might be done: by the perfect art of the silent mimes, and Aurelian Bentley was master of that art. By the gestures, by the facial implications, by great silent acting this might be done. Was there any witticism that Adeline Addams could not express with her talented, high society face? Was there any devastating riposte that she could not give with her autocratic hands? It was never tested, but Aurelian believed that she was pretty good.

On the lower level, *An Evening in Newport* was a one-sided duel between Mistress Adeline Addams of Newport, playing the role of Mistress Adela Adams of Newport, and Clarinda Calliope, playing the role of Rosaleen O'Keene, a low, vicious, ignorant, filthy, bad-mannered, fifth parlor maid newly arrived from Ireland. It was a stacked set in favor of Adeline-Adela.

On the higher level, the drama was the passionate portrayal of the total love of a beautiful and wealthy and intelligent and charming and aristocratic young lady (Adeline-Adela) for a man of surpassing genius and ineffable charm, a man of poise and power and heroic gifts, a man the like of whom will hardly appear once in a century. The drama was supposed to take on a note of hushed wonder whenever this man was mentioned, or so the libretto said. The libretto does not identify this exceptional man, but our own opinion is that the librettist, Aurelian Bentley, intended this hardly-once-in-a-century man, the object of the torrid and devoted love of Miss Adeline Addams, to be himself, Aurelian Bentley.

But *An Evening in Newport,* intended to be the surpassing climax of that first and still unsurpassed television series, was never produced.

13. *Pettifoggers of Philadelphia* is the noncanonical, apocryphal, thirteenth apocalypse of *The Wonderful World of Aurelian Bentley,* that first and greatest television series. There is no libretto to it. There is no formal production, and it does not carry the Bentley "Seal of Production." But it does repose in one of the old television receivers, the one that was Aurelian's own control receiver, the one that was in Aurelian's own luxurious den where he spent so many

hectic hours with Clarinda Calliope and later with Adeline Addams. It reposes there, and it may be seen and heard there.

Though Bentley was already dead when these scenes were ordered and live-presented, yet he walks in them and talks in them. The experience of hearing the thoughts and words of a hovering dead man spoken out loud and of seeing him as if in the flesh is a shattering but dramatic one.

The setting and sole scene of *Pettifoggers of Philadelphia* is that same luxurious den of Aurelian Bentley's, first placed under court seal, but then opened for a meeting which, as one of the parties to it stated, could not validly be held anywhere else. A probate judge was present, and pettifoggers representing several of the parties, and two of the parties themselves. It was a hearing on the disposition of the estate of Aurelian Bentley, or what might be left of that estate, he having died without having made a will. But one of the parties, Clarinda Calliope, insisted that Bentley *had* made a will, that the will was in this particular room and no other, that the will in fact *was* this room and the eared and tongued walls of it.

There seemed to be several meetings in this room superimposed on one another, and they cannot be sorted out. To sort them out would have been to destroy their effect, however, for they achieved syntheses of their several aspects and became the true meeting that never really took place but which contained all the other meetings in one theatrical unity.

The pettifogger of a second cousin once removed was there to present the claim of that distant person, as next in kin, to the estate of Aurelian Bentley.

The pettifogger of Adeline Addams of Newport was there to present the claim of Adeline to the estate, claims based on an *irrefutable promise*. This irrefutable promise was the marriage license for Aurelian Bentley and Adeline Addams. It was not signed or witnessed, of course. The marriage, the pettifogger said, had been scheduled to take place on a certain night after the presentation of an opera, that was contained in a television drama, that was contained in a riddle. But Aurelian Bentley had been killed during that opera, which voided the prospect of marriage, but did not void the promise.

There were pettifoggers there for the different creditors. And all the pettifoggers were from Philadelphia.

And there was Clarinda Calliope representing herself (as Portia, she insisted, and not as pettifogger), and she claimed rights by a promise too big and too intricate to be put on paper.

There was the probate judge of the private hearing who ambled around the luxurious den flipping a silver dollar in the air and humming the *McGinty's Saloon Waltz*.

"Oh, stop flipping that silly silver dollar and get on with the matter of the probate," Miss Adeline Addams complained to that nitwit judge.

"The silver dollar is the matter of the probate," the judge said. "The dollar is important. It is the soul and body of what this is all about."

The piles of paper began to accumulate on the tables there. There were the documents and attestations of the distant next of kin, of Adeline Addams, and of the creditors in their severalty. And not one scrap of paper did Clarinda Calliope put forward.

"Enough, enough," said the judge after the flood of paper had narrowed down to a trickle. "Stop the paper," but he didn't stop flipping that silver dollar or humming the *McGinty's Saloon Waltz*. "All a-sea that's going a-sea. Miss Calliope, it is time you laid a little evidence on the table if you are to be a party of these hearings."

"My evidence is too large and too living to lay on the table," Clarinda said. "But listen, and perhaps look! Due to the magic of the selenium 'slow response' principle, and to the walls of this very room being wired parallel to the receiver in this room, we may be able to bring to you a veritable reconstruction of past words and avowals and persons."

And pretty soon the voice of the once-in-a-century man began, ghostly at first, and then gradually taking on flesh.

"Oh, Aurelian!" Adeline Addams squealed. "Where *are* you?"

"He is here present, in this room where he spent so many wonderful hours with me," Clarinda said. "All right, Aurie baby, talk a little bit clearer and start materializing."

"All these things I will give you, Clarie," came the voice of Aurelian Bentley, and Bentley was there in shadow form himself. "No one else would give you so much. No one else would ever care so much . . . trust me, Clarie."

Aurelian Bentley was standing there solidly now. It was a three-dimensional projection or re-creation of him, coming into focus from all the eared and eyed and remembering walls of the room that was wired in parallel to the television receiver. Aurelian stood in the midst of them there in his own luxurious den.

"Clarie, I will do handsomely by you . . . a million dollars, my love, and I will give it to you." Oh, these were startling and convincing words coming from the living ghost there!

"I swear to you, Clarie . . . I will buy any island or group of islands in the Pacific Ocean for you . . . Hawaii, Samoa, Fiji. Name it and it's yours."

What man ever made such tall promises and with such obvious sincerity?

"Not on paper, not on air, Clarie, but in real life. I will make you the real and living queen."

If they will not listen to one risen from the dead, whom will they listen to?

"Clarie, believe me, believe me, believe me! I will do all things for you. I promise it." How are you going to top something like that?

"I leave you . . . my kingdom, ah, estate, Clarie. My word is good for that."

It was all in the bag, and the drawstring was being tightened on the bag.

"I hereby attest that . . . my estate . . . belongs to you. Let the eared walls of this room be witnesses to what I say, Clarie. If the walls of this room will swear to it, then surely they will be believed."

The image of Aurelian Bentley disappeared, and his sound was extinguished with a sharp snipping sound. Adeline Addams was putting a scissors back into her handbag.

"I've meant to find out what that wire there was for several times," she said. "That sort of shuts it all off when the wire is cut, doesn't it?"

"Here, here, you are guilty of destroying my evidence," Clarinda Calliope said. "You can go to prison for that! You can burn in fire for that!"

A sudden flaming hay wagon with a wild woman driving it rushed into the room and seemed about to destroy everyone in the room. Everyone cringed from it except Clarinda and the probate judge. The flaming hay wagon did crash into all the people of the room, but it did them no damage. It was only a scene from one of the earlier plays. You didn't think that Clarinda had only one circuit in that room, did you? But several of the persons were shaken by the threat.

"Good show," said the probate judge. "I guess it wins, what there is left to win."

"No, no," Adeline cried. "You can't give her the *estate?*"

"What's left of it, sure," said the judge, still flipping the silver dollar.

"It isn't the principle either," said Clarinda, "it's the dollar." She plucked the silver dollar out of the air as the probate judge was still flipping it.

"This *is* the entire residue of the estate, isn't it?" she asked to be sure.

"Right, Calliope, right," the judge said. "That's all that was left of it."

He continued to flip an invisible coin into the air, and he whistled the last, sad bars of the *McGinty's Saloon Waltz*.

"Anybody know where a good actress can get a job?" Clarinda asked. "Going rates, two dollars a day per role." She swept out of the room with head and spirits high. She was a consummate actress.

The other persons fade out into indistinct sounds and indistinct shadows in the old kerosene-powered television receiver.

The prospects of retrieval and revival of the first and greatest of all television series, *The Wonderful World of Aurelian Bentley,* recorded and produced in the year 1873, is in grave danger.

The only true and complete version of the series reposes in one single television receiver, Aurelian Bentley's own control receiver, the one that he kept in his own luxurious den where he spent so many happy hours with his ladies. The original librettos are stored in this set: they are, in fact, a part of this set and they may not, for inexplicable reasons, be removed to any great distance from it.

All the deep and ever-growing side talk, "slow talk," is in this set. (All the other sets are mute.) All the final drama *Pettifoggers of Philadelphia* is recorded in this set and is in none of the others. *There is a whole golden era of television recorded in this set.*

I bought this old kerosene-burning treasure from its last owner (he did not know what it was: I told him that it was a chestnut roaster) for eighteen dollars. Now, by a vexing coincidence, this last owner has inherited forty acres of land with a fine stand of chestnut trees, and he wants the chestnut roaster back. And he has the law on his side.

I bought it from him, and I paid him for it, of course. But the   I 13 check I gave him for it was hotter than a selenium rectifier on a shorted circuit. I have to make up the eighteen dollars or lose the receiver and its stored wealth.

I have raised thirteen dollars and fifty cents from three friends and one enemy. I still need four dollars and a half. Oh wait, wait, here is ninety-eight cents in pennies brought in by the "Children for the Wonderful World of Aurelian Bentley Preservation Fund." I still need three dollars and fifty-two cents. Anyone wishing to contribute to this fund had best do so quickly before this golden era of television is forever lost. Due to the fussiness of the government, contributions are not tax-deductible.

It is worth preserving as a remnant of that early era when there were giants on the earth. And, if it is preserved, someday someone will gaze into the old kerosene-powered receiver and cry out in astonishment in the words of the Greatest Bard:

"—what poet-race
Shot such Cyclopean arches at the stars?"